CLOSE YOUR EYES

By the same author

Swung
Distance
Ménage

CLOSE YOUR EYES

EWAN MORRISON

JONATHAN CAPE
LONDON

Published by Jonathan Cape 2012

2 4 6 8 10 9 7 5 3 1

First published in Great Britain in 2012 by
Jonathan Cape
Random House, 20 Vauxhall Bridge Road,
London SW1V 2SA

www.vintage-books.co.uk

Addresses for companies within The Random House Group Limited
can be found at: www.randomhouse.co.uk/offices.htm

The Random House Group Limited Reg. No. 954009

A CIP catalogue record for this book is available from the British Library

ISBN 9780224096232

The Random House Group Limited supports The Forest Stewardship Council
(FSC®), the leading international forest certification organisation. Our books
carrying the FSC label are printed on FSC® certified paper.
FSC is the only forest certification scheme endorsed by the leading
environmental organisations, including Greenpeace.
Our paper procurement policy can be found
at www.randomhouse.co.uk/environment

MIX
Paper from
responsible sources
FSC® C016897

Typeset by Palimpsest Book Production Limited,
Falkirk, Stirlingshire

Printed and bound in Great Britain by
Clays Ltd, St Ives PLC

For Edna, David and Glenna

Acknowledgements

This book could not have been written without the generous assistance of the Scottish Arts Council/ Creative Scotland; through the Edinburgh City of Literature/UNESCO Writers' Exchange to the Sydney Writers' Festival; and the Writer's Centre Varuna Fellowship, New South Wales.

Can ye no hush yer weepin'?
A' the wee lambs are sleepin'
Birdies are nestlin', nestlin' the gither
Dream Angus is hirplin' oer the heather

Dreams to sell, fine dreams to sell
Angus is here wi' dreams to sell
Hush my wee bairnie an' sleep without fear
Dream Angus has brought you a dream my dear

Hear the curlew cryin' o
An' the echoes dyin' o
Even the birdies and the beasties are sleepin'
But my bonny bairn is weepin' weepin'

Dreams to sell, fine dreams to sell
Angus is here wi' dreams to sell
Hush my wee bairnie an' sleep without fear
Dream Angus has brought you a dream my dear

'Dream Angus'
Traditional Scottish folk lullaby, 1850

home

THE MOMENT BEFORE you lose someone, the last moment you had together, people always say, is an image, this image that stays with you for ever. But it was a song. Or rather, her singing along to a tape as we drove through a blizzard. *The Long and Winding Road*. Driving through the night with the spiralling snow in her headlights. *The Fool on the Hill.* Maybe it was, I'm not sure, that last night with her. *A Day in the Life.* Me mesmerised by the tunnel of white, pulling us in, and her voice lulling me to sleep. *Let It Be*.

It might not even have been that album, I don't know for sure, maybe it's just the word beetle – singing along to the Beatles in the VW Beetle. I used to like that, me beside her in the front seat heading south. Two or three in the morning, athough the time was always only what she told me it was because I didn't have a watch and she had never taught me how to read the time because in the commune the days were measured in light and dark and not hours, these inventions of men. And night looks pretty much the same, whether it's eleven or four and you are ten or twelve and it's always south, through the Highlands, although you could never see them, the high lands, not at night. And my first dad's cups and plates and sculptures he'd made himself, from the clay dug from the fields, fired in the oven Angus'd built himself, filling the back seats, packed in old boxes. Driving south to Edinburgh or Glasgow. Always south, through the night because we had to be there early, because it was too far for a kid to travel without sleeping, I guess. She was going to sell Angus's ceramics, the ones she helped him make that she let me paint flowers on. A wasted trip

3

like all the others. Craft fairs and no one ever bought a thing, or maybe just an ashtray, out of politeness or embarrassment or pity, because ashtrays were the cheapest. She never sang on the way back home.

Let It Be. I know it must seem funny that she was still listening to this stuff from '68 in '81. We were, but it was our music. Both sides of the double album meant you were at Inverness. She used to just flip the tape over when it was done and play it again. I never made it much past twice without dozing off. *Octopus's Garden* was my favourite but she said Ringo was a sell-out. She liked John best, John Lennon. He was shot dead in New York, she told me, by someone who thought he was the real John Lennon and that the real one was an impostor and a sell-out. She said we would never sell out. *All You Need Is Love.*

Her long black hair in the dark and not being able to see her properly. She was this profile, always, in that last year, lit by what was oncoming, driving on into the dark. It went all the way down her back, her hair was so long she could sit on it. It covered her body when she was naked and she liked that, to be naked. She looked like a fairy and an elf and a witch, like in the books she showed me. Galadriel from *Lord of the Rings* and the Wicked Witch of the North. Her cheekbones, her neck bones, her pelvis, a woman of bones and eyes that grew bigger and darker the skinnier she got and she said it was the vegan diet, but in that last year I never saw her eat a thing. Everyone told her she was a beauty, cats and chicks, mostly cats. We used to say words like that, these words for guys. I'd wake beside them sometimes, after our drives. All of them long-haired, like her, naked and smiling and singing. Everyone used to sing all the time.

Her hands on the steering wheel. They never seemed to fit her body. Strong, from throwing pots, digging, planting,

4

building. Like a man's hands, like Pete's, my second dad. She said I shouldn't call him Dad. Everyone we lived with were our brothers and sisters, she said. Mummy. Mumma. She preferred me calling her Jenna. She only let me call her Mum when the others weren't around, like in the car. But I remember turning to her and whispering the word to the side of her face because she was singing and couldn't hear me and looking at the road and couldn't see me. Mum. And her sensing my eyes and talking without turning. She could always tell when I was watching her, when I was trying to say something and not saying it.

'Shh. It's a long drive,' she would say, always. 'Listen to the music, close your eyes.'

No, it couldn't have been her last night. If it was it wouldn't have been the Beatles. She'd stopped singing by then and Lennon's death, she said, was really a murder, the FBI, the CIA, like JFK, like Malcolm X. All these people whose names were just letters to me who lived in a place called the USA.

They told me she died in the second or third week. September 1981. Between the twelfth and the nineteenth. Her car skidded off the road, over a cliff, at this place called the Struie, the border between Caithness and Sutherland, fifty miles from anywhere, a natural border where the flatlands turned to mountains. It was a steep decline, trucks went over the edge all the time, and an unpopulated area, and her car had been under the water maybe a week, which was why it took them so long to find it, but not her. The waves, they said, the currents. The car doors burst open on the impact, my grandfather said, a two-hundred-foot drop. She must have been thrown out when it hit. It was the gradient. They should have built a bridge.

She drove me to my first father's house then she headed south and skidded in the snow. This is the story I was told and that I've told myself for years. But snow in September?

5

It might just be a whole bunch of other times I've put together, years apart. Or maybe there was no snow but there was singing, she was singing again, just for that one night, because she knew it would be our last. Because she wanted me to go to sleep, for everything to be OK again. I don't know why I'm trying to put these things together now, nearly twenty-seven, twenty-eight years later. It's something to do with this thing that happens to me. The first time maybe I can seem to recall it happening was in her car. Like the snowflakes were singing and it was cold outside but my toes were warm. And her voice was warm but her face cold. Things not matching up. Out of sync. My senses and thoughts belonging to two different people. The way I feel most times now. Usually when something is about to go wrong.

*

Open your eyes. See, everything is as it should be. The plastic elephant, the roundabout, slide, climbing frame, rubberised concrete. Think about that. It stops them hurting themselves when they come down too fast. Try to stay awake. Focus. Look at the people. The mother over there in retro hippie gear putting a baby on a baby swing. Hippie gear in 2009. Things come around, let it go. Don't judge, you're going to be fine. Boy or girl? Girl, not in pink but still you can tell. How old? Three months. Must be. A little girl three months old. Voices.

'That's what they do in Germany.'

'Really? I heard something like it in Sweden.'

They are talking beside you. Joan and Lisa. Your neigh-bourhood friends. Their children are beautiful. *Other mothers can be your closest allies during this challenging time.* Try to stop staring at the mother pushing her child backwards and forwards on the swing, pulling faces, trying to get her baby to laugh. *Your child should be at least six*

6

months before being allowed to play on swings and slides and even then the head must be supported. The baby's head flops backwards and forwards with each push, hands barely gripping the plastic security bar. Can only be three months – *Your baby can sit upright only with support.* No, you're not going to get up from the bench and tell the stupid fucking idiot that until six months the infant brain is floating in protective fluid and that sudden movements can— You can't. Can't move. You are so tired and your eyes are closing again. Stop it. Focus on their voices. Lisa, Joan.

'Glass, bottles, cans and newspapers all separately.'

'We should do that here, definitely. Don't you think, Emma?'

Silence. What? Who? They must be waiting for you to talk.

'Sorry,' you say. 'I was just . . .'

'Like they do in Germany. Don't you think it would be good here?'

Something about recycling. Your mother never bought anything plastic and had a compost heap thirty years before they became fashionable. You can still smell it, your fear of the rats. Wake up. They want an opinion. You used to have one on everything. It was your job. Don't think about your job. Don't let the stupid designer hippie upset you, pushing her child too hard on the swing. Jesus, hasn't she read the manuals? *Sudden movements such as swinging or shaking can produce haemorrhaging or frontal lobe damage.* Maybe not a mother – a nanny then. Student nanny. Just a job to her, this is why you said to Josh you'd never have a nanny. Stop staring. Lisa and Joan are waiting for you to speak. Speak then. Show them you still can. 'Yes,' you say. 'No, I mean . . .'

The shriek tears through you. *You will be able to discern the sound of your own child's screams above those of others from a distance of a hundred yards.* Little Sasa, in her

carrycot at your feet, crying again. Like she does every time
you are about to open your mouth to try to speak. Every
time you close your eyes to sleep. Like she knows.

'Shh, Sasa, shh.'

She wants your breast. You can feel your milk weeping
into the breast pads but she is too old now and must learn.
*Six to eight months is the ideal time for weaning your baby
off the breast. You can retard your child's development by
prolonging breastfeeding.* Josh has moved on to another
manual. Your breast pads are soaking. It's natural they say,
in his. Your child cries – you feed. But it has gone on for
too long. She sucks so hard. You are so tired but shouldn't
be. His manual says different things so he knows better.
The Best Start in Life it's called. Your mother would have
dismissed it as capitalist propaganda. You've read it three
times, compared it to your own, tried to bury the contra-
dictions. Page after page then again and again. It's what
you do to try to get to sleep. Memorise the methods for
being a good mother. When that doesn't work you put
your headphones on in bed beside him and listen to your
relaxation CD. It never wakes him, the hiss from your headphones. You have four of these CDs from the Self-Help
section in Waterstone's and they all start with the words
'Close your eyes'.

No sleep again last night. You have to learn again. How
to do this thing that normal people do.

'Shh, Sasa, shh.'

'Three times a week she comes now.'

'God, that's fantastic, mine never does. What's your
dad think about it?'

'Just bloody glad to get her out of the house, I think.'

Something else they're laughing about now. This is
what happens. One of you tries to speak, a baby cries, you
change the subject. You can't keep up. Sasa resents it all
because she has no words. The screaming in your spine;

breasts, swelling like a bruise; the wet patch growing on your blouse. You can tell they're looking at you with that look. Lisa, Joan. Pity. Because you can't cope and they can. Grannies. They're talking about Joan's mother. You can't talk about your mother. They've stopped asking because the few things you told them seemed to scare them. You need to have friends like this, everyone needs friends. You love your friends.

Sasa, stop screaming, please.

She won't stop till she gets what she wants. Eight months. *Your baby needs less sleep and may be awake for eleven hours every day. She may wake three or four times in the night.* She's struggling with the straps now, trying to get out, but this is her sleep time. Week two of Sleep Therapy and she is only allowed one daytime nap. *Has tremendous belief in her own abilities and is increasingly frustrated when she finds she can't achieve her goals.*

'Shh, sleepyhead. Close your eyes. Please, Sasa, please.'

Both their babies are dozing in their carrycots. Hands out to their sides. Little angels. Lisa and Joan are good mothers. Joan is your godmother. If you could sleep you would like to wake up as Lisa or Joan.

'Baby Sasa, shh, Mummy loves you.'

But you *are* a good mother. You are doing so well together. *Take time out to appreciate your progress.* She is being tried on solids now. Mashed banana and apple, liquidised pork and chicken soup. She must learn that she's not part of you. She must learn how to eat, sleep, she must stop screaming and reaching for your breasts. She must just stop.

'To the pictures last night and Vietnamese at that new place.'

'And she what, she sleeps in the spare room or what?'

'On the sofa bed, she prefers it. Better for her back, she says.'

Joan's mother, yes. Try to tell Joan that it's wonderful

9

that her mother is there to help, that it's fantastic that she's getting out now, really having a romantic and engaging life again with her hubby, Ray, now that her mother is baby-sitting so much and really that must be the meaning of family, three generations together.

Sasa's screams drown out your words. Fucking hell. *Look down at your baby and feel love for her. Look at her little face.* She doesn't look like you at all. Your mother's eyes, his chin. When he tells you it's all OK, you want to stab him in the fucking eye.

They are not talking now because of Sasa. Lisa and Joan. They sleep, their babies; they are asleep right now. They play, they laugh, at regular times. One nap in the day and then right through the night. These incredible mothers. They are so strong. You love them. You love your child. You love your husband and your lovely big house. You are not going to end up like your mother.

It's no good. Sasa has woken up the other two, Tom and Sophie, and now they're all crying. Focus. Think posi-tive. Look at Lisa and Joan picking their kids up. Don't look at the nanny and the swing. The stupid idiot. Can't anyone see? Pushing her kid like that, she's going to kill the baby. Sasa's screams getting louder. Someone has to do something. These idiots you call friends, look at them inanely chatting while the slave-labour nanny tries to kill the kid. Run up and take the baby off the swing.

You are on your feet, but the pain shoots through your pelvis. You must remember to rise slowly. Pelvic floor muscles torn in labour. Emergency Caesarean. Another step. Sasa shrieking. You turn and Joan and Lisa are staring at you. What are you doing? Did they really think you were walking away, just walking away from your own child.

Show what a good mother you are. Take your index finger, bend it and give Sasa the knuckle to suck on. Josh doesn't believe in dummies. Turn your kid into a dummy, he says. She is biting so hard, but it's OK. She's not doing it deliberately. She would never want to hurt her mother.

It happening again, though, isn't it? The pain in your knuckle as she bites, and you're staring at a perfectly happy private play park in the nicest part of Islington. Look up and out. Lisa and Joan and the nanny and the laughing kids on the swings and remind yourself that this is what you wanted. You planned this child. You love her. The pain shoots through your knuckle to your back to your breasts. You could pick her up, put her on the swings, push her hard. Higher. Harder. She could make you do it. Or walk. Leave her here, like your mother left you. You want to cry, but your breasts are all that weep. *Talk to your child. Your gentle voice will reassure her.*

'Please, baby, please, Mummy loves you. Please, for fuck's sake, shut the fuck up!'

*

The 21st of September 1981 was the date of the story in the *Dornoch Times*. WOMAN DIES IN ROAD ACCIDENT. Not 'local woman' because they hated the hippies from Ithaca and weren't going to mention that place in their paper. The accident happened the week before, it could have been longer. It was only a weekly publication and the place was on the border so it wasn't really local news. That was what they said when I called them. They didn't have an online archive but the local library had all the papers going back to the forties. Four hundred miles away. A two-day drive.

Sorry. I get distracted. If that was her last night, if I was eleven, then there was no snow, and her hair would have been shaved off too and no pots in the back. Just books and flyers and pamphlets; CND and Gandhi and passive resistance. She'd smashed all the pots by then.

And if she was singing then it would only have been because she was angry with me and it was better than talking and I didn't want to talk either and she wouldn't answer my questions, like where the hell are we going anyway, you stupid cow. She used to say music had power, like this weapon for good in the world. But her singing that night, it was maybe a way to shut me up. She blamed me for everything.

I'm sure she was singing though. If it wasn't the Beatles then it was maybe one of her old folk songs. *Dream Angus*? My first dad was called Angus. *Dream Angus is here with dreams to sell.* She told me he'd sold out too, when he left the commune in '78. It was Angus she left me with that night.

Just these flashes. I would fall asleep in her car and she would lift me out and carry me, holding my whole weight, through the cold, covering me from the rain and singing to me. Her mouth against my head, little kisses and her breath in my ear. The sound of the saliva on her lips. The feel of her chest filling and emptying against mine. The rhythm of her walk and song. And I would wake up in places, strange and alien, and I'd be scared at first because she wasn't there but then I'd hear her voice as she cooked the breakfast I could smell in some kitchen I couldn't see and I would open my eyes on the face of the man or woman I'd woken next to and knew it wasn't scary but OK because I could still hear her singing.

She wasn't there that morning when I woke at Angus's place in Thorster. Or was it Tulloch? Sorry, I get everything mixed up.

I do remember, though, on that last night – snowflakes or *Dream Angus* or not – really having to fight sleep. The rhythm of the car and her voice. Because it was all so perfect and I knew if I fell asleep she would stop singing and if I could just stay awake there would be more and

12

her face and her voice and the road, they would all come together and stay together and everything would make sense.

Hush me my dearie. Don't sleep by yoursell.

'Yoursell' was an old Scottish word for yourself. But I can't remember the words. Maybe 'and sleep by yoursell'. 'Hush me my dearie.' It doesn't make sense. Why tell a kid to sleep by themselves? I don't know, because I closed my eyes, like she said I should. And those other fragments, possibly imagined. Being carried by her, through the wet and the night. These things maybe from other times. She must have laid me on his bed and said goodbye. I can only pretend to remember any of this. She was going off, alone, to start a new life or to die or to be killed. The government were chasing us. I don't know. I have too many versions of the story.

*

7.02. It's best not to deny it. His energy exhausts you. Admit it, then let it go. Think of the good things he's done today. He's fed Sasa, played with her on the floor, he's bathing her now, chatting away with her. *Every day activities like bathtime can be stimulating learning experiences for your baby.* He is a good father, the best. You can hear her laughter all the way through here in the kitchen. He doesn't coo-chee-coo her; his manuals say it's better for child development to talk to them like they're adults already.

'Clever girl. Go on, take the sponge. You can wash yourself. Have you got it? Go on, hold it, squeeze. That's it. Clever girl.'

He's worried that her hand–eye coordination is not as good as Jobe's or Arturo's. That she is a bit behind. You have told him so many times that girls develop these things later but have an earlier grasp of words, names.

13

Her first word was Dah. The manual says this is not a reflection of the child's preference for one parent over another. D is easier to pronounce than M. That's all. She has no name for you.

Admit it. You could scream when he is with her and you just have to sit and wait. She came from you. Your body. Is you. You need space from her, you demand it of him, she drives you crazy, but still, every second she is away, you feel alone, more alone than before, and you had her so as not to feel alone again. You don't, you can't, resent your husband for being with her. Even though he keeps her up late and she wakes early, grumpy from not having slept enough. Face it, the fact. You are still there, aren't you? In those first hours. Crying at the wonder of her. Holding her to you. Weeping over her tiny fingers clutching yours, her mouth reaching for your breast. You would love to live there for ever, wouldn't you? Born again with your newborn. It pains you, this separation, as she grows and passes from the body of the mother to the language of the father, as the manuals say is necessary. When you are separated every joint and muscle aches. The lungs, the heart, they race. It's hormones, the books say, but it's more, you know this. You had her to stop the panic. You must never tell your daughter of your mother's anxiety attacks. Nights you sit silent watching her breathing in sleep. Worrying that she'll stop if you leave the room. Face it. You are finding it hard to sleep in your bed with him, because you need to feel her at your breast, her fast little breaths, her tiny lungs, breathing in your scent as you smell her head and cling to her, not too tight, just right, trying to pull her back into you again. The way her mouth always finds your nipple and that moment of aching. That gratification and the pain all at once when she is feeding, like you were once told sex should be. You slept better when you were with her every night. Now that you are separated, in bed with your husband, you can't.

7.08. He told you, you should take the weight off your feet, take a nap. He is such a generous, caring man. But you can't. You've told him this. Do what you always do. Keep busy. Sterilise the changing area, get the nappy ready and the wipes. Make a list of things to get from the twenty-four-hour Sainsbury's. Take the Aveda Vacuum Breast Pump and disassemble it. The handle, the bottle, the plastic breast pad, the suction valve. Rinse your old milk from it and place it inside the matching Aveda Prima Steam Sterilising Unit and put in half a cup of water. You are there now in the kitchen. It takes twelve minutes to sterilise the pump. Your baby manual tells you you don't have to do this any more, Sasa's antibodies are strong enough to deal with hostile germs. Josh insists it's better to be safe than sorry. Your mother, it was told, breastfed you for three years. You must stop thinking about her.

Raspberries, he's doing that thing he does. You can hear them. He must have her out of the bath, wrapped in her towel, lifting her up and blowing kisses on her tummy, fart noises. She giggles and screeches every time. Then there's the silence, then he does it again. If he doesn't stop now, she'll laugh herself into hiccups. She'll be too excited to go down tonight. *Typical signs of overstimulation include a high level of activity, a disrupted sleep pattern, irritability and unpredictable levels of concentration.* Fucking idiot. He gets her excited and who has to deal with it? He comes in, out of nowhere, he calls it work, he has no idea what work is, after you've been with her all day, no naps, he gets her excited, he's not the one that gets woken three times a night. His stupid smiling face when he gets her laughing.

You love your husband. He is everything a woman could want. Educated, sensitive, a good listener, principal

15

breadwinner, but respects and encourages your career. He does all the cooking. He designed the kitchen and bought all the Le Creuset pots. He massages your shoulders and pelvis in bed at night with lavender-scented Body Shop oil. You chose him, did your research. *Loving the New Man. Children for Beginners.* You read from the manuals together. *The Working Family, Planning Life Together.* Remind yourself that you are making progress. You are *Partners in Progress* like the new advert at work says. Don't think about work. You must stop checking your emails. You must reply soon and tell them you need a little more time. You did maternity leave, then sickness leave, you are running out of leaves.

7.28. Nine minutes to go till the sterilising steamer is finished. You swear it was nine minutes last time you looked. Keep busy. There's his copy of the *Guardian* on the kitchen table but you know it will only upset you. Afghanistan and your mother and the peace camp at Faslane. The caffeine in a cup of tea might keep you up. You can't have a glass of wine because it passes into her milk. His copy of *The Best Start in Life* is on the table with his paperwork. You could reread the chapter on Sleep Therapy again, but you know it by heart. You're going to try it again tonight, together. Attempt number ten, not picking her up when she wakes, but sitting with her through her screams till she falls asleep. *The New Home Doctor* is on the table too. Don't pick it up. You know what happens when you do.

It started with colic, months ago. You read that it was a natural non-life-threatening condition that would pass, and kept on going, turning the pages in bed, so quietly, so as not to wake him. You knew it was wrong but couldn't help yourself. Past C to D to Dementia to Depression to Endocrinal Spasmosis to Fibroids to Gastroenteritis to Hepatitis B, through J, K, L, M, N, O to Post-Natal Depression.

16

He says it can't be. That it would have happened just after Sasa was born. Unless it's some hormone change that's come about since you started reducing her feeds. 'We,' he says. You haven't got to 'W' yet. 'Double you.' Last week, in secret, you went from P to S. Sleep Deprivation.

After 72 hours of broken sleep, sleeping less than three hours at any one time, you may lose your sense of time and space. Perception starts to fail and things may seem out of sync. Sleep deprivation has also been used in reconditioning, also known as neural reprogramming or brainwashing.

Suicidal Thoughts was on the next page. You told yourself you wouldn't read it. Your mother did not commit suicide.

Page 237. *In an effort to suppress evaluative awareness and shut down her emotions, the suicide narrows her mental focus. The resulting state is a kind of numbness characterised by rigid and concrete thinking, focus on the here and now. It is clear that many victims have no concrete plan for killing themselves. Many road accidents may in fact be suicidal acts on impulse.*

You will not read it again tonight as he sleeps. You will not think about her postcard, hidden in the glove compartment of the car, that proves it's all a lie. The postmark date, two weeks after they told you she was dead. The postcard you found at Grandpa's house.

Out of the corner of your eye, through the kitchen doorway, his big dark form is carrying her tiny white towel body into the bedroom. The giggling is still going on. Focus. Seven minutes till the steamer is done. Two minutes for it to cool down, one to reassemble the pump then fifteen to express your milk. Five to decant it into the vacuum-sealed plastic sachets that go inside the sterilised bottles. Then it will be 7.35. Sasa's story time.

Six minutes. Watching the steam leak out from the

steamer. Pick up *Toddler Taming*. Get with the plan. Good, yes. Page 182. *Some babies like a steady background noise such as a washing machine. If all else fails, most babies will drop off to sleep in the car.* If all else fails. She'll wake at two then at four and she'll be too angry to go back to sleep. Tonight will be the same. You will have to do what you always have to. Wrap her up warm, put her in the carrycot, carry her to the Subaru and drive her round the block. Round and round till she stops screaming then falls asleep. Then round two more times, just to make sure, then carry her back to her cot. Little Sasa. Little Ailsa. Named after an island in Scotland because he has this romantic thing about your Scottishness. Your years in Ithaca you've simplified to some witty dismissive anecdotes. You never told him that it still exists, that its name throws you into panic, that the postcard tells you she is still alive.

Four minutes. What year is this? Two thousand and eight, nine.

It's happening again. 'Ten Green Bottles' he's singing to her. *And if one green bottle should accidentally fall.* You are staring at the steamer, the Alessi bottle opener, the Sabatier knives, the Guzzini cutlery. It's as if the kitchen is singing. Like the picture from one channel and the sound from another. He does crash noises when a bottle falls. Stare at his half-empty Chardonnay bottle on top of the fridge and try to stop thinking about smashing it. You haven't had a glass of wine in over a year. He doesn't know about your drinking and how you gave it up for him. About hash and speed and LSD. N is for neurosis. *Neurotics try to build utopias based on denial – one thing goes wrong then they regress and destroy all they have built.* You should have told him more. *Communicate with your partner about your past and your fears.* It's too late now.

'Rowan, the steamer!'

18

Who is this voice who talks to you all the time? This woman who calls you Rowan? Emma is your name now.

Thirty, forty seconds then the steamer clicks off. Take off the lid, don't scald your fingers, then take the pieces out. The suction cup is at the front, it's made of a soft plastic that simulates the touch of a baby's mouth and has nodules that stimulate the breast when you depress the vacuum pump lever.

You have assembled it and placed it on your breast and depressed the suction handle. But it's not working. So sore. Breasts aching, full to bursting, but nothing coming out. Her gums have damaged your nipples. You worry that they might bleed again. You don't want to see blood in the milk, or pus. *The sound of your baby crying or the sight of her face may help in starting the lactating process. Focus on her face.* Go over to the big bookshelf by his PC and take Sasa's photo down. Sit with it in front of you. Focus on her pretty face, her little blonde curls, so like his, and the dark eyes that run in the family on your mother's side. Start pumping. Yes, that's right.

Something seems to snap, burst, a sharp pain, then the milk shoots out, thin at first, yellowish, then getting thicker. Never white like cow's milk. More like sperm. It took so long to conceive her. Nine months and so many false starts. You bought a manual for that too. Idiot self-help addict. The self must be annihilated, your mother said.

Count the pumps. Focus away the pain. Eight, nine, ten. His voice singing from next door. Now it's one man went to mow. 7.41. Does he really think he can teach her how to count? For fuck's sake. Seventeen, eighteen, nineteen. Went to mow a meadow. Two men, one man and his dog.

He doesn't know how it feels, pumping yourself into a plastic container. Twenty-two, twenty-three, twenty-four. It's happening again. Your milk spraying and three men, two men, one man and his dog. The sight of your child's face in a photograph. Spot, a bottle of pop, an old tin can for a frying pan. Words and pictures mixing up. Sasa's farm animals on the floor, pigs in pink, cows in brown. We have become as plastic as the products we consume, your mother said. Went to mow a meadow.

'She's down.'

You look up and he's smiling at you in the kitchen doorway. Very proud of himself. His pinstripe shirt wet where she's splashed him in the bath or maybe it's sick. He's so tall, so good-looking, so much younger than you. He could have been a model, he looks like Clark Kent or a Calvin Klein advert.

'Went out like a light,' he says.

'Wow,' you say. 'How d'you do it, Superdad?'

But he really is. He has a way with her. He takes a seat beside you and watches you expressing, smiling to himself. *Tell your partner when you are uncomfortable. He must take time to understand the respectful distance from the maternal body. Communicate your need for private space.* But still, it's not that he's staring. You would feel as bad if you were doing it alone in a blackened room. You have not really touched, not in that way, since the first trimester. *Your focus may move to your baby and away from your partner. Don't worry, this will pass.*

He's smiling at you, grinning. He marvels at your breasts, they are amazing to him. He tells you how he loves them, now they're so much bigger. But every time he even touches them they start weeping. Last week he kissed your nipples and they sprayed his face and then he kissed you and you tasted your milk on his mouth. It made you gag. He said it tasted sweet. You have been postponing weaning Sasa so you don't have to touch him.

'Tea? Decaf?' he asks.

You shake your head. You want him out of the room. 'No, OK, yeah, camomile.' That way at least he'll be through

20

the alcove and you can turn your back on him. Squeeze harder, faster, to get it done. Count the pumps – thirty-five, thirty-six, thirty-seven. You are the same age now that your mother was when she died.

Only 200 mg. His back is to you now in the kitchen. It's 7.59. By the time you've eaten and had a bath and he's given you your shoulder massage it will be nine.

'Hey, when you thinking about going back to work?' he calls through. You can't tell him that you suspect your periods of sickness were not hormones but nausea over the job. Writing promo copy for corporations that suck the life from the earth. You can't go back. You don't want to be stuck at home being a mother. You don't want to have sex again ever. You don't know what you want. To just close your eyes and sleep. 'A couple of weeks, then we'll see,' you say. Just listen to you. A week, a day, is too far to see ahead. He talks always in the future tense. About when Sasa's at school, and what school, and catchment areas. And when she's at university and up and gone and then we will have 'our special time'.

Twenty more pumps to go. Fifty-three, fifty-four, fifty-five. He calls through, 'If she wakes tonight I'll take care of it, OK?' Look at him so happy in his designer kitchen. His inane textbook platitudes, his deodorised smell, his pinstriped shirts with baby sick. Everything your mother would have despised.

You love him so much. Sixty-three, sixty-four. Make her go away. Sixty-five, sixty-six, sixty-seven.

*

'It's me, Angus,' he said, the man I woke beside. But his face wasn't what I thought my first dad's should be. Bearded, sweaty. Jenna had gone away for a couple of days, he said, and I could stay as long as I liked and we'd have the coolest time, then she'd pick me up, and did I like KitKats and did I like Jimi? I looked out the window and it looked like nowhere. Bricks facing the window. He made me camomile tea with honey and put on some Hendrix. His whole place was full of crap, posters and flyers and stinking old clothes lying on the ground. His cat pissed everywhere and he smoked weed and no one else ever came round. I really tried to put his face into the old photographs but he didn't look like my dad. I couldn't sleep on the crummy sofa he'd made up for me. He'd get high and walk around with nothing on. He expected me to do the same but I had sore growing breasts and I had to hide them from him. He showed me photographs of him with my mum in the old field at Ithaca with all the others, when I was just a bump in my mummy's tummy. Seven hippies in mud, by a fence, all smiling, my mother holding her gut. He tried to sing me to sleep but he didn't know the words to *Dream Angus*. I couldn't sleep. Not for days. I kept asking him when she was coming back and he'd tell me to chill, it was cool, we were all family. Then one morning the doorbell went and I ran to it but it was some other face at the door. She had a clipboard and bent down to speak to me and reached out to shake my hand and told me her name was Julie. He wasn't there when I turned to look for him. She stank of cigarettes and chips and her hand was damp and weak, like she was sick or scared. She said we were going to be friends now and if I could get in the car with her she'd let me meet all her other friends that worked in something called Social Services.

*

Her screams wake you and you are staring at the back of his head. The clock says it's 12.02. You haven't slept more than two hours. He has work in the morning. You must quieten her so she will not wake him. Pull the sheets off, gently. Tiptoe through.

Little Sasa, standing upright in the cot, trying to escape, her foot caught in the bars. Poor baby, you have to free her. She reaches for you, face wet with tears, but you are not to hold her. Mmm sounds, muh, muh, mah.

'Please, baby, please.'

Her little fists and feet kicking, she's going to hurt herself.

'Sleep, baby, sleep.'

It's starting. The textbook tantrum. She's getting closer and closer to the point of hyperventilation. You want to pick her up, rock her to sleep, to have her face close to yours and stare into her eyes and scream so loud she'll be startled and stare back at you with her big hurt eyes that are not yours. The Top Ten Tips. Run through the Top Tips for Tots.

1. *Make a big effort to keep control of your temper. Don't feel guilty.* If you could just get away for a few days. Just somewhere by yourself and sleep.

2. *Get help. If possible, let another person spend time with your crying baby. This could be your partner, a friend or a relative. You'll be able to cope more after you've had a break.* Maybe Charlie, go and see Charlie. She'd understand. Sleep for a few days at Charlie's.

3. *Under no circumstances indulge yourself by picking her up. If you do then she will learn that she can get attention on demand by crying and you will have aggravated the problem.* Or some hotel, somewhere, anywhere. No friends around, no chat, mobiles. Sleep all day and all night, then come back.

A noise. You turn. He's there behind you, rubbing his eyes. Your copy of *Toddler Taming* in his hand. He kisses your forehead.

'Mmm, s'OK, babe, get some shut-eye,' he says.

'OK, OK, I'll go back . . . to . . .'

'Hello, baby Sasa, you look very sleepy.' She is quietened as he talks to her. 'You're going to be a good girl tonight, aren't you, Sas, and go to sleepyland, so that Mummy and Daddy can sleep too?'

She's whimpering now, not yelling. Dahh . . . dahh. You are still stuck there in the doorway. How can he do this? One word from him and she calms. This bare-chested, worked-out man with your instruction manual in his hand, whispering secret intimacies to her. Turn. Go to bed.

You are standing before the fridge staring at your many bottles of expressed milk. How did you get here? Why this shivering? Shut the fridge door. Quiet now. Her whimpering has stopped. There's no need to panic. Why the hell are you running back through the corridor?

Close your eyes. You didn't see what you just saw. He's picked her up. Cradling her in his arms, cooing at her, smiling up at you.

'Jesus, Josh, what the fuck are you doing?'

It's like he's been slapped. Calm down. Don't shout at him, it will only upset her more.

'You're not supposed to. You promised. Now we'll have to start all over again.'

'Oh, c'mon, I mean, just look at her sad little face . . .'

'You promised and now you've gone and . . . for fuck's sake!'

'Shh, you'll make her more upset.'

'Don't quote the fucking book at me.'

Don't look at them. It's not true. He's not cuddling her like he's protecting her from you.

'I just can't . . . I'm sorry . . . losing it . . . I'm sorry.'

He's looking at you the way Lisa and Joan do. Sasa too. With pity.

'S'OK, babe, go back to bed, I'll sleep on the sofa bed.'

24

His voice so gentle, so calm. 'Go and catch up on kip, eh? I'll take care of her tonight.'

Nod your head, don't weep. He's right. You've been bad again. Go back to your bed that you no longer share. Lie down. Close your eyes. But how can you sleep? There are things to do. More lists. Emailing work. Telling them you'll be back the week after. Some more cleaning. You'll be up for hours. You might as well get dressed.

*

She left me in the first week of September and I remember the Social Services woman apologising for not getting to me sooner because of the weekend. So that must have been the weekend of the second week. The 12th, so my mother must have left me sometime between the 8th and the 10th. The article, dated the 21st said that she'd probably died the week before.

But then there was the postcard.

It was in this box. My nana, my mother's mother, died not so long ago, held out till she was almost ninety. You know, getting the last word and all that. There was the usual clearing out the house and there were these bits and pieces from my mum in an old crisp box in the attic. I must admit, I'd long since got over dreading just such a find. But it took me almost a month to even bring myself to look through that box.

It wasn't much, some old records and books, some lists and things, sketch pads full of quotations and scribbles. Hippie shit basically. But then it fell out of this book – *Ariel* by Sylvia Plath – this postcard with a picture of Dounreay Nuclear Power Station on the front. It made sense. It was postmarked from Caithness, which is where the power station was and the commune.

It was addressed to Nana and Papa. I did my research after that. Thought it was some kind of suicide note. And

25

what I know now is that suicide notes are not what you'd expect. You think they'd be all romantic – I can't take it any more, and all that – but the books say they're actually, usually, pretty banal, full of instructions on how to tell those left what to do and I'm sorry about the electricity bill and don't forget to feed the cat. Things like that. But the card was pretty upbeat.

> Mom and Pop – We're fine. Rowan is with her dad. Have to go away for a while. Please send some money. Usual amount. Usual account. Sorry again.
> Love Jenna xx

Suicides always say sorry but this didn't seem like sorry for everything, more just like sorry for the inconvenience. The words 'usual' and 'again'. And suicides don't ask for money. After the excitement wore off it upset me. Because it meant what they said had been true. Just this tragic road accident. And that gutted me for months. But then the postmark. I hadn't even looked at it at first. The 29th of September 1981. It was mailed two, almost three weeks after her supposed, her so-called accident.

And there were other things too. The fact that Papa never went to her funeral, and I could find no record of such an event.

And then there was this self-help guide for carers of children who'd been abandoned, which I came across among their things. This chapter 'The Lesser Lie'. About how – and there was a long tradition of this, especially in romantic literature and among the parents of mothers who abandoned their kids, since they'd been brought up with these old books and these old values, basically, books like *East Lynne* and *Anna Karenina* – how the grandparents would tell the child in their care that the mother was dead, because they thought that was the lesser lie. You know, to protect the child. And how because of their values, the shame of it all, their daughter had become dead to them anyway, after doing this inhuman thing. How they even went to great lengths, like changing phone numbers, like moving house, like Karenin did, to protect the child from any possible encounter with the mother because mothers often did that, tried to come back. Like Anna did.

That was when I knew, because they did move house with me, and Papa always took the phone off the hook at night and Nana did have a copy of *Anna Karenina* and I once saw her cry when the movie came on TV, then Papa shut it off and said it was well past time for bed, young lady.

*

A weight, an adult weight, on the edge of your bed, a woman, somehow sensed, waking you.

Turn on the light. Laugh at how silly the thought was. The clock says 2.15. You have slept for over an hour. See, no one here. You're only shivering because the heating goes off in the middle of the night. It's OK. You must have dozed off with your clothes still on. Why isn't he in bed beside you?

Put on your trainers, support your lower back as you bend over. Sit there on the edge of the bed. Take a moment. The white walls offset by the beige curtains. Everything is fine. This is your white room. No sound in the house. Focus on your breathing and you will stop shivering. No sounds of crying. Walk the corridor. It's fine, see. He's asleep on the sofa bed. Her room, see, she's fast asleep. Watch Sasa sleeping. See, everything is in its place. All closed eyes, all sleeping. Go back to bed.

But you are clumsy as you turn, you stagger and bump into her door. The noise wakes her and then it starts again. The crying.

27

'Dah, Dah.'

Shut up, shut up, shut the fuck up. You didn't think that.

'Shh, baby, shh.'

You don't want him to wake. To go through the whole process again. You are not going to pick her up and shake her.

Your breasts are weeping. Hold her. Listen to your body. You have maternal feelings. There's more pain in watching her cry. You love her so much. Yes, pick her up. The screams stop, slowly. Hiccupping now, sobbing.

'Shh, Sasa, Mummy loves you.'

Her breathing calms in your arms. Shh, tell her shh. Feel how perfect she is. Little perfect person, no past, all is future. Wait till her eyes close then sing to her, rock her backwards and forwards.

The words come from nowhere. The song.

*Dreams to sell, fine dreams to sell, Angus is here wi'
dreams to sell.* Again and again. Because you only know the chorus and have lost the rest. She's closing her sleepy eyes. Rock her backwards and forwards. *Dreams to sell.* It's fine, going to be fine. You love her so much. Sweet baby Sasa. Go to sleep now. Focus away the back pain and slowly lower her into her cot. Don't take down the safety side because the latch will make a noise and any sound can wake her. It's OK. Bend over taking her whole weight. Bearable. Lower her head down onto the mattress, gently. Slowly move your fingers from under her. Shh, there, shh, shh. Step back on tippy-toes. So quiet. Shh. She's in sleepy-land. Good. Look at her face. As unspoiled as a blank page. None of your mother's genes. *Dream Angus is here with dreams to sell.* Shh. Turn and tiptoe out of the room. Not a sound.

One foot out of the door and she rolls over and it starts. A whimper. A yell. A scream ripping through your scars.

*Some babies like the sound of a washing machine. The
hum of the motor and the gentle movement. If all else fails
try the car.*

She struggles against the safety straps as you strap her
into the carrycot. Wriggling, screaming. You carry her
through to the kitchen and pick up the car keys without
waking Josh. You carry her to the door and open it as quiet
as quiet can be, locking it behind you. Round the block
eight or nine times in the car will do. Your eyes heavy with
her weight. Strap the carrycot into the passenger's seat beside
you. She is not supposed to go in the front seat until she
is eighteen months but you won't be able to bear the sound
of her screaming behind you. You can watch her from the
front. Keys, ignition, the engine silencing her screams for a
second. Shh, baby, shh.

You turn the second corner and a taxi is blocking the
road, double-parked, hazard lights on. Screaming. Reverse
and drive further out, towards the petrol station, the twenty-
four-hour Sainsbury's. The faster way is the expressway.
You can get the groceries tonight. Kill two birds with one
stone.

Screaming.

*If you're suffering from sleep deprivation you should
seek immediate medical help. You should not attempt to
operate machinery or drive.*

The road is deserted. Lights lighting nothing. You will
be fine, the passing lights are not lulling you to sleep. Think
of something, anything. Page 317. Sleep Deprivation.
Junction 12 forty yards. The filter lane. The shopping mall
to your right. She doesn't love you, never did.

'Shh, baby, shh.'

The rhythm of the road. The change in the hum as
the texture changes beneath the wheels. You are staring
at the junction. You should be signalling. Mirror, signal,
manoeuvre.

29

Spends up to a fifth of her waking time staring and observing. Fifty miles an hour. A sign. *Should not attempt to operate machinery or drive a vehicle.* Keep a safe distance. You've missed the turn-off. Junction 13 then. The roundabout, then double back. Check her beside you. She's struggling with the seat belt. Making a gnuh-gnuh, sound. Little muscles. Little anger staring at you. *Loses her temper easily.* The roundabout ahead. Central lane. Go down to fourth, to third. No cars around. *Stares at others her own age but does not interact with them.*

No point stopping at Sainsbury's if she's still crying. Left-hand lane, straight on. Next roundabout, Junction 14, then double back. The speeding lights in a rhythm.

Hush me my dearie. Her voice pushing you to accelerate faster. The signs telling you to slow down. Fifty-five, sixty. Your mother would be sixty now. *Many road accidents are believed to be suicides.* Roadworks ahead. Decrease your speed. Sasa screaming louder. The lanes merging. *A mother can recognise her child's cries from a hundred yards.* You're indicating and go to turn. But an immense juggernaut is beside you. Page 357. You move past Sleep Deprivation through to Snoring to Stretch Marks to Suicidal Tendencies. You and her together in the car. 1981. He won't let you in. You must be in his blind spot. Screaming. Your lane is going to end, orange cones heading fast at you. He must let you merge. The postcard in the glove compartment. Sixty feet, till the end. Can't he see you? Accelerate past him. Fifty feet. Postmarked the 29th. *Dreams to sell, fine dreams to sell.* Your lane ends in forty, thirty. The 29th of September. Sasa screaming. You're walled in by metal. *Angus is here with dreams to sell.* Speeding sixty, seventy. You won't make it past him in time. Snowflakes in the windscreen. Twenty feet, ten. *Hush me my dearie.*

Stop.

Feet hit brakes, eyes flash open.

30

You come to rest on the hard shoulder. The mass of the juggernaut's wind, throwing you. Shuddering, shivering. Put the hazards on. Look down at her so quiet beside you. Her quiet face now lit by red flashing on off, on off. 'Mmmm,' she says, 'muh muh.'

'Mum,' you say. 'Mummy.'

Somehow you make it home, unlock the front door and carry her in. You lay her gently beside him on the sofa bed. She snuggles up into his arms without waking him.

You pick up your keys from where you set them down and go to the door. Tiptoe quietly. You came so close. *In times of exhaustion, a female friend can be your closest ally.* You once had a friend, the only person you told. Charlie. Get back in the car and drive to her. Josh will understand. Charlie will let you sleep. One night you'll be away, that's all.

the road

SHE DROVE BACK that night to Angus's to find that her daughter had been placed in care. She called her parents and found that they'd taken her in. But after the long drive south, outside the door to her old home, standing in the private garden in St John's Wood, she could not find the strength to knock.

She would pick her time and place. She got any job she could, the first that came up. Office temping in Hackney and a one-bedroom in Dalston. She would have liked to have lived closer so she could watch her daughter every day, but couldn't afford the rent. After three months she got herself a night job, cleaning offices in Knightswood, and spent her days working out her daughter's daily movements. She waited across the road from the big private school that her parents had first sent her to, Compton Hall, and watched her daughter being dropped off and picked up by her grand-parents. From a discreet distance she watched her playing hockey in the park and smoking in the playground. She followed her as she went shopping with her new friends, and climbed onto buses and trains, into cars and taxis – waiting for the opportunity she needed to put her plan into action.

She would walk up to her when she was alone, explain quietly, and if that didn't work, grab her, force her into the car, drive her north.

She didn't want to be recognised, not until her plan was complete. She dyed her hair blonde and wore sunglasses. She was constantly tired from the night work and started to lose confidence. And her daughter was changing too,

35

becoming exactly the kind of obnoxious private schoolgirl she herself had once been. A year went by, then two, and she watched day by day as her daughter drifted away. After three years she had a real day job and had cut back to spying once a week. Another year and it was every fortnight. Her daughter had changed so much, her skirt was too short and she worried about the company she was keeping. Her daughter had become a punk, a Rastafarian, then a goth. She bought the records to try to understand. She told herself that her daughter's anger was merely a fashionable thing and no reflection on what had happened. She worried that her daughter would drop out like she had.

But still, she saw the way her daughter was with others and it brought something like a smile. Always in the middle of it, always they came to hear what she had to say and laughed because she had what looked like irreverence. Years passed and she herself had never graduated but she hid herself at the back of the university hall and watched as her daughter climbed to the podium and accepted her BA Hons with no gown but with fishnets and black lipstick and blew the sad old professors a kiss and waved at the crowd. There was a moment, then, when her daughter looked straight into her, through a hundred people. And she ran.

She took it as a sign. A decade more, almost two, and she had made friends with friends of friends of her daughter's friends but kept her distance. She heard her daughter was married and about to have a baby. She spied on the husband, she thought him unsuitable and worried that he couldn't possibly understand how complicated her daughter was, that maybe her daughter had been cynical in her choice. He was a dull man, daily dreary nice. She worried that her daughter hadn't told him the truth about her past, and that this was her fault. She taught herself to stop worrying. She sent a baby present with no card or name but with an X for a kiss.

Then, before the child was even weaned, she heard that her daughter had left suddenly, one night, as she herself had done. Everyone was talking about it, and she felt guilty because she knew. She knew instinctively where her daughter had gone. North, to find her. The absurdity of it. She had to follow her daughter as her daughter searched for her. She would find her beneath the tree she planted on the day of her birth, the one that she had named her after. The rowan tree in the place called Ithaca.

This is just a story, a comfort, a lie. There are other versions, memorised, re-ordered then abandoned. The details change over time. The endings. They always begin with the same words: she drove.

*

You have left the North Circular. Escaped the circle. Lights overhead, in a straight line. You pray for a junction, a bridge, something other than these miles and miles of spotlit sameness that lull you to sleep. Concentrate. Gears, clutch, brake, fifth to fourth, three hundred yards to roundabout, down to third.

Sasa is safe now with him. She is not safe with you. You always knew this. Keep on.

Lights glaring in the rear-view. Some man wanting to overtake, forcing you into the slow lane. Watch him passing. 4 x 4. Yuppie fuck. You must stay awake. It is late, too late, after three. Your husband will wake when Sasa does and find you gone. You must send a message to his mobile. *Had to do this, don't worry, back tomorrow. Sorry, love you.* Words will be found.

This next breath you take is your own, feel it, own it, call it you. Too long you have put this off. Your mother lied so you could live, now you must find her so that you in turn can be a mother. The lesser lie, yes, everything is connecting again. Charlie loved your mother, Charlie will help you find your mother.

*

Two weeks after she drove away, I was stuck on a train with Papa and taken back to their nice big mansion and their finishing school for refined ladies. Nana said my mum had gone there too, so I was their second chance at finishing. Compton Hall had a speech-making society, a choir and hockey club, but I knew where I had to go, my three weeks in social care had taught me more than any school. Strike at the heart of the State, Pete once said.

The girls' toilets. I'd heard the stories, the new girls always got bullied, heads down the toilet. Nothing compared to school at Wyster. Easy meat, really. I spent a couple of days in there smoking till the seniors came round. Waiting for them. Knowing what had to be done. This girl called Charlotte had this racket going with the first years, pocketing their pocket money. Big bully, tight-lipped, nasty, pucker-pucker little fucker. A racket – jolly hockey sticks and tennis – a tennis racket.

'We are all equal,' my mum once said and that made me so angry. Brewing over all the old lies, waiting for the third-formers, smoking one fag after another. We are sisters. Respect the sisterhood.

'Which one of you is Charlotte?' I asked, when they tried to grab me, and that got them, made them pause, then I reached forward to shake her hand and twisted it up her back. She was lucky I missed the eyeball, they said. The cigarette hit her eyelid. When she got back from hospital she had an eyepatch and I met her in the toilets and we didn't speak but I gave her a fag and then she put out her hand and her posh voice made me laugh. She said, 'Charlie – Charlotte is so square, don't you think?' And it was a question and when someone asks you a question about themselves you have power. From then on, me and Charlie were the sisterhood. We were too scared to use the knife I had in my back pocket so we stubbed fags out on our palms, not blood brothers, but blisters, blister sisters. 'What's your name?' she said and I had to think. There was a girl, they broke her tooth, the seniors. Head down the toilet. A little weedy thing two classes above me. Emma was her name. It made more sense than my real one. So I told Charlie that I wanted to change, and she took my hand, 'Nice to meet you . . . Emma.'

The blister on hers and mine weeping into each other, then I could see the pain on her face and feel it in my hand and I knew. And that eye, that one eye, the other covered in the patch.

She never grassed on me. They asked Nana and Papa about the fag and the name change but I opened the letters before they got them and wrote back, faking their signatures. They even changed it on the school register. Idiots. It was that easy, our little private joke. From then on I was Emma and Charlie was the only person that knew my real name.

*

You must apologise when you see her. You and your 4 x 4 and your plans for 2.5 kids. Charlie stood there at your wedding reception, all alone in that ill-fitting hired dress, hiding her tattoos and piercings, and you didn't make time to speak to her. You only invited her because your husband asked why your friends' list was non-existent. You never thought she would actually turn up. Throughout, you prayed she wouldn't get drunk and open her mouth. That horrible thing you said to her, just to shut her up – 'So, when are you planning on having a family?'

Charlie loved your mum, she asked you again and again to tell her everything. And you did and when you ran out you made stuff up. And Charlie was so stoned she couldn't remember. You told her – she drove away and killed herself – she left and joined the Sandinistas – she slashed her throat in the desert in Morocco. It was so cool for Charlie with her Putney parents and her trust fund. She became a terrorist – she was a friend of Patty Hearst – she blew herself up with a home-made bomb. This was when it started, when you lost it, in the Charlie years, living off your grandparents, stealing their booze, fuelling the cult of your mother. And so you told her – she went macrobiotic in Iceland and died of malnutrition – she bought a ticket to New York and hung out in Warhol's factory and did backing vocals for the Ramones – she had a black lover who was a pimp – she moved to Berlin and joined the Red Army Faction – she was the lover of Joan Baez – she moved to California and started a free love commune with Timothy Leary and was arrested for trying to put LSD into the water system – she fucked Dylan and Crosby, Stills and Nash, all three – she read Sylvia Plath and did the first ever recorded literary copycat suicide. This was where you lost it. That look on Charlie's face that always wanted more. Turning your mother into story after story.

But then, on your sixteenth birthday, there were questions about your future and so the past started to haunt again. That week gap between her leaving and her so-called death. The stories no longer helped. Every new one contradicted the last and the questions you woke to every day split you in two – which was worse? – her abandonment or her death? The two questions took you in opposite directions. One towards self-pity, the other towards grief. Neither could fill the hole. Everything is connected, your mother once told you. So you put the two questions together, made one the consequence of the other and came up with the solution: suicide. She abandoned you and couldn't face herself after that. Five years and

40

a hundred stories later and you worked this out. One story about her death to let you live. It was clear-cut. A beginning, middle and end. A moral to it. Your reason to wake, eat, study. At once an alibi and a motivating force. No ambiguity. No doubts. Your sad music. You studied suicides. You read your mother's beloved Plath and discovered that Hughes's second wife, Assia Weevil, took their child with her when she killed herself. You became obsessed with details. On the 23rd of February 1965, Plath put her children to bed, called a neighbour to say come round early next morning. She put two little pots of milk by their beds for her children's breakfast. She went into the kitchen, soaked some tea towels, rolled them up and stuffed them under the door and taped the doors so the gas wouldn't leak through. Weevil crushed forty sleeping tablets and put them into some hot chocolate. Her daughter always had hot chocolate before bed. They drank the hot chocolate together and Assia lay down beside her.

Your ability to study detail did not go unnoticed in school. It was all that interested you, it saved you from being expelled. You spotted an important omission in the national curriculum about Plath. You told the class exactly how it was she died. You quoted 'Lady Lazarus' at them off the top of your head.

And how Charlie was obsessed with you. Developing theories about suicide. You had evidence to back it up. All your mother's heroes died or killed themselves. Plath, Hendrix, Jim Morrison, Malcolm X, Tim Buckley, John Lennon, Nick Drake, Brian Jones, JFK, Janis Joplin. You theorised it as a symptom of history. Idealism leads to death. You and Charlie developed a cult of hippie-hating. Artists, poets, idealists, all the butt of your teenage scorn. Even the music you listened to confirmed this. In those later years at uni it was grunge and Nirvana. Cobain and Courtney Love both had hippie parents. The hatred in their lyrics, 'Rape Me', 'Doll Parts'. The two of you memorised all the songs.

41

People feared you when you were together, the angry girls giving the finger, waiting for that provocation, that sexist comment, that accusation that you were dykes so you could throw drink in their faces, and run and hide and kiss.

But then, in the last year of your Masters, the suicide of Cobain brought your mother back again in waking thoughts. You remembered that you'd made yourself forget and didn't know for sure. Unlike Plath, unlike Joplin, there were no facts, not even an exact date for her death. You could not face your final thesis, you delayed for a year, you told everyone you were sick. When you finally graduated, after filling two hundred pages with other people's words, you could find nothing to connect who you were supposed to be with anything like a future. You moved from temp job to temp job from lover to lover and came to realise that repetition does not make up for the lack. That it is hard to live without a narrative, to wake every day to only questions and no guide. You told yourself again and again the story. But the truth was – you were only here because she didn't love you enough to take you with her. She made you hate the days between the 8th and the 21st of September. She made you purge every bit of her from yourself. She made you fear the face that looked back at you sometimes; when hungover, you would catch yourself in the mirror and glimpse her beneath the layers of make-up. You stopped eating and started cutting yourself.

The stories rushed at you again. Where did she go that night? She went to Ithaca, who did she see, she saw Eva, she saw Pete. Where was she hiding now? The stories multiplied and they gave you hope. But hope, you found, was harder to live with. Charlie fed the stories but you had to move on. Leave Charlie behind. Get a job. Get a life.

But Charlie was right. The postcard is there in the glove compartment. You'll show it to her and you'll sit together and cry and laugh and drown the silence of years apart with wine and Nirvana and Hole. Be so fucking good to hear them again. Keep on going. Junction 12. Read the signs. The road so straight and empty. Hard not to let your mind wander. Focus.

Luton. Leighton Buzzard. Toddington. Junction 13 north to Milton Keynes. Lights and road. Road lights. You have to stay awake. That's it. Hold the wheel straight. Fifty minutes and there will be Cobain and Charlie. Turn on the radio, anything to stop this talking to yourself. 'Shout going out to the dezzic posse.' 'Gimme dat booty.' Change the stations. One finger. Keep your eye on the road. Talk, so much talk. 'Of mass destruction, a spokensman said.' 'Farside crew. Spinning at Apocalyse Friday night.' 'Comeback album later in the year.' 'Shake ya thang, babay, shake it.' 'Me and ma bitches.' A shake through the car. The things on the side. Sleeping policemen, catseyes, speed control bumps. You were swerving off. Open your eyes, steer back in, hold it straight on the straight road, leave it on talk radio, you can shout back at it and it will keep you awake. The straight roads have the most fatalities because people get bored and tired more easily. Live for a reason, your mother said – die for a cause. Turn off the radio.

The M1. Only twenty minutes till you see Charlie. You hope she still has the same address. She will. She was going nowhere last time you saw her. Junction 13. Three more miles to Milton Keynes. You are wide awake now. Lucid. You are the car. The air conditioning the same temperature as your breath, the tension in your foot like the pressure in the pedal pushing back. The power steering delicate to every touch. Hands, eyes, arms, feet, gears. Euphoria of speed. Floating past the other cars. Flying free in the fast lane.

*

She drove that night after she dropped you at Angus's and skidded off the road. She was so lucky, she told herself again and again in that hour while she waited shivering by the roadside, thumb in the air, to have jumped clear just before it slid into the gully. An HGV took her to Inverness and she spent a night trembling as the adrenalin wore off, telling herself it was a wake-up call and so she must retrace. From there she hitched back to London to seek out the people she'd been involved with in the squatting scene. She went round the old places, the anarchist bookshops, the dive bars, the vegetarian cafes, asking for them by name. She was running out of money, and slept in cheap hostels. She was about to give up when she was approached by one of them. He'd heard she was asking around. She was not to say their names in public. She understood. In the years she'd been in the commune they'd moved on, they explained, become increasingly politicised, become affiliated with the Angry Brigade, involved with the bombing at the home of the Minister for Housing in '71. They were convinced the Secret Services were hunting them down. They had learned how to create fake identities. They'd splintered into smaller groups. Had gone undercover working in low-profile day jobs in administration and the private sector while they made plans for further actions. She did like they did and got a quiet job where no one would find her, cash in hand. She grew her hair back into a less threatening style. She bought second-hand clothes that had originally come from Marks & Spencer. The conflict, they said, had spread, become multinational. They had to target the Americans. Her knowledge of Scotland was useful, they said. There were three US nuclear bases in remote parts of the highlands. They had access to explosives. She wanted to become involved but hesitated when they asked her. She spent a week listening to her old tapes. Thinking it through. There was this song she listened to again and again. *Woodstock* by Joni Mitchell, the words over and over said we must return to the garden. She thought about her garden, the plants dying, the jets flying over, how it was a crime to bring a child into a world that you yourself despised.

She signed up for an action, a bomb to be planted by a perimeter fence, she was to be the driver. After, they would have a new identity for her and she would not be able to contact anyone she had known before.

*

But her face when she sees you, peering round the chained gap in the door, clutching her tattered dressing gown round her neck, shivering. It's like she's ten years older and doesn't recognise you.

'Charlie . . .'

'Jesus, what you . . . what time it is? Come in, Jesus, Rowan, what the hell you doing here?'

You are shaking, like her, as you stand there in the tiny living room of the council flat she chose over her inheritance. The words welling. You want just to hold her, gush them out, but you can't when she's pottering about like this. Turning on the lights, the heating, putting on the kettle, lighting a rollie for herself, asking you if you want one, apologising that she forgot you don't smoke now.

The postcard inside your coat pocket. You can't wait for her to hold it in her hands. To hold you when you tell her.

You say sorry. You should have called. It must be 3 a.m. at least. She is busy, not hearing. Your eyes drift over to the sofa. To just lie down. Explain in the morning. If you could just close your eyes. Charlie. It's so good just to see you again. I'm sorry about the . . . but she's in the kitchen and maybe can't hear. The thing, the sofa, is covered in stuff. So her. Papers, an Open University textbook, child psychology, a wrapper for a big chocolate bar, her ashtray full of rollie butts, cat hair everywhere. She's started painting

45

the walls in blue, it's only halfway done, there's patterned seventies wallpaper underneath. Some drawings by kids in crayon tacked up with tape. A little person and a big person and a house, flowers in the garden and a big yellow sun. The smile on the little person's face has been gone over four or five times. The colouring-in goes over the edges. The fingers are reaching for each other but not touching. Yes, that's right – she teaches disturbed children now. Close your eyes, breathe and take in the smells of Charlie. Something brushes against your leg. You recoil. Her cat. It's OK. She's a cat person. She told you you were a dog. And a monkey. Year of the monkey.

She's calling through from the kitchen about how you look well, and she's sorry about the mess. One sugar, right? And don't mind Winston, he's second-hand, feral but friendly, picked him up at the pound last month – needed a hip replacement and has no teeth. She's feeding him mashed vegetables. A vegetarian cat. Fuck. Just so her. So incredibly her. Still picking up strays. All of it insane and sad and wonderful and so Charlie. You sit among her papers and books and plans for making a small difference in a world that doesn't care and stroke her second-hand cat named after a Conservative prime minister.

Pick the right moment to tell her about the postcard.

'Hole,' you call through. 'You still got Hole?'

'What was that, sweetie?'

So then you're singing, because it's easier than explaining, like the way you were before, just into things together and when you were stuck for words you just sang. The intro, the drums and guitar, right there in your head. Then Courtney's vocals. This song maybe about rape or maybe about love. 'You know, fucking *Doll Parts*.' You're shouting. Laughing at the stupidity of shouting.

'Oh that. Yeah,' she says. 'On tape somewhere. Try under the . . . In a box or . . . It's in a box somewhere.'

46

What where? You are up, the excitement cutting through the exhaustion, eyes scanning the room. She's been in boxes since you can recall. So incredibly amazingly Charlie. Her crazy Afghan dressing-gown thing and her clogs and you could weep.

'Isn't it a bit late for Courtney Love?' she calls through but still you're singing, searching through the boxes. Big Black, Nirvana, Millions of Dead Cops, Psychic TV, Foetus, Ministry, Galaxie 500, the Happy Mondays, the Pastels and Dead Kennedys. It's all there. Lost years in a box.

She's calls through from the kitchen. 'There's no sugar. Is honey OK, honey?' You call through, laughing at her little joke, 'OK, honey.' The box under the stereo. On your hands and knees. Dust and Jesus and Mary Chain and big balls of fluff and cat hair everywhere and the Renegades and Fugazi and Suicide all with handwritten Gothic lettering and stars and kisses on the tape covers she used to make herself. Hundreds of them. Codeine and the Pixies and the Mission. 'You were such an old goth!' you say, laughing. 'Kurt is here,' you shout through, 'but can't find fucking Courtney!' 'God,' you call, 'it's just so fucking amazing, like there's times when I just so needed to hear all this stuff and I think maybe I could get them again on MP3 but it's kind of sad, don't you think, re-buying all your old tapes from like twenty years ago? And Josh wouldn't understand anyway. He likes Moby. Can you believe that? Fucking Moby. I mean, a few tracks are OK but . . .'

She's standing behind you with two mugs of tea and you didn't realise and were still shouting. 'Here you go,' she says. 'Thanks, babe,' you say quietly like her. 'I really can't find Hole.' She puts the cup down beside you. You were both in love with Courtney. You were in love with Charlie. Close your eyes and sing.

'Rowan!' she says with an expression you haven't heard from her before. 'I need you to tell me what's going on.'

47

Open your arms. Tell her. Everything. Show her the postcard.

'You remember how you said the whole thing was staged. Right. Like there were no dental records, like how the body was just some corpse they bought and dressed up like Kurt, right, like how he's still alive somewhere like Elvis. Well – I think she still is.'

That's it, reach into the pocket, take it out.

'I found this.'

She doesn't take the postcard. She leads you by the elbow back to the sofa.

'How's Ailsa? Is everything OK?'

'The dates are all wrong. It says the twenty-ninth of September.'

Her hand firmly on your shoulder. You suddenly feel your body and it aches. Your throbbing breasts. The postcard trembling in your hand. You see yourself for a second as she must. Your hair a mess, your jumper with baby sick on it, you have no socks, your house trainers.

'Why don't you just tell me what happened tonight?' she says, talking to you like your shrink.

'Hey, remember when we burned our hands together and got high and kissed and . . .?'

She waits for you to run out. Her Elvis clock ticking above the big bookshelf. Her smoke in the air.

'Maybe you should lie down,' she says.

'Yes, yes, can I? Can I please? Just do that, can I stay for just a few nights and crash.'

She clears the teacups and ashtray as you shiver. She pulls out the sofa bed and gets the bedding things. And you say sorry so many times and thank you, thanks, and tell her that she's your best friend in the world and you want her to stop moving around so fast so you can just talk. Then she's giving you some kind of tablet. Valerian, she says, organic, natural aids to sleep and tucking you in and taking off your

48

trainers and your head is on the pillow and your eyes, Rowan, so fast, are falling.

A voice in the distance as you drift off, the tablet still in your hand.

She's talking to someone and you can't hear the other person. Something's wrong. Her voice from the corridor.

'Yeah. Some Valium.'

Who is she talking to?

'Yeah, sure, absolutely. I agree. But she's sleeping now.'

Whispering about you on the phone.

'OK, tomorrow. Seven thirty is pushing it cos I have to be at work. I don't want to leave her alone. If you can get here for about seven-ish.'

You're up. Staggering, woozy, tripping over your trainers, the damp pill dropping from your hand.

'Who? Who?'

Her face when she sees you. Not hers.

'You need to lie down,' she says. And she's got the phone in her hand, hiding it behind her back.

'Who, who was it?'

'You're not well,' she says. 'Lie down, it's OK.'

Then you're reaching for it, the phone, pulling it from her. And she falls backwards and her face as she falls is unlike anyone you've ever seen. Furious, feral. And then the phone is to your ear, but the line is dead.

She's up on her feet and a voice is screaming that she should understand because she's single and she's never trusted men and she was right all along about the phoney wedding and how could she call him and she's a stinking fucking hypocrite. These words like a soundtrack. Out of sync. Coming from your mouth.

'Shh,' she says. 'You're OK. Shh. Lie down, close your eyes.'

No, you will not. Not ever again. You see it all now. Fuck you. And you think you're safe here with your fucking toothless cat and you're do-gooding psychology textbooks because you're a nice person and if everyone was more like you then the world would be a better place. It's not OK. It has never been OK, and every little thing you try to do, to make it OK, only makes it worse. You're a sad, lonely cow, and all of this is nothing, nothing.

'Shh, it's fine. Are you on any other medication?' she says, holding you tight, repeating the question. And you are struggling then as she tries to restrain you. And you are back in the toilets on that first day at school but this time you are breaking away, diving, out the door, falling through her garden. Keys. Car door, seat belt, ignition, heart racing.

Her blinds pulled back watching you. On her phone again. Her face in the rear-view mirror, getting smaller and smaller, as your foot pushes down on the accelerator.

*

She drove that night, south, for an hour, crying, then stopping in a lay-by. It seemed absurd to her, as the natural border grew above her and the hills became steeper, to be leaving everything she had tried to build. She stepped out of the car, to clear her eyes, to get a grip. The handbrake never worked anyway and she'd forgotten to leave it in gear. Fumbling to get a hold, to hold it back as its weight pulled it over the cliff, she found herself, minutes later, laughing at how the car seemed like some crazy metaphor for her life. The dumb stupid weight always heading towards an edge. As she watched it fall into the waves she knew there was nowhere to run and so decided to go back.

Two hours waiting on the A9 and the few cars that passed wanted nothing to do with her, then a local man, in his fifties, stopped. He had too many questions, she lied and told him she was a tourist, a hitchhiker.

The A9 then the B-roads, then the roads without names, single-track, the passing places, the dirt. Eva in her white robes took her in. Eva got her a caravan sharing with two others who were younger. She sat with them for two weeks not eating or speaking. One night, when they went out, she took a razor to her hair. Tufts of it left among little clots of blood. Eva advised her not to call a doctor as she didn't believe in Western medicine. Four nights later one of the caravan kids rang emergency. She'd had a nervous breakdown, the doctor said. She needed to be institutionalised. Eva said no, nursed her herself, and when she couldn't, she sent others, strangers who sat with her holding her hand, talking in Eva's words. Psychiatry was oppressive, Eva said. And the past and the future. She would get better only by living in the now. All will be well because you are with us now. One day at a time. One meal at a time. When you are cured, only then, should you return to your daughter.

Thirty years later she was still in Ithaca. Living in one of the old caravans. The few that saw her said she wore a crystal round her neck and a crucifix and a mandala. She believed the spirit would provide for her and cleanse her of her sins. She lived on little more than bread and vegetable soup and water. She looked much older than she was. Hunchbacked, her clothes threadbare. Sleeping in the rusted caravan that became hers alone, praying, meditating, speaking to no one. Eva let her stay because Eva felt guilty. Eva let her stay on the condition that she took no part in community life until she was ready, and she was not ready. Almost thirty years. Walking slowly to the vegetable caravan each day, slowly boiling her carrots and leeks to make the soup, slowly forcing the spoon to her mouth. Closing her eyes and swallowing as the bare minimum of nutrition passed into her and she tried not to gag. As she reminded herself to swallow she told herself not to think of the child. That, as Eva said, the past like the future was oppressive.

Every day she chanted a mantra and focused on the now. Since her menopause she had been feeling more emotional. She did not drink alcohol or smoke, Eva had helped her leave such poisons behind. Her one indulgence was an old radio-tape player. She listened to it for half an hour a day so as to conserve the batteries. She never listened to the news because it exhausted her. She had three or four old tapes. Hendrix, Joplin, Baez. Joni Mitchell. It was the old Joni album she sang along to most because Joni had abandoned her daughter too. She sang along to *Clouds* as she stared out of her window, waiting for some change, for those days when the grey Caithness clouds cleared and there would be a flash of true sky. Her voice was still strong, they said on the rare occasions that she turned up in the sanctuary to sing the old religious songs and the new New Age ones. Coloratura soprano, the song-leader said she was, and so clear and true. She knew that when she sang she would cry, so she mostly stayed away and sang only to herself in her caravan and told herself that one day like Joni Mitchell she would be reconciled with her daughter and there would be no blame or guilt. They would sing like they once had. In the car. Then when the half-hour was up she would turn off the tape and tell herself, like Eva told her, that she was not ready, there was much of the past still within her. She tried to be in the now. The now of the one bowl of soup and the old clothes and the caravan with the frozen condensation. She wondered how old her daughter was, how old she herself was, she had lost all sense of time. When these thoughts troubled her she would chant the mantra that Eva had taught her. A song without a tune. Nine words and only three notes. Three times three. 'We are together, all is well, in our world.' In the last year she found the courage to go back to the sanctuary once a day and sing. Some of the others had complained, years before, that she led and did not join. They had been intimidated by the power of her voice. She taught herself to restrain the urge and to merge, invisible, to not rise and soar above the others as she sang.

*

The sound of cars. Sunlight shouting through eyelids. Your limbs, aching hot. Wake up, Rowan. Open your eyes.

The wallpaper is peach. The furniture is veneered pine. There are sachets of tea and coffee and sugar, brown and white, and NutraSweet by the mirror. Scan the room. The bedside table has sharp edges, at about her eye level. There are two wall sockets without safety covers that she could poke things into. The flex from the tiny kettle is dangling and she could pull it down onto herself. The room is not child-safe.

Pull back the curtain. Look. Six lanes of traffic. You must be in a motorway motel. Try to remember. Your mobile says 15.30. It says you have twelve messages. What day is it? You left on Wednesday night.

You try to scroll through the menu but it won't let you see the date till you have opened your new messages. Cars whistle past, low rumble of trucks. Idiot, what a state you are, sleeping in your jeans. Your credit card is beside the bed on the unit, with what looks like five or six hundred in twenties. Think. Vague memory of a cash machine, the stale wind of passing trucks pushing you. Of looking over your shoulder to see if it was safe. An empty car park. Three cards. Two credit, one Switch. Taking out everything you could on all of them.

Your phone keeps beeping. Your gut is empty, your breasts ache, you have what feels like a hangover. You can't recall drinking. You must read your messages, they will tell you what to do next.

First message. Josh.

Babe, whats going on? Tell me where U R I will come and get U. Luv U XXX

Second. *Please pick up yr fone.*

Your eyes scan. The TV is on. Some kind of on-screen menu. You can watch *The Dukes of Hazzard* for £5.95 or *Teenage Tits and Ass* for £7.95.

Spoke to Charlie. Am taking week off work. Where R U now? Will come and get U. Pleez call me. Love U so much. XXX

Nothing you can see out the window tells you where you are. Could be America. Germany. Hard to tell how far you travelled. Manchester. Newcastle. No memory of checking in. The swipe of the card, the polite smiles, the effort involved.

I understand. U need time out. Sasa OK. Come home. I will take care of her. Rest here w/us. Please come home. Love you XX

A pedestrian overpass. Pizza Hut. Junction 21. A sign for a Quality Inn. You must be in the Quality Inn.

Please tell me U are OK. My mother is coming to take care of Sas. Can be w/u today. Where R U? Please call. I understand. Luv U XXX

Why is it you feel nothing?

Friday, the date says on the TV. Not possible, but no memory. You have to eat. A packet of Bourbon biscuits on the side by the tiny kettle. Tear the packet open. Eat, Rowan, get back your strength.

His texts. His sense that this can be healed. His sense of propriety. His solidity. His way of joking out of a problem. The way he says, 'Cheer up, it's not the end of the world.' The way he folds towels, newspapers. His righteous obsession with recycling. His anxiety over his receding hairline. His *Best of the 80s* CDs. His scowl when he senses he's done wrong. The way he always jokes about your hairs in the plughole but takes them out anyway. His interest in learning the names of wines

54

and where the grapes come from. His collection of Penguin Classics that he'll never read. His home abdonimator. His insistence that being positive makes everything OK. His 'taste' in movies. His gifts of flowers. His conversations about how much cars are damaging the ozone layer. His choice of a sports utility vehicle because it was safer with a child in the back. His big manly shoulders. His understanding of childhood trauma which comes from books. The way he talks so much about how he adores silence. His secret masturbation routines. The fact that he washes up as he cooks. The way he boasts of his little successes as a father at dinner parties.

U R not well. Dr Foster says it may B Depleted Mother syndrome. Tell me where U R. We'll work thru this together. Luv U XXX.

The way he always says we – 'We think this.' 'We always shop there.' 'We love this, don't we, love?' His back massages, which are too brisk. His listening-sympathetically face. His enthusiasm for his career. His schedules for trying to have sex again. The fact that he never, not for a second, doubts the foundation on which all this is built.

Why won't U speak to me? PICK UP. U need time to consider this. I understand. Baby, please, just pick up. XXX

His political views, which are what he read yesterday. The fact that he calls himself a feminist. His 'Child on Board' windscreen sticker. His unflinching faith that the future will be even better. The way he repeats his phrases and each time makes it sound like he's thought them for the first time. The way he always finds other people's opinions 'interesting'. The way he bounces round Sainsbury's and always treats himself to a 'little something'. That he can quote from *Star Wars* movies and do the voices and thinks this cute.

Four more messages. You should call him. Tell him you're OK. Text him at least. Your phone is low on power, the charger is in the car. But you feel nothing. You read this somewhere. One of the manuals. D for Depression. How the emotions shut down. The final state is not one of trauma but of detachment. You become body, just eating, breathing. The money on the bedside unit. Enough to eat, to sleep, just a bit longer. Go back to bed. Take off your jeans. Turn off the phone, conserve energy. Lie down, Rowan. Close your eyes. Think about Josh. Forgive Josh. You love him. Sleep.

*

She could not sleep, she drove, as she had to every night, fearful of rest. At every turn she sensed their black cars hiding just beyond sight. She kept the documents close to her at all times, knowing that if she stopped for one moment, they would snatch them from her. She drove east, trying to shake them off but always they haunted her rear view mirror.

She had to get south, to the news people, to print the results of her investigation: the covert manufacturing of weapons, the illegal dumping of radioactive isotopes in the sea, the leukaemia clusters among the local children, the government cover-up.

She sensed the reason they had not arrested her yet was her daughter, asleep beside her in the car. She feared the danger she was placing the child in.

She dropped her at her father's and wrote a postcard, to say she was on her way, south. Then it was the long road through the silent mountains, alone.

As darkness fell, with no oncoming lights in sight, they accelerated beyond and forced her into the ditch. They shot her twice in the head at close range. They placed her papers into prepared bags and sealed them.

Unlike anti-nuclear politician William Macrae in 1985, no body was left to be discovered in a car at a remote location, placed in a certain way to make it look like suicide. Unlike activist Hilda Murrel in 1984, no mutilated body

was found hidden in a copse across a field from the abandoned car. No risk was taken with the body. It too, like the
papers, was placed in a prepared bag, and at a later date,
destroyed.

*

You were in your thirties. Ten years wasted going in circles.
You'd been through shrinks like men, like drinks. The NHS
psychologist was a behaviourist and told you that the past
was no excuse. He recommended a number of self-help
manuals to help you deal with your array of behavioural
problems. One for the eating disorder, another for the sleep,
one for the self-esteem deficit, one for helping you find
meaningful work, and another for relating to men in non-
destructive ways. They made you laugh at first, these stupid
books telling you to take small simple steps. *If you have
trouble eating alone, go to a busy restaurant. If you have
trouble sleeping* . . . Your shrink told you that the past is
only a story you tell yourself so you can build a future, that
the future can be built on small stories. A better car, a few
drinks less a week, losing a few pounds, setting a schedule
for eating, planning for a better home, starting a career, a
more meaningful relationship. You followed the steps and
they led you to Josh.

You finally found work with an advertising agency.
Nothing glamorous. A proofreader. Your background in fact-
finding, in close reading, in finding mistakes was of use.
At first it was commas in the wrong place, grammatical
errors and the misuse of parentheses in low-profile sales
catalogues. Your relationships with men were the same.
Cautious corrections of other people's sentences. No over-
view of paragraphs. You took them one word at a time,
ever-vigilant for the overuse of clichés. The self-help actually
helped. Small steps. You survived minute to minute then

hour to hour. You did not need to believe in what you were doing, or to question. *Small changes in your behaviour can become permanent through repetition.* Josh was your immediate superior. A copywriter for the agency. He was impressed by your ability to work hard, to focus, to work late. He didn't see your fear of going home to an empty flat or your rituals of eating, sleeping, not drinking. He saw only commitment to work. He moved you up the ladder onto paragraphs, you got to delete entire sections of other people's writing. He welcomed your critical comments, your ironic, negative take. He said you were very *now*.

Small steps and no direction but still you moved forward. You found yourself at the age of thirty-three with a career as a copywriter. You found yourself falling for your boss. Your mother had been reduced to a few witty one-liners and it was ironic that you'd found a life in advertising. It was the time of irony. Everything was laughter in spite of itself: clothes, haircuts, adverts. This was very Gen-X. You learned to say words that you feared by putting them in quotation marks. Together you and Josh originated the concept of an anti-ad for a soft drink. It started off as a joke. A couple on a candlelit date holding hands are served Diet Coke instead of wine. The actress turns to the camera and says, 'Wait, I think we're in an advert.' It won an award and suddenly all of the ad agencies were making anti-ads. You went to an expensive candlelit restaurant together and he said the words that you feared most by putting them in inverted commas: 'Wait, I think we're falling in love.'

You bought books on relationships and sharing intimacy. One night you confessed to him that you were addicted to self-help. He said you should write a self-help book for self-help addicts and this made you laugh. He took the fear from many words. Always in quotation marks, he talked of moving in together, of a future. You joked that no one believed in these things, that you couldn't see further than tomorrow and even that scared you. That commitment leads to abandonment. Ideals to death. You told him that your books said you should never want someone else to save you. He held your hands and said the words without quotation marks: 'Marry me.'

Your wedding speech was sincere. It was unusual, they said, for a woman to make a speech and your work friends told you that you were the last person they thought would ever get hitched. Charlie left as the speech started. People were moved to tears. Halfway through the speech it hit you. That your mother and father were never married, that if you could do this and pull it off then she would be gone, for ever.

But then it was hard – the expensive apartment, the SUV, the upwardly mobile friends and dinner parties. The irony was disappearing. You were torn and tearing in two and it started again. The hole in the place where your centre should be. You decided it was time to have a baby.

*

She drove around for days, lost in doubt, then returned to Ithaca. She pretended to be there to visit Eva and other old friends. She bided her time, taking part in the Eastern Dance Workshops although it was hard to dance with her mind focused on only that one thing. She knew where it was. They didn't like having it around, they were against violence of any kind, but it was deemed necessary in the event of a horse or goat breaking a leg, or some other incurable injury. She knew where it was hidden, she'd polished it and put it back in its place so many times. In fifteen years there had never been cause to use it but it was still there, wrapped in gauze in the old cupboard in the basement. The self-subsistence handbook recommended that it be primed and ready. She hid it in a canvas bag, sneaking it past them. It was big, had to be for the horses. She drove south into the mountains, to be alone with it, to stare it in the face. It was there beside her on the passenger seat where her daughter had sat. She tucked the gauze round it, to keep it hidden and warm. She got out of her car when the road ran out and the hills rose around her. She walked with it for miles, through heather and bracken, over streams that wet her feet, carefully holding it against her breast, thinking it over, feeling its growing weight. She kept on further into the hills. These things that had names she'd once learned when she first came to Scotland, Maiden's Pap, Morven and Suilven. Terrifying volcanic peaks three thousand feet high which laughed in the face of all any human had endeavoured to do with them, to climb and conquer, to write poetry or song. Her feet sank deep into the bog and she had second thoughts. The sound of a curlew then, a solitary moorland bird circling overhead, swooping at her, defending her eggs, making her think of her child. Its voice like a song, curlew, curlew. She tried to run from the mother bird, across the moors, tripping in the peat bog, her legs soaked, stumbling, holding it tighter to her breast as she fell. Throwing herself onto her back, cradling it to keep it dry. Whispering to it. She stayed where she fell, sat there for minute after minute. Her bones sinking into herself, her skin cold and wet as the mud. We are together and all is well in our world, she whispered as she rocked it in her arms. She unwrapped it from the gauze and put it gently to her lips, holding the handle firmly between her knees, her thumb cocking it, her forefinger circling the trigger. The curlew flew overhead singing its song. She started to cry, the metal rattling against her teeth, her hand shaking. She lowered it, to steady herself. The shot deafened her, the lead whistling through her hair, the curlew, flying in fear, her ears ringing, echoing into mute silence. She got to her feet, marvelling at how she couldn't even hear her own laughter. She threw the gun into a peat bog and watched it slowly sink. The final place of its trace. It rained and she let the rain run to her bones and cursed at the mountains and laughed at them but there was not even an echo.

She ran stumbling back to her car, as if the grey granite itself was chasing her. Inside, she felt safer behind the glass. Ashamed and shivering, she turned the key in the ignition, the radio started up and her hearing returned, a mess of broken signals. She drove south until she found voices that were unbroken, and in those hundred miles, she found herself glad to be back in the world that she'd hated. She was grateful for the stupid car and the petrol, for the heating and the sound of human voices, singing stupid songs on the advertisements for pointless things. She was glad.

*

You are stumbling through the car park to where you think the public toilet is. Three hundred miles and another service station you have put between you and where you should be, thirty text messages you have deleted without reading. Listen, your daughter is crying. Go home and feed. Let Sasa hear your voice. Selfish uncaring inhuman.

The milk sacks are hardening as breastfeeding has ceased. Your breasts are so swollen, rigid, milk curdling inside, hardening like cheese, nipples throbbing, full to bursting, but what you feel is empty.

There's only enough of your milk in the fridge for one day's feed, only two days' worth in the freezer. You've been away three. You tried mixing her feeds with formula before but she wouldn't take it, she wanted only mummy milk. He'll be up now, it must be that time when she wakes, that's why your breasts are screaming. You are still on her clock, her body time. He'll be up now defrosting your milk in the microwave. Heating it up too hot. Killing the nutrients, scalding her mouth. What were you thinking? You don't think, Rowan, that's your fucking problem. You feel too much and then you shut it down, all of it. Piece of shit. Call yourself a mother?

Call him now. Tell him he must remember to test the milk on the back of his hand, not take it straight from the microwave and put it in her mouth. Call him, he's going to scald her. He doesn't know what to do. Tell him to put the milk back into the freezer first. Idiot male. How will he cope waiting ten, fifteen minutes for it to cool down, trying to calm her down? How will he cope with the screaming? Call him, you fuck. He'll speak to you so gently, no recriminations, his voice will be so tired, so slow. You'll hear her screaming in the background. You won't be able not to cry. There will be his silence and then he'll say, 'Baby, please, whatever I've done I'm sorry, can you just come back, please? Right now.' And you will. You will tell him where you are even though you're not sure, you'll say sorry, sorry. He will put her in her car seat and drive through the night and she will fall asleep with the rhythm of the wheels and he will come and get you with her in his arms and you will cry and say, sorry, baby, and reach for her, not him, and bring her to your breast. To feed.

You are going to vomit.

It's OK. Support yourself against the toilet wall. The empty gut full of acid hormone rush. It's OK if you can't puke. Calm down. You need to feed her just one more time. Your breast is like rock, you are hard and heartless. You know what to do to make it soft again. Close your eyes. Do what you have to do to make it stop. There is nothing like that feeling. You will kill for it; how can anyone think themselves alive if they have not felt it?

Take your left breast in your hand firmly, summon her face. Squeeze slowly, firmly, down towards the nipple. It's sore. Yes. That's it. Squeeze harder as you move slowly towards your nipple. You're not falling, it's OK. Rest your head on the tiles. You're doing so well. You are a good mother. Close your eyes. Think of those first moments.

All the terminology, the classes, the training videos with an NHS room half full of other mothers on orange plastic seats who had failed too, watching the video 'Latching on'. *The entire areola should be in the mouth, not just the nipple. The head should be supported at the right angle so that the baby should have no fear of choking.* The week spent crying because she wouldn't take your milk.

Think of her face. How you did it together.

If you are full- or soft-breasted then it may be that your baby cannot breathe when feeding as your breast may be covering her nostrils.

Getting angrier and angrier at the videos, the midwives, the trainee nurses so much younger than you and already so tired of having to do this, so routine, as they touched your breasts and held her head, who had only read the same manuals and watched the same videos as you. Your breast aching as she screamed. If they would just let you go home, you were sure she would feed, but they wouldn't let you, they said you had to be monitored, they took your blood, and she took no milk. The nurses telling you she was losing weight, only a day or so more they said and then you'll have to give up and get her on the bottle. The fear of being just like those poor mothers, the social scum. Watching her rooting for your nipple then her rejection of you as you fumbled. The panic each time, then the exhaustion. Sleeping not sleeping in your hospital bed, waking every time she moved, trying again, failing. *Hold the areola between two fingers in a scissors shape and squeeze outwards while holding your breast back.*

That's it. Get it out of you. There'll be no more pain. Aim at the toilet. Don't make a mess now.

Then it happened, for no reason you could work out, after a week of exhaustion and failure. She woke beside you, and without even trying, her mouth so wide. 'Clamped on,' the nurse said as she passed by. 'Good for you, well done.' The joy, the rush of it, the rhythmic suck, feeling you were filling up, not emptying, and she *did* love you. Because you were so scared, weren't you, that already she'd rejected you, that you have PND and you should never have read about it. Brimming and bursting with love for her as she drank from you in gurgling, greedy gulps. Closing your eyes, holding her so tight but gentle. Just right, in some way, your body telling you, your arms just right, her head just so, so right. No pain in your back, in your wound or breast. Hearing her sucking swallowing, this joy bursting from your nipple to spine, to head, toes. Feelings, thousands of them, welling up behind your closed eyelids. Together in the gentle dark heartbeat heat of feeding. Singing to her as you fed. Falling asleep with her. No worry of smothering her. Of rolling over onto her. No words or books to tell you what was right. Sleeping in some position that seemed so perfect like her fingers, toes, mouth, her eyes still closed. Waking sated, full, whole, staring at her dreaming face, which knew nothing more then than your voice, smell, breast. Happy to be only that, wanting never to be more than that again. Holding her head to your nose, drinking in the sweet smell of your birth, still there on her skin. Thanking her for that. Stroking her face, waiting for her to wake so you could feed again.

That's it. It's flowing now. Don't spill your milk over the edge of the toilet bowl. Watch the water turning white. The smell of her mixing with bleach, with urine. Let it go. Squeeze her out. You are not fit. It's not safe for her to be with you. No tears, only wet hands, nipple. Don't think of the picture, of this woman, late at night in some motorway service station milking herself into a toilet. Poor baby, please forgive Mummy, she has to be away for a few days, then she'll come home.

Outside the trucks throw stale hot wind, gusts of fast food. Your eyes scan the site with sudden hunger. Beyond the car park is Pizza Hut, but its lights are off. To your left, a games arcade and an arrowed skywards sign – McDonald's 24 Hours. Go now, feed.

You pass the empty arcade, shadows passing, sounds of punches, screams, tyres screeching, machine guns, spacecraft. You follow the arrow up the steps over the overpass. You are not afraid, as you perhaps should be, a woman alone with so much money in her pocket, the flashing neon, the torn linoleum, the gangs with knives, lurking. You have no fear. All this seems in some way like a memory. Predetermined, déjà vu. You have never stopped at one of these places before. Josh doesn't believe in franchises or fast food and avoids the urban poor. But there is no threat, only concrete and glass and this empty pain in your gut, driving you on.

The sign on the motorway says Glasgow 14 miles.

Coming down the steps on the other side, the déjà vu again. A sign that says Open All Night, next to a red plastic bin, the old seventies wall tiles. You have been here before.

Put all the things together, Rowan, make them connect, the picture and the taste with the money. Buy the meat, take a seat, look at the advert for the burger as you put it in your mouth.

Chewing and staring at the sign that says Welcome Inn, across the motorway. Why are you smiling? Why this stupid grin growing on your face as you gorge on this thing your husband says is full of nothing, but tastes like the first thing you've really tasted in so long? They call it a Happy Meal. Maybe you are that stupid. Look at you, laughing at the huge empty spaces between the six or seven others eating, all alone at their own tables beneath the same neon lights, each afraid to look up as you roar like a madwoman.

And this place. It's possible she came here, exactly

here on that last night. For the first time in many years she ate a burger of beef and she didn't think about her daughter and capitalism and the rainforests and the cars and the toxins, she thought only of pickles and ketchup and how amazing they tasted. She sat here and licked the mayo from her fingers, and laughed, about how this thing that had come to stand for all that was evil was just this simple stupid lump of meat that tasted so sweet.

She stopped here, at this table, and ate and laughed and that gave her the strength to go on. You know this because this voice, Rowan, that's been telling you what to do, all this time, that led you to this place, is talking now and telling you all this. She is alive, you know this, because this voice who calls you You is hers.

Your road again. The dual carriageway then the cars jostling for dominance as the road narrows. As the distance behind you grows in weight with each mile, what you need is just to follow. Be safe, keep your distance, judge your speed by the car in front. Let them pull you on. Don't look back or question. But all cars are vanishing now and you are alone as the cold mountains rise around you. You check the rear-view mirror but all is black. You beg for another light to come and lead you on. It cannot be long now till the sun rises, till Ithaca. Just a few more miles, before you can close your eyes.

*

They drove north, four hundred miles from London, in the spring of 1971. The VW kept breaking down and they had to stop to pump up one of the caravan tyres that had a slow leak, and so that Jenna could pee at the roadside, because I was pushing down on her bladder. It took them three days and they often thought about turning back.

I remember the stories only because they told them again and again to everyone that came to Ithaca over the years. All of them sitting round the big pine table in the barn, telling, retelling, laughing, joking, holding hands. The visitors sometimes wept when they heard.

For three days they took turns driving, apart from Jenna who got to sit in the passenger seat because she was heavy with me. There was Eva, Pete, Mike, Jenna and Angus. Tessa was in the back in the caravan nursing Jono, who was one. She was in there with a woman called Petra. A week later a man called Sean joined them from Edinburgh. Those were the eight founding members. They all had their own part of the story, they all told each other's. No one ever said this was 'me', 'what I did'.

Angus was the fixer, he could mend anything. He'd been training to be a mechanic but got into the whole LSD and folk-music scene and dropped out in '68, then spent two years fixing up squats in Brixton and Hackney. He could hot-wire electricity and do plumbing. He'd welded the chasis of the caravan the week before they left, cut a hole in the roof and covered it in perspex, so they could lie in there and look out at the stars as they drove north. His story was always details about the car. How they were stuck in this lay-by on this single-track road somewhere near Inverness and he had to take the damned radiator out. A whole day they sat there, miles from anywhere while he cleaned it, prayed for it, kicked it and refitted it. I like to picture this farmer in a tractor, nearly skidding off the road as he passed the long-haired hippies holding hands in a ditch asking the sky to breathe life into a bright yellow VW van with wood panelling.

Angus held the radiator together with wires he'd stripped from the heating system and elastic from my mother's bra – or so the story goes. They all said how if it wasn't for Angus, the crofts would never have had roofs or water, how they probably would've abandoned the place after that first long hard winter. Thirty Coca-Cola cans became a long gutter to feed the fresh-water tank. Car wheels became stools. How his makeshift magic of exchangeable things held their brave new world together.

Eva's story was of her first sight of Ithaca. She'd tell them all of how she'd travelled the world, searching for herself, living in communes in Holland and California, Big Sur, Freihaus, in kibbutzim in the desert, but nothing had prepared her for the bleakness of the Caithness landscape. That final hour driving through it, the trees thinning out, the moorland stretching out to the horizon, the empty sky as grey as lead, as if it was pushing the land flat. Her growing despair that it had all been a mistake. The three crofts and the ruined laird's mansion, all the roofs broken beneath the falling rain, all abandoned for a hundred years. The silence as they stopped the car, in shock, and heard nothing but wind in their ears, no trace of man. More than any sight it was that soundless sound, like a breath or voice, Eva said, telling her that this was the place. That was when the name came to her. It came from Greek mythology. It meant home, after a long voyage, the return to home. They would often tell Eva's tale in poetic ways, talking of spirit, the ideal, the vision. My mother once said that Eva was actually very practical, that if it hadn't been for Eva's organisational skills and contacts they'd never have been able to buy the land. Eva never gave many details about her years before. It was much later when I discovered Eva had been left half a million when her South African father died and that she had left two children and a husband behind to find herself.

Tessa, all the men loved Tessa. She would talk about the squats and the pigs and the parties in London and how she didn't care where she was as long as it was away from the suburbs and her plastic fascist parents. She told this story of her first morning in Ithaca. How she woke in the caravan and the birds were singing and she felt the pull of the landscape. She walked out across the moors and there on the horizon was a gypsy and his horse in silhouette against the rising sun. The accidental wonder of it. She did a dance there in the mud and rain, naked, for herself and all women everywhere, an ancient rite that she'd discovered in her psyche. A bird circling and calling out to her as she danced for joy. The others joked that she was indeed a gypsy, always running off to party when there was work to be done.

Pete would never talk about things, not real things but Bakunin, Trotsky, Marcuse and revolutionary poetry. He'd lecture, not talk. Tessa always teased him, saying he was on the run, just like her. She liked to boast that he'd been involved with the Angry Brigade bombings in '71, though he always denied it. Tessa's favourite story was the time they finally managed to get Pete to cook for them all. Lentil bake with vegetables from the garden. And he'd left the ends of the carrots on, and there was still mud on them in the pot and they had to add curry powder and ketchup to give it any kind of taste and everyone had diarrhoea for days after and Tessa thought they'd had dysentery because she discovered Pete had been dumping human waste in the compost.

All the stories about Pete always got them laughing. Like the time he was digging in the garden and he cut through the pipe to the septic tank and how the sewage leaked into the water supply and they had piss coming through the taps. Yeah, yeah, yeah, he would say and they would hug him and joke that Marxists were banned from the kitchen. Pete was the only one that eventually got a real job – as a standby teacher in Wyster. He never talked about the school or the kids there, or even his own kids. That seems strange to me now, that Pete and Tessa never really mentioned Jono or little Saphie.

Jono. John – O. I don't know why Tessa named him

that. Maybe just her posh public-school voice. A cute way of saying John. We lived near John o' Groats. Or maybe it was John Zero. They believed in Year Zero. Believed they could change the world, one child at a time.

Petra didn't last. Eva would explain that Petra and Sean's croft had always been a problem. How they'd looked for other permanent members to fill the space and maybe twenty had come and gone again within three or four years. How communal living was too much for most people. Tessa would joke about Petra and her 'experiments'. Eva would always interrupt before the details got out and explain that in the first few years they'd all learned a lot about personal boundaries and responsibility. My mother told me Petra had been, in some way, Eva's lover for a while, that Tessa and Pete and Petra had been a ménage of sorts. But really I was too young to remember even Petra's face – she was just a story. A cautionary tale.

Mike, the musician, would always tell tales of the folk festival. His plans for making it better and bigger for next year, the Scottish Woodstock. Mike always talked about my mum's singing – there had been this one time, he'd been fucked up, losing faith, there had been fights over the garden and he admitted he hadn't been pulling his weight. He was about to walk, then, this one morning, he came into the kitchen and heard my mum singing to herself. How her voice made him stay.

'Bullshit,' my mother would say. 'You were hungry and horny, that was all!' She would always try to talk plainly about the day-to-day things – whose turn it was to do the bloody dishes, the difficulties of maintaining the cleaning rota. She became shy when others told her story, the one they all loved to tell more than any other. The story of my birth.

It took place on the very same table we all ate from. There was no doctor or midwife or painkillers, just some home-brew and weed and the old *Home Doctor* manual.

70

The labour was long and they were all there together, the eight, throughout the night. Eva and Tessa on either side of my mother holding her hands. Mike playing the guitar, Angus reading from the manual. Eva always liked to tell of how it came to her. Jenna was screaming with pain and so she had this idea then to sing through the contractions, to focus on the breathing. Pete would interrupt then, telling of how after eight hours of pacing he'd gone out to walk, and smoked some weed then kept on walking, early in the morning, the sun was coming up. There was dew on the heather. He headed back for a sleep, but as he got closer to the barn he could hear it. The voices of all the others, singing *Kumbaya* at the top of their lungs. Tessa would always interrupt him then – It wasn't *Kumbaya* it was the fucking Stones. Eva said it was an old folk song. Mike said it was a Woody Guthrie.

He came through the door into the croft and, just like it was meant to be, the song was nearly over and out popped this little screaming creature, as perfect as a poem. Tessa would always cry at that part of the story and Eva would take their hands in hers and say, 'She was a gift to us all.' My mother would interrupt, saying, 'Actually, I can't remember a bloody thing,' and squeeze my hand under the table because she knew it was embarrassing for me.

The details of every story changed. They would argue over what was really true and about many, many other things, but over the years and conflicts, somehow retelling their stories to others always brought them together again. And always the stories ended with Jenna and my birth and her voice. Singing through the pain.

ithaca

THE MORNING LIGHT. The leaves on the trees take flight as you approach. Black crows, leaving the branches bare. There never used to be trees or crows here. The horizon, a flat line now, telling you you are near the end. The windscreen wipers say, Yes no yes no stay go stay go. Slow and turn the double bend, as it was. There is a sign. There never used to be a sign.

ITHACA INSTITUTE.

Twelve miles. The grey leaden sky of Caithness, forcing you to look down to the speeding ground. Mile after mile. Another and there it is, as it always was, on the right. RAF Delta. No Cold War now but they have not left.

No sounds, not now. Turn off the heater just to make sure. No sound of jets. But look, razor wire, security surveillance camera, perimeter fence, blast-proof gate. No sight of the jets. All as it should be. We are one and all is well in our world. Another sign – ITHACA INSTITUTE 5 miles. Slow to the bends down to fourth. Empty horizon like it was, like it should be.

Ithaca. The hippies gave everything pretentious names, stolen from poetry, from myth. The commune in New York called the Motherfuckers had armed patrols outside their squat to protect hippies from violence and were shut down amid accusations of rape. Just a few more miles. Kommune 12 Berlin. One of the leaders, Deanna, left her bourgeois husband and three children to create the commune. Another sign.

ITHACA INSTITUTE 2 miles. A graphic of a tree, a rowan tree.

Second on the left. Your mother and Eva planted the

tree when you were born. In Haight-Ashbury three of the first-generation women left their children to be free and live communally. 'There can be no abstract liberation of society without a concrete liberation of life in all its intimate, everyday facets.'

Joni Mitchell had her only child adopted so she could find herself.

Your mother knew all the words to all the songs on the first two albums. You bought *Clouds* again in your twenties. You told yourself it was therapy. To make yourself listen again and feel nothing.

A few miles. You will find Eva. Evil Eva. Odysseus left Ithaca and his wife and brought destruction on his return.

You will hit her with it, corner her and force it from her. You will. But you will have to be clever. So protective they are, the New Agers. Such reverence they have for her. You will have to plan it carefully. Will have to win her confidence. Spend a day or two pretending to be one of them then get her alone in a room. Tell her who you are and she will see it on your face. That you will do what you have to, to get the truth from her. By any means necessary.

The road is wet. Down to third, careful now. The Freihaus community in Hamburg was based upon the spiritual leader abandoning her three children. She renamed herself Alpha.

Somewhere quiet you will let Eva lead you. For a walk into her beloved nature. You will pin her down, hands at her throat. You will force it out of her lungs, the lying dying old cunt.

Slow down on the bends. It all makes sense now.

One mile. 'The bourgeois family unit is an oppressive patriarchal construct.' The last turn, a big sign. There it is no mud now, no dirt track. Look at it. Really. The sign says WELCOME TO ITHACA.

Smooth tarmac road. See it. General Office, it says, 100 yards. Pete and Tessa's old croft. To your left, the field of peat bog. Thirty caravans now, concrete beneath. To the right the same. How many people? One caravan painted with a sunset. But a hundred others, new, of shining metal. More.

Look, nothing is the same. Your croft, where you slept, were sick, danced, played – the sign now says Community Centre. Jono's tree house, gone. Guests' Car Park now it says. Tarmacadam round the tree. The big house is called Information Centre. Angus's workshop – the Arts Centre now. The field beyond – the sign says Eco Village. Look at the houses built there. How many? Twenty, thirty? Made of wood. The solar panels on the roofs. Why didn't you know? How many people? A hundred, two? A woman walks past in a sarong. Another in jeans and hiking gear.

It says Car Park so you park the car. You do what you're told. You can't offend Eva. You are . . . you are scared of seeing her now. Sit in the car. You are safe behind the windscreen, the heating on, the engine still running. Close your eyes. The voice will tell you what to do. Breathe. Try to focus on the now. Just breathe. Get out of the car or turn round and go.

You doubt now why you came. People your age dressed like hippies, they come out of the eco-shop with baskets not bags of food. An ancient woman walking by. Grey hair, grey skin. Smiling with her basket of vegetables. If she was here from the start you would have known her. She is Tessa or Eva or your mother. How would you even know?

The doorway of your old croft has a sign that says Reception. It would be so easy now to turn the wheel. Go back.

Her first teeth are growing. Her milk teeth and you are not there. He must have been calling, texting, panicking. Your mobile must stay off. Two days here and then you will go home and explain. You need this like a tree needs water, like a . . . You hate similes and metaphors. Nothing is like anything. Everything is what it is. Just that and nothing more. Metaphors were the problem. Your mother raised you as a metaphor. You were not her child, you were the future, the brave new world. When people reduce you to a metaphor they fail to see what you are. They blame you for not coming close to poetry.

You've been sitting here in the car park for too long. People are staring at you in your evil SUV. Put your hand on the door handle. Your foot outside. Cold rush of air. Smells of peat burning. People waving to each other, smiling. Long-haired. Like it was but not.

Your feet on tarmac where none should be. Look at it now. There are fences and properties. Tourists shopping in the Craft Centre that was once your play home. Look at it now. The same branded sign everywhere, the same shape as the logo. Your tree, Rowan.

You have to see your tree. There are twenty, thirty caravans in the way. Behind the ceramic workshop is where your tree should be.

Eva always said this place was like a plant. If it can't grow then it will die. It has grown. But not in the way your mother said it should.

You head to your right, towards the river, but there is a new building in the way. A sign. Administration, it says. Ten steps from here must be your tree. The other side, maybe follow the mosaic path. Feet in front of you suddenly. Sandals.

'Can I help you?'

A woman's voice, not Eva's. Look up. She is fifty, in black slacks washed grey, like Eva must be now . . .

'The tree,' you say. 'I'm looking for . . .'

'Ah yes,' she says, smiling. 'The heart chakra. It's just round the back in the herb garden.'

You can't meet her eye. Heart chakra, and the compost heap is the pelvic chakra, and how many other fucking chakras are there? You thank her and keep going.

There it is, Rowan, your naming tree. The flowers dead around it. It is no longer your tree. The lovely bleeding heart of the community sucking the fucking life from the flowers. Its roots digging up the mosaic path. A swing hanging from it now. You walk over the flowers and touch the swing, too high for Sasa. Don't think of Sasa. No sound of children here, not like there used to be. This swing is for adults. Discover the child within, Eva said. You push it and watch it move backwards and forwards. The tree now so big. Old as an old lady. Climb onto it. Feel your age. Swing and try to recall what you used to sing when you used to swing.

Strawberry Fields Forever, I am the Walrus, Rocky Raccoon.

Look at you. It's always the same, trying to make yourself feel something where nothing is. Stupid fucking tree. Must be nice for the tourists. Bloody hippies. You wish they'd cut it down. Build a multiplex cinema here, shopping malls. Anger is good, use it while it lasts. Go to reception, now. Demand to see Eva.

Close your eyes for a second, take a deep breath, hold it. You're going to be OK, open your eyes, then enter. It's OK. There is a door now. Open the door. Read the signs. Pass the immense yukka plants, the paintings in rainbow colours of spirals, of sunsets. Stand at reception. An old woman is there behind the desk at a PC. Could be Eva. Look away. A sign on the back wall says 'Peace' with hand-drawn flowers. Slow down, take a good look at her. No make-up, no bra, like Eva, but too tall. She looks up at you with a smile like Eva's, like she's been expecting you.

'You're here for Sharing Week,' she says, not asking but telling.

'Actually . . .' Find the words. 'Just here to see Eva, is she . . . available?'

'You've signed up for Sharing Week?'

It's OK, the rise in her voice at the end that turns a sentence into a question. She's foreign, French. They do that. Calm down. You're not scared of her smile, which seems like another question.

'If you haven't booked I'm sorry but we only take advance bookings.'

Of course, they screen people. Spiritual background, psychological, earnings.

'I've been here before,' you say, almost saying too much.

You will have to leave now. Because of her smile that has changed again. She is on to you.

'You've done courses here before?'

Quick. Look around, the back wall, the flyers, anything. One reads 'Spiritual Awareness Week'.

'Spiritual Awareness.'

'Ah,' she says and smiles to herself. 'Your name?' Don't be scared of her smile. 'Actually, if I could just see Eva . . . when's she free?'

'Everyone wants to see Eva,' she says and her smile turns into something else again as she turns from you and clicks the mouse to open what can only be a list.

'Name?' she says again.

If you tell her your real name she will know. In the beginning there were four couples, one kid, one expected. In the beginning was the word and the word was Rowan. Eva named you not your own mother. Eva is your naming mother. The good mother. God the mother. Remind yourself, this woman wasn't here then, she won't know. Think. Quick. She'll want your credit card. The name on your credit card, the forename you changed by deed poll aged twenty-one. The name of your husband that you took aged thirty-five.

'Emma,' you say. 'Emma Phillips.'

A moment of typing, waiting, shaking her head and tutting to herself.

'It was a while back. But Eva knows me.' You almost say twenty-five, thirty. 'Ten years ago,' you say.

'Technology.' She sighs. 'What, what the heck? It's crashed again.'

'Oh God, yeah,' you say. 'Like every time I touch one it just wants to keel over and die.' It's coming out a laugh, nervous.

'Sorry. Phillips, was it?' she says.

You are getting nowhere. You know how to do it, speak their language. Take out your credit card. Cough, make her look up and see it. You do. She does.

'Well, you're in luck. We've had a cancellation,' she says. 'You are here for Sharing Week, yes?'

'Yes,' you say, 'absolutely.' You try to smile back with a smile like hers.

'Let me check the rooms,' she says, as she leans over and takes your card. 'Sometimes,' she says, 'it takes people a long time. I came here in 'eighty-nine; it took me all of six years to return.' And her smile has changed again as she swipes your card without telling you how much.

You are in. Just wait. Avoid her eyes. The noticeboard says – *Reiki, Guided Meditation, Shiatsu Massage. Hi, my name is Jodi, I am from Sweden and I have for first time found my life. I would like to stay. Rates negotiable.*

The old woman fumbling with the keyboard, sighing over the printout signing slip as it chugs out, her movements as slow as the machine. Then, God – an apparition.

She is coming down the stairs, old woman in flowery multicoloured cotton. She smiles at you with Eva's smile. It says you're not one of us, not yet, but you will be in time. We will show you. You are here, we are all here together. Another woman over there at the noticeboard is now smiling too. Fifty, sixty, in khaki slacks. Look at you now, they seem to say. The smiles on their mouths but their eyes not smiling at all. Their soft fluid steps as they pass. Their slow turn of the head as they walk so quietly away, as if on air, towards the garden or wherever, which will be somewhere that leads them back here to find you again, a day or two later, to give you the same smile which asks you, so quietly, if you belong. And in a day or two if you are still here then there will be names, and touches and the promise of love without names and when you join us, you will no longer need a name and a time to check in or to check the time because you are one with us and then you will be able to smile at the new people in this way and welcome them and know that they will not be able to leave because they have fallen under the power of that smile.

Just sign the printout. Your hand isn't shaking. Don't even look at how much it costs. It's still working, he hasn't shut down your shared account yet. Don't think about him. Keep smiling, sign the name you taught yourself to sign, hand it back to her.

'Thank you and welcome to Sharing Week,' she says.

'So what do we do in Sharing Week?' You nervous fool. 'Sorry, of course . . . I can't wait to start sharing!'

'Starts at eleven thirty.' She smiles. 'Here's your schedule.' And she passes you a nicely made full-colour brochure called *The Ithaca Experience*.

'Wow, great,' you say. 'Thanks, really appreciate you doing this for me.' You are talking too fast, like some idiot from the city.

'Enjoy your sharing time,' she says. 'Eleven thirty in Orchid on the second floor. The others are waiting in the Lilac Room, just through there.' She raises her hand, not her finger, so slowly, like pointing was wrong. Her hand drifts through the air, like what is out there is part of her too. 'You might want to put your bags in your room, or have some quiet time to yourself, or make yourself some tea in the kitchen, you're in Lily on the second floor.'

'Right, great, thanks so much.'

Lily. Of course. Rooms have names not numbers. They don't believe in numbers. You have no bags. You hope she doesn't see the hesitation that betrays you, your phoney smile, your ulterior motive.

Tonight you will walk the caravans. Knock on doors. Will ask the people you meet, discreetly. You could ask her now, this old woman. Jenna, you could say it. Is Jenna here? She would be about sixty-five now. Jenna Mathews.

Go now, to the place she waved to. It was where you built your nuclear bunker, which your mother said was cool and how clever you were. The room beneath the stairs. Five people sitting there on big sofas now. Try not to stare. A man with a ponytail, one with a bald head, two young women, one older, taller.

You enter. But it stops you a few feet in, the first thing you see. The photograph of Eva. Five feet from the sofa. A shrine of plants and crystals and fruit beneath. Her hair is white, her cheekbones chiselled, as they were, her features more gaunt but there are no lines in the impossible ageless airbrushed skin. Her Californian smile and shining eyes. You look into that perfect face and know that you were wrong to come here, that no matter how much you delve and intrude and plead, for every question you ask, person after person, you will receive only that smile.

*

We were playing 'houses'. Me and Jono and Saphie and Sally and Tom and some of the other kids and most of the grown-ups too. And it wasn't really playing because what we were doing was helping to build the real houses. Carrying bricks and sticks and mixing cement and paint. There were no dolls, no Barbies or Sindys, and when we fed our dolls we were really helping to make the food that fed us all. That's what I mean by playing houses. 'I played in my house' doesn't sound right. I could say 'we played in our house', but even that would be wrong. Because the houses weren't even finished and no one owned them, and we moved from one to the next, the kids and the grown-ups, sleeping anywhere we wanted. Even 'dolls' would be wrong. Whatever they were – a bundle of sticks, a bag of rice with a face painted on – these things never stayed what they were for long before they were turned into other things. You see, even the grammar breaks down. Even saying I. I still find it hard. It has always felt not like a thing in itself but something left after a We has been broken.

Every story told so far has to have a protagonist, a goal, obstacles to be overcome. Stories of the outside world, of the heroic Western male and conflict, Eva said. We never went there. We made up our own.

There were no heroes, no real identifiable differences between people. The obstacles were a form of play and the goal was just being together, trying to keep that moment for as long as possible. Of course there were troubles later, but before there were days, years, undifferentiated, without a story. Or maybe I was too young to know. The years when we played at houses with real bricks, when I played at being mummy with a real baby.

Little Saphie was Jono's little sister. There was another baby there too, for a while, called Toby. I must have been under five, because it was before the school started. Me and Jono and Sally and Tom used to take turns carrying the babies and washing them, changing their terry-towelling nappies. I'm sorry. There are too many characters, and if I describe them all, it will start again. You'll be looking for differences. But the names don't even matter because in some very real way we were all the same. I could tell you that Saphie had red hair and freckles and that Pete was her dad and he often laughed about how he was raven black and Tessa was natural blonde and so Saphie must have come from the milkman, and you might find conflict in that but it was never a problem for Pete. I could say we taught Saphie how to walk, but even that would be wrong. Saphie taught herself and we were just there to catch her. And no one taught us anything unless it was useful. Any parental influence on a child is harmful, a child must learn that a knife is sharp by cutting herself – that is what they said, when we came to them with splinters and cuts and burns.

One of us would cry and one of the grown-ups would hold us. Maybe Tessa or Eva or Petra or Jenna or Angus or Pete or Mike. I could say my mother always held me but that would be a lie, just making it sound like a family drama. Nuclear family. Someone held us and we stopped crying, we all had eight parents each.

I recall how we learned to stop Saphie crying by putting her fingers in our mouths and going, 'Am gonna getcha, gonna eatcha.' Or biting her feet or chewing at her tummy, like Tessa did when she was mad funny, 'Yum yum, fresh baby, yum yum,' all slurpy noises and big crazy Tessa laughs. Or making up silly rhyming songs to sing her to sleep. The weight of her in my arms and having to work out how many more steps I could carry her across the mud before I would have to pass her to Jono or Tom or Sal. Her face the day she ate all that jam. Counting her freckles. I'm sorry this is not a story, just fragments. I can't even say fragments of happy times because we didn't even realise then that we were happy. I could tell you I'm being nostalgic, that it was a time of some kind of idyll but that too would be a betrayal. It would come across as kitsch, as sentimental – framed by a story of the now in which such things are lost.

It's no good. If I'm going to try to tell you it needs conflict.

It came when Jono had to go to school. He was a year older than me. We'd been through town before but I guess I'd never really understood. Tessa said it was where the plastic people lived. There was me and Jono and baby Saphie and my mother in the Beetle.

It was like a fairy story, a story about aliens, what she told us as we drove. The houses that all looked the same. One male, one female, in each, with two children, one car, one washing machine, one fridge, one TV. Hundreds of them all the same in every street. I was laughing. 'One washing machine in each house! Why?' 'They're just like that, they don't think,' my mother said. 'In hundreds of towns it's all the same.'

We drove past the school and it looked grey and dark, blocking out the light. She told me and Jono that we'd have to sit separately at our own desks, like everyone else. She was sorry that we had to go. She'd wanted us to learn in our own time in our own special way but the government insisted. She seemed distracted, she didn't like driving through the town.

And the cars everywhere with just one person in each. A man polishing his bright silver one with shiny wheels, shouting at his kids to stand back from the hose. And fences and hedges around houses and name plaques. The women on the high street in high heels with their babies in their own individual prams.

Plastic mothers, she said, were fiercely competitive, setting neighbour against neighbour, child against child. Overprotective of their offspring and stifling. One fridge, one bath, one garage, a trip to the supermarket once a week. This was what they called maternal love. There was a song about it. She sang it to us as we drove.

86

Little boxes on the hillside
Little boxes made of ticky tacky

She kept saying sorry, but we weren't to worry. School would be an adventure. The locals had a really beautiful accent and we would make lots of new friends and who knew maybe even start speaking like them and then we could teach her all the new words.

And they all play on the golf course
And drink their martinis dry
And they all have pretty children
And the children go to school

There was an old lady washing her windows with an apron on. She had garden gnomes and a little wishing well made out of plastic.

We passed a play park. All the kids alone on the swings and climbing frames. Jono wanted to get out but my mother said no because just look at those straight plastic mommas worrying over all their perfect plastic kiddies, making sure they didn't fall, or play with any of the other kids. The smell of all that plastic, she said, God, it made her sick.

And the children go to summer camp
And then to the university

Talking about mothers always seemed to set Jenna off. She'd raise her voice and say all this grown-up stuff then go quiet for a long time. I remember when I was older, she hugged me and told me about when she got her period, what her mother said. Her mother's 'serves you right' face – 'Now you'll know what suffering is.' How mothers love to blame their daughters for the years they sacrificed for them. Their long sighs of 'if only' after the third gin and tonic. How her mother did the dishes every night even though they had a dishwasher, then would complain about how the detergent was ageing her hands. How she fussed over trivial things – preaching it in fact because she'd forced herself to accept so little and felt everyone should do the same. Valium junkies, secret alcoholics. The suppressed hatred that scored the face with lines that were then hidden behind the layers of something called blusher.

Where they were put in boxes
And they come out all the same

My mother said sorry for the bad trip and we'd stop off and get some ice cream as a treat.

There's a green one and a pink one
And a blue one and a yellow one.
And they're all made out of tacky tacky
And they all look just the same

This was all something to do with why she preferred to be called Jenna, not Jennifer, her christened name, not Mother, not Mum. But when I went to school and brought my new friends to Ithaca, she said, it would be OK to call her Mum in front of them because they wouldn't understand.

We got a pink ice cream and a green one and a yellow one, and she told us to keep it secret because ice cream wasn't allowed in Ithaca. As we rode back home, singing along, I remember thinking that she'd got the words a bit wrong because the houses weren't green and blue and pink. They were just grey.

And maybe I've got this all wrong. Maybe it wasn't my mother at all, but Tessa who drove us that day. In a very real way it doesn't matter. You see, I would have to lie, even

88

to myself, to say it was her, it was she, to split us all up into 'I's.

*

You are standing in the room, where no room was before, watching them as they wait.

'It's only by going into yourself that you can find self-lessness – is what Gurdjieff says. Have you read him?'

The accent, Swedish, German. The bald-headed forty-something on the sofa. You should make the effort to introduce yourself, to sit with them and share. But the voices, recounting what brought them here, their spiritual CVs.

'Oh yeah, the whole Russian American tradition, it's so fascinating, the turn of the century,' says the American ponytail. The men talking to the men.

The wallpaper is in pastel shades, fake Victorian cornicing. A stack of books to the side. *Selfless Love, The Garden, The Story of Ithaca, Ithaca – Return to the Source.* All books by Eva. They talk of Eva in excited voices.

'My God, I read it as soon as it came out in 'ninety-one. *The Garden,* my God, that book, she saved my life.' The American again.

'It was nineteen eighty-nine, for me.' A woman, foreign, her voice snapping the words out.

'Really, I'm . . . sorry, you're from?'

'Sweden.'

'Really, in translation in Swedish, it came out in Sweden back then?' His accent. Canadian.

'Yes, nineteen eighty-nine.'

'Really. Sorry, how do you say "Garden"? I mean, in Swedish.'

They say she walks through the garden every day. She may be visiting the lecture on Wednesday. They have

89

travelled to hear her from Hamburg, Los Angeles, Sydney, Amsterdam.

They don't know. The place where they sit, where there were no floorboards before. The windows they look out of. Which you and Jono used to smash for fun. You all left. The children. You could tell them about little Saphie and Jono and lap-dancing and smack.

Be calm. Try to sit beside them on the big sofa and exchange names beneath the smiling photograph of Eva. Smile when they ask you where you are from. You could tell them how you used to play here. How Eva called you her child – you are all my children. How she rarely touched you, though she touched your mother. Kissed her, held her, stroking her head in the aftermath of the rage. How after Eva left her alone you had to comfort her. Aged ten, mothering your mother.

How long can you stand there silent? Run over what to say to them – Hi, you here for Sharing Week? Hi, my name is . . .

The ponytail is talking now. Canadian or Californian? How he left his job in finance to come here, the woman is interrupting again, big, Dutch, yah yah, she says, she left her job to come here, and how already, this space, even after half an hour, she feels the change. And he's interrupting her saying that it wasn't just his job that he left, but his wife and kids. 'Leavin' it all behind,' he says.

The silence hanging then. And you're thinking of a song your mother used to sing, *Leavin' It All Behind*. Something like that. Dylan. No, it was an album, *Bringin' It All Back Home*.

Stop thinking about home. Sasa is so young, she won't remember Mummy's little holiday. Josh has been away for longer before with work. You should text him, not call him, you can't bear his voice. Not yet – text him and turn it off before he can ring back. *Back in 2 days. Sorry. X.* Should

90

you put an X or two Xs or none? You must remember to charge the mobile in the car, then go for your walk and start your enquiries. Maybe later, once you've had a rest. Look for her after.

Look at you now. Still halfway between the photo and the sofa with the sharers. It's OK, they're not staring at you.

'I love very much Eva book, *mia fidanzata, scusa non mia sposo,* how you say, we live together.'

'Your fiancé?' – the American ponytail.

'No, no, but like that, maybe is not same in Eengleesh. Mia.'

'Boyfriend. Right?'

'Whatever.' She says the Italian or Spanish, spitting the Americanism back in his face. 'I . . . I no tell him I come. I am actress, I want to be. I come here to decide . . . what I do.'

Nothing has changed. They still come here to escape lovers and find a greater love.

'We're all here for that,' says the big woman, interrupting with her slow voice, her accent – Dutch, you think. They have to be authorities on everything.

'No, no, yeah, yeah,' says ponytail. '*Je comprends,*' he says, although no one speaks French.

She spoke many languages. Your mother. When foreigners came she would ask them to sing folk songs from their country then she would memorise them, then teach you and the other kids.

'My wife too, cos, *c'est la même,* you know, she wouldn't have understood. Is the same, no? *Comprendez? Capiche?*'

The Italian gets up abruptly and stands there behind you. She's going to speak to you. She's pretty, mid to late twenties, her skin dark, eyes black, full of fight. Not like the others. You hadn't thought of it, that there might be another like you. How long can she stand there behind you

91

not speaking? You can hear her breathing. She walks on but her image stays with you. Her dyed-red short-cropped hair, her loose-fitting faded men's clothes that speak of being an artist, an anarchist before, of ten years of trying everything, drugs, men, women. Even though she has gone, you are blushing. If you stay a day or two you must avoid her.

You walk away from the sharing group. Across the floor to the door, over the thick pile carpet, trying to feel the beams beneath, which you and Jono used to jump between. Pete had said the place was dangerous, it could come down at any time. Four steps to the door. The rats must still be there beneath. You never saw a rat. Jono said he had. Jono died of an overdose in 1999 someone said. A lie maybe. Like the ones about your mother. A day or two and you will find them. Both. Here.

A voice behind. 'So how the hell is Sweden these days? I used to do a lot of conferences in Helsinki.' The fool American.

Go to your room, Rowan. Lily is its name the woman said. Upstairs. Go to Lily.

To your right the staircase. A broken frame it was. You had to jump and pull yourself up on the fourth step, the first three missing. Balancing so the wood wouldn't break. Lily.

It's all flowers and trees, Jono said. Morphine is natural, it comes from poppies. South America. They give people morphine in hospitals when they're going to die, he said in his stuttering way. Six parts morphine equal one of heroin. Funny, he said. Mushrooms are like acid. His dad, Pete, told him all this.

The carpeted steps where none should be. Another smiling fifty-year-old woman, passing you. Up there, above the second floor, the room at the top was Jono's secret place, his porno stash, the women spreading themselves across the dusty floor. The room where you first touched a cock.

'Sanctuary' the sign says now.

I am open twenty-four hours a day. You are welcome to use me for your silent meditation. Please book in advance. If your meditation requires movement, dance, chanting, etc, please ask your focus leader to allocate you another room. No shoes please. Please do not enter when the green light is on as others will be inside and should not be disturbed.

You turn away. Bedroom, corridor, no numbers, just names. Petunia, Carnation, Snowdrop, Bluebell. There is no room here called Poppy or Mushroom or Hemp or Peyote. No one knows about Pete or Jono.

As you turn the last step a withered yukka on the table facing you has a sign.

My name is Lo-Pi. I am sick right now. Please don't feed me. There is someone special who cares for me every day. I need time. I am getting better. Peace.

You feel suddenly sick. Your mother can't be here, how could anyone survive here for long?

The toilet has a name sign, it is called Rose. The name is written in pink swirling felt tip with flowers crawling round the letters in green and yellow.

You are not having a panic attack. Push, go inside. Don't think of the words 'choke', 'vomit'. Hold the sides of the toilet bowl and focus on something. The sign on the cistern.

My name is Dahlia. I am the toilet angel. I ask that you dispose of tampons or towels in the container provided.

Puke, cry, get it done. The angels will protect you. Blow your nose on the eco-friendly toilet paper.

Please be considerate towards the needs of our ecological septic tank. Peace.

Eva's voice everywhere. Focus on something else. The bath has a sign and a name.

I am Iris, the bath angel. Please ensure that you respect me and the wishes of others. Please don't use me after 9 p.m.

*or before 6 a.m. Don't fill me too full and please make sure
that you clean me after you leave. Peace.*

Sasa in her little bath. Holding her head so she won't
sink under. Her giggling with the splashes. Your mother
bathed you in the sink. She loved you. She sang you to
sleep. *Dream Angus.* You would pretend you'd had night-
mares just so she would sing it to you.

Dream Angus is here with dreams to sell.

Puke it up, you'll feel better for it.

The wad of recycled toilet paper in your hand, wet
with the saliva. Should you flush? Please God, godless
fucking angel of the shit and tampons, help, help, please,
here now in this toilet that was never a toilet.

This toilet that was named by Eva the same way that
she named all the children of your generation, the same
way she named you – after a plant.

*

Oh, whit'll we dae wae the herrin's heid
Oh, whit'll we dae wae the herrin's heid
We'll mak it a loaf an sell it for breed
Herrin's heid, loaves o' breed, an' aw sorts o' things

It was summer of the folk festival, '78. She'd been rehearsing
for months with Mike and Angus. The name of their band
was JAM: Jenna Angus Mike. She'd designed the posters
herself and we coloured them in with Tessa and went round
the towns trying to get the local shops to put them up in
their windows. Jono didn't want to do it. Kids will only
laugh at us, he said. They didn't laugh but I saw them
whisper about Jenna and her long hair and follow us from
shop to shop. Most of the shopkeepers said no thank you
or that there wasn't enough space in the windows even
though there always was. They all had this other poster

94

up, not hand-painted like my mum's but glossy with a photograph. Some man with a big smile and a Stetson and a bright yellow cowboy outfit. His name was written in stars. Donnie Dallas and the Rhinestone Cowboys. Pete said it was probably because of the nuclear base, the fucking Americans.

My mother spent months in the local library, dragging me along while she dug out these old books and copied the words by hand. Local folk songs about the fishing, hundreds of years old. She bought a record by Jean Redpath and taught herself how to sing along to the old Scottish words. Jean and Judy Collins and Joni Mitchell and Jenna, all Js, Angus used to say, his thumb up in the air. 'Jenna,' he'd shout. 'Some day soon!' It was the name of a song by Judy. Some day soon, they all believed, the world would say Jenna's name in the same breath as the other great Js.

She practised so hard, she made me correct her when she got the words wrong. Over and over.

> *Oh, whit'll we do wae the herrin's bellie*
> *Oh, whit'll we do way the herrin's bellie*
> *We'll mak it a lassie and christen her Nellie*

She said the locals would love it. To hear their own old songs sung again. That Eva was wrong to give up on them. That it was so important to reach out to people, that we weren't living in a vacuum. The herrin's song, she said. It was just like what we were doing in Ithaca. It had an ecological message, it was about recycling, using every part of a fish.

> *Herrin's fins – needles and pins*
> *Herrin's back – laddie called Jack*
> *Herrin's eyes – puddin's and pies*
> *For aw the fish that swim in the sea*

95

The herrin is the fish for me
Sing fa la la lido, fa la la lido, fa la la liday

If they could start the folk revival in Caithness, like
Dylan had done in America, then the locals would see them
differently. I couldn't help but think this was all something
to do with Jono, like she was trying to get the commune to
mix with the locals for his sake, but then again, his beatings
were a secret, he'd made me swear on her life.

She'd mailed posters down south, she'd contacted all
the newspapers in Scotland. The debut of JAM. She said
they needed a hundred people to come to break even, and
told me what that meant and how she'd put money into it
so they could get a PA system and some recording equipment and the other folk bands from down south had to be
paid travel expenses, and the ones from Shetland had to
come by boat and that wasn't cheap. She figured that maybe
sixty locals would come then maybe seventy or eighty from
down south. If they got two hundred people then they would
have some profit to put into the garden.

She learned *Aw' the Week yer Man's Awa* and *Wild
Mountain Thyme* and *Copper Kettle* by Joan Baez, even
though Joan was American and America was the evil empire,
like Donnie Dallas and the Rhinestone Cowboys. She practised every minute while washing, weeding, digging,
cooking. Always stopping herself when she hit a wrong note
or forgot the words, asking me what they were then starting
again.

The week before the festival she dragged us round the
shops in Wyster again, trying to sell tickets. Some older
kids started following us and shouting, 'Tinks!' She said,
'Turn the other cheek.' The only one that bought a ticket
was the man in the grocer's but that was only because she
bought a huge box of tea bags and some butter. In the other
shops most of our posters had been taken down or had the

other one stuck on top. Everywhere we went Donnie Dallas was smiling back at us from under his Stetson with a big red banner that read SOLD OUT. I tried to hide behind her big dress in the grocer's while this rough-looking girl and her gang peered through the window pointing at my mum's sandals, laughing and giving us the two fingers. Jono said her name was Debbie.

We all painted big banners with flowers and stars and decorated Eva's big barn with long paper chains of people holding hands. They came from down south, in vans and caravans and a big bus painted with a CND sign and brought presents of pans and handmade pots and plates and a toilet bowl and some shovels and food, lots of it, jam and cakes and seeds and beans and huge bags of lentils and rice and things to drink and smoke and little pills like paper. They came with stories of Pictish burial chambers and earth goddesses and ghosts of kings. They came down from the islands and talked of the growing folk scene. JAM were going to open the festival, playing before Peerie Jane, the big five-piece from Shetland who'd been on the radio. They turned up with their fiddles and the banjos and accordions and flutes. There were maybe thirty of them in the bands, with maybe another twelve or so that came with them, girlfriends and friends. My mother was too embarrassed to ask them to pay.

Not one single local turned up, not even the grocer. The local paper said Donnie Dallas was playing to crowds of nine hundred every night. A gang of ten local kids had beaten Jono up and chased him out of town shouting, 'Hippies, go home!'

Mike was sitting on the stage Angus had built, frantically tuning his banjo. Angus was drinking and laughing with Peerie Jane. I found my mother in the kitchen, bent over on herself, holding her head, her face hidden by her long black hair. I stood there at the door, not sure if I should disturb her, but she looked up, and opened her arms for me. 'Donnie Bloody Dallas,' she said.

She stood on the stage and thanked the twelve in her audience for coming. She thanked all of us kids for our wonderful decorations and Eva for her financial support. She apologised for the long journey they must have had, and for the weather, for her nerves, and for her accent which wasn't authentically Scottish. She cleared her throat and looked down at me and Jono with his big black eye.

'This is an old local song,' she said and Mike struck the chord. She closed her eyes and sang every word perfectly, every note. She was good. But her voice wasn't as strong as it had been the week before, in the garden, in the kitchen. Her voice had a tremble in it.

*

Lily is open. There is movement inside. There is nowhere else to go, only the car. You stand and read the sign on the door. *Lily is sponsored by generous contributions from the participants of Gay Awareness Week.* You peer inside and it is her. The dark eyes. The Italian.

'Ciao, bella.'

'Ciao.'

She's unpacking an old army rucksack covered in badges. Go in, find your bed. Are they numbered, named, which one? There are three. A map lies open on one, by a large expensive suitcase. The only free bed is by the window.

'Man,' she says. 'These fucking people. Pah; raising her hand, palm upwards, like throwing the air over her shoulder, shaking her head. 'Know watta mean?'

You are too tired to interpret. They say 'Know watta mean' in London. It means you're part of the same gang. Shh, Rowan. Stop thinking. Sit on the bed, make it yours. Rest.

98

'You are funny,' she says. '*Non, scuse* . . . fun,' she says. 'My Eengleesh – I think we have fun together, you and me here, uh?'

Your smile, so pathetic against the strength of hers. She is very pretty, sitting on her bed, facing you, her bare feet curled beneath her, like she could explode into action any second. Apologise, tell her you are too tired, too fucked up. If she could, could she just let you just lie down, not talk?

'That American, blah blah blah blah, the Dutch too, ees funny, no?'

She is psychic. Psychotic. Smiling. Looking for a good fight. A good friend, only one, in the whole world. You must have lost all your friends in the last few days.

She's putting on the voice of the big Dutch.

'I haf dun these courses before, yah, I vood like to find myself, yah, I haf tried in Sydney und California und Freiburg to find myself, uh.'

She explodes in laughter. She exhausts you.

'They must be rich, uh?'

You nod. 'Yes.'

'Yes, yes.' She is bouncing on her bed. She wants to be your new Charlie. Say nothing.

'Are you Sagittarius? I am, I could see, I saw you, yes?'

The carpet is sand-coloured, it must be the same in all the rooms. This dizziness. It might be that there's no pattern to focus on, or that for the first time in hours you realise that you haven't, not even for a second, really thought about Sasa.

It's 10.45 a.m. She will be in her peak alertness period. Trying to crawl, putting everything into her mouth to learn what it is. Combs, mobile phones, pens, books, shoelaces, DVD covers.

'I'm sorry, I just need to . . .'

Screaming when he takes them away from her. Telling

99

her, 'No.' You agreed on this. There are rules. A child doesn't have to learn what pain is by hurting herself.

'I'm so tired, I just . . .'

Is he even there? Has he got a new nanny? Did he get an agency? Did he read the chapter on vetting nannies? Did he take time off work? Please, God, let him be there with her now and not some minimum-wage illegal worker.

Get up now. Walk past the excited Italian. Back to the car park. Plug the mobile into the car, check your messages. He must be insane with worry. How could you do this to him?

You must have stood too quickly. You are going to vomit. You have to lie down. Close your eyes.

'Ees OK,' she says. 'I see you – I am same, ees gonna be OK.' She says, 'I want to leave today but I stay cos of you, we will be friends, uh?'

You can't speak. Curl up. There, that's better. Close your eyes.

'*Capito tutto*,' she whispers. Her mouth must be close to your ear. Her hands on your shoulder. A squeeze. Deep. 'I feel it,' she whispers. 'Right there, ees sore. We do this, you help me too, uh, we be friends now, seesters.'

You clutch your knees tighter. Willing her away. Then you hear the door close and she is gone and you are alone. 'We are seesters.' Jono smeared his burst blister into yours because blister rhymed with sister and blood didn't rhyme with brother; you stage-dived to a song called *Sister* and Charlie caught you; your mother hugged you when you had your first period and said, 'We are all sisters now.' You hug yourself, 'sister' screaming in your ears.

*

The festival went on for five days more but she didn't sing again. No point crying over spilt milk, she said.

The guys in the bands were funny, always picking us up, me and Jono and little Saphie, swinging us around to the music. Their vans got stuck in the mud and they were always covered in it, dancing in it. There was one guy who walked around with nothing on but mud. He had scary eyes and was always eating. They were all eating all the time, which was why I hardly saw my mother. Days went by and she came into the caravan long after it was dark and I'd reach for her but each time she was tired and hardly spoke and smelt of food.

I never saw much of Angus either. He was chilling, Jenna said, while she made huge pots of soup and hundreds of biscuits. He'd earned it, she said, after working so hard all year on the roofs and the plumbing and the garden and the band. But I knew the real reason. She hadn't spoken to him since they argued after the first night with the band. And Jono hardly saw Tessa, his mum, because, Pete said, she loved music and always went a bit daft this time of year with the sun that never seemed to set. But we did, one night, me and Jono, see Tessa dancing. She had her top off and all the men were clapping as she twirled round and round the barn, her big breasts swinging. There was this other guy, skinny-looking, who had a camera and was filming everybody. He didn't look like the others, his hair was short.

I can't recall any words said, or what arguments there were. There was this big Welsh guy with so much hair he looked like a Santa Claus and a monkey at the same time. Byron, he called himself. He was a guitarist, and he had goats like we did, a goat farm in Wales, and two kids, real kids not baby goats. Skye, a big girl, and Rosie, who was my age. We never saw their mum. I think she was maybe one of the other women that helped my mother in the kitchen.

Byron wanted to us to perform a play, he said. Me and Skye and Rosie and Jono and all the other kids. It was supposed to be about nature. Skye said he was an arsehole because when she went to school and they did plays there was always some words to learn and a story. But he just wanted us to make it up because the mind of a child was a beautiful thing. Skye said he was a wanker, she was a teenager and never told us what her words meant though we copied them a lot and laughed when we said them to the grown-ups then ran away. He was her dad but she never let him kiss her like he kissed us and she didn't want to be stuck with little kids either in some stupid fucking play. Byron got us to dress up. Helped us on with our costumes. We only had faerie ones, and Jono had a cowboy one but he said cowboys were for kids and he didn't want to dress up any more. Byron said we looked great so it would be a story about faeries and did we know they were all around us and were really just pagan gods that had been forced underground? He told us to improvise as he sat there on his caravan step smoking, but we didn't know what to do, so instead he put on some music and turned it up loud. *Foxy Lady*. And he went back inside and took off his clothes, but we didn't mind, we saw naked adults all the time, we just giggled and danced around, shouting, 'Foxy, foxy lady.' Wow, he said, great, now pretend to be foxes. So we crept around with our fingers out like claws in the mud, trying to be as sly as foxes with our faerie costumes on, shouting, 'Foxy lady,' every time the record said it. Jono got in a huff, said it was stupid, we couldn't be foxes and faeries at the same time. He called us little babies and went off to look for Skye. No one ever saw our faerie play apart from Byron. I remember feeling weird about the way he spoke so quietly to us like it was secret and bounced us on his knee.

Jono came back one night and said he had a real secret — Skye was kissing a grown-up and I should come and see. Saphie woke up and wanted to come too but Jono said no because she was just four and that wasn't even half of thirteen. So we snuck out, me and Jono, round the back of the barn, past the caravans. The man was there again with the camera, he tried to film us but we ran past. Jono said he was from the CIA. We ran and jumped over the stream but I fell in. Shh, Jono said, shh, and pulled me onto the other bank and said, 'Wuh, we . . . ha . . . have to be . . . spuh . . . spies.' His stutter started round about then. My mother said it was all because of school, because he had two different worlds, two separate languages in his head at the same time. And when he struggled, we shouldn't try to correct him, or guess what he meant, no matter how awful it made us feel, because it would only make him more tongue-tied and more cross. Patience and love, she said, would mend him.

The lights from the bonfire made the trees look scary. Like they were moving. I wanted to go inside Eva's barn but Jono said no. 'Shh, Skuh . . . Sky kih . . . kissin, cuh . . . come on.' He led me round the back of Eva's and it was dark and I was cold and shivering but he took my hand and showed me how to creep. 'Like foxes?' I asked, but he said nothing.

He ran to the back of the barn like a cop, his two fingers pointed in the air like a gun. He waved his other hand for me to come and I hid behind him, copying the gun shape. 'The cuh . . . cuh . . . coast is clear.' It was too dark to see much. There was noise, like someone moving, a twig breaking. We stood there behind his tree, really still. 'Cuh . . . c'mon,' he said, with an American accent, and he ran, stooped down, like he was dodging bullets.

He threw himself to the ground. I tried to copy and jabbed my toe and whined at him. 'Shh . . . shut up,' he said, 'or you . . . you duh . . . dead.' It took him a long time to say but I worked out that if they caught us they'd do interrogations.

103

'Shh, loo . . . look.' And he pointed. We were in the shadow of Eva's croft, but I could almost make it out. A man was grunting like he was lifting something heavy and a woman like she was in pain. She had long hair, not like Skye at all. The man was on top, wrestling with her. Jono slumped down beside me, but I couldn't stop staring. An elbow, a leg, two other legs around a bare back.

'We should call the police,' I whispered but he wasn't listening. 'Jon Jo,' I said to him like Tessa did sometimes when she was cross. I stood up. 'This is no fun,' I said.

'Sh . . . uut up.' He pulled me down, but before he did I saw.

The woman's face looking up. She covered her breasts, she couldn't see me, but I could see her. It was her.

Jono ran off, not even trying to hide himself. I could hear them behind me getting up, talking, as we ran. The light from the bonfire was dazzling my eyes. The shadows dancing round.

'Jono,' I shouted, over the music. 'It's OK. It's all right, come back! It was only your mum.'

I looked for him in all the usual hiding places, by the stream and the sheds, calling his name, but he had vanished.

I knew Jenna would still be in the kitchen and I needed a hug so I ran in. He was there, by the range, crying in her arms. Her eyes told me to stay away for a bit. Holding him like he was a little baby.

'It was just Tessa,' I said to her.

'Wah . . . wasn't,' he said. His head between her breasts, crybaby.

'Was!'

He turned, furious. 'Was your dah . . . dahhh . . . dad,' he said.

Maybe I felt jealous. I tried to make myself cry so she'd open her arms for me. 'Shh, shh, tell me,' she said. So I started.

When I'd finished, Angus and Tessa wandered past the kitchen, mud-stained and laughing, holding hands.

'I see,' she said, so quietly, and held us close and kissed our heads. 'I see.' But when I looked up at her she had her eyes closed. 'Shh,' she said. 'I see I see I see.'

*

'Please make sure your mobile phones are turned off. We have Internet access in the Cyber Room but we'd recommend that if you're to get the most out of your Sharing Week you resist the urge to contact people outside. We would also ask that you show emotional restraint in your interactions with each other and respect each other's need for solitude.'

You came to the meeting room named Orchid, just as your brochure said you should. You arrived a little late after running back to the car with the mobile, trying to work out how to charge the battery from the engine. Worrying, wondering if the engine had to be turned on for it to work, tearing through the glove compartment, under the seats for instructions, then giving up. All the other seats in the circle were already taken by the time you got there. There was only one left empty, between the Italian and the Focus Leader. She reached out to touch you as you sat, grinning, '*Ciao, Cara Mia.*' In an hour when it is done the mobile will be charged and then you can call him. Sit and observe, kill the time.

The Focus Leader has now introduced herself as Tamara. She is maybe twenty-eight, a natural blonde, pretty, denims, T-shirt, no bra, sitting in her Zen pose, her bare feet tucked under her thighs on the standard office-type chair. There is a big candle on the tiny table in the centre. Rainbow-patterned, like the ones from the Body Shop. Burning. Scentless. Her accent. Taught English by Americans. She is not a leader really, she says, her task is to introduce

105

you each to the concept of sharing and to help you through the process of opening up to each other. She doesn't want to hear of past problems, just names. 'This is not a therapy session, just a game, beautiful in its simplicity. The first in a series of sharing games which might seem silly and which some of us might struggle with at first but which are intended to establish a new kind of connection.

'Please say your names and one sentence about where you are from and why you are here. You say this only so you can leave it behind. And then say, "And this is my friend," and name the person who went before you. First of all, I want you all to hold hands.' She pauses, smiles. 'Go on. It's not so hard.'

Titters and giggles. The Italian is already grabbing for you. Her grip tight, her palm moist. Tamara reaches for your other hand, her hold weak, dry. Human Resources. You played a similar game in your first week at work. Some here look vaguely corporate. It makes sense. Just get it done.

'I'll go first.' Tamara closes her eyes, takes a deep breath, then opens her eyes and speaks on the outward breath.

'My name is Tamara and I am from Tampere, Finland, and I came here five years ago after the death of a close friend woke me to the gift that is life. My name is Tamara. Like that.' The smile, the way she pushes it round the circle, giving it to everyone. It doesn't quite add up – like she was happy about a death.

'We go round the circle – to you,' she says, 'and your name is?' For a second, the fear. You are sitting next to her by accident. Don't panic, go first, easier that way, get it done. But she turns her head the other way, so you will be last in the circle.

'Sorry, Heidi.' The middle-aged skinny woman sitting next to her on the left.

'Start with a "Hi, my name is Heidi . . ."' Tamara

whispers and the others giggle and titter, already rehearsing their one-line lives.

'OK, hi, my name is Heidi, I know it's stupid to be from Sweden with this name.' She laughs to herself. She sounds American like Tamara. The woman beside her with the London haircut hugs her feet beneath in imitation of the scary Italian, whose hand gives you little excited childish squeezes.

'I come here because –' She looks to Tamara. Tamara has her eyes closed. 'I . . . I would like to be in community, to be really together, to eat together, every day. I think is not natural to eat alone. We are by nature, animals.'

She stares at Tamara, waiting for her to open her eyes. So slowly Tamara does and smiles Eva's smile – 'Your name again and then "and this is my friend Tamara".'

'Yes, yes, sorry, and my name is Heidi and this is my friend Tamara.'

Tamara nods, doesn't say, 'Next,' but already the twenty-something London haircut is twitching. The designer army slacks, eyebrow and lip piercings, tattoo visible on one shoulder.

'Hi, my name is Jules.' Her accent. You were right. You hate that, when you are right about people. Phoney norf Lundun accent.

'Cos of the trees and wot we're doin' to the planet. I mean, fucksake. Like global warming, right, and the flood, cos, I mean, we're all gonna, sooner or later . . . Knowwhatta mean? We gotta do sumfing.'

Tamara raises her hand from her knee. Everyone's eyes on her.

'Jules,' she says. 'WE,' she says louder. 'I should have said this before.' And smiles to herself. 'Eva said something beautiful once about "we".' She takes a deep breath and closes her eyes then another breath and then the smile. 'I wish to be We, because I suffer being I. But We is not Me, is not I, and we can only ever start to be a We from an I.'

Someone, a man, hums from across the room.

'Yeah, but I was just—'

'When we use "we" we forget the "I", and the "I" is like the eye. It sees and it does not blame. We is blame. I personally find it of value to say I when I talk of my own experience and then one day hope that I might meet other Is who may become a we.' She opens her eyes and looks at Jules.

'Right, right, sorry. Yeah, I'm Jules . . . my name is Jules and these are my friends Heidi and, sorry, Tam?'

'Tamara.'

'Like tomorrow.'

'Yes.'

The words, the circle, the rules. You know this. They make you sleep communally, they get you up after five hours and subject you to rigorous group exercises. Break down the ego. Get you crying with strangers. The CIA did it first. Eva was a CIA plant. Communal living was an mind-control experiment funded by the Americans. You read it on a conspiracy website. They had to break up the anarchist/communist cells. The Cold War. Why do you think Eva picked a site so close to a US Army base? Where did Eva get the money from when the commune faltered? Eva was a plant. What plant are you today? We don't say we, we say I, I, I. The American way.

'Hi, my name is Marianne, I live in a commune in Vrije huis, Holland.' The big Dutch. 'It start in 'eighty-five, is uh, uh . . . intentional community, yes? Bigger than this but uh . . . we have some problems, jah? Uh . . . I just come here to see how things you do, to see, to learn, also how we do things better, maybe in Vrije huis. Uh, I have been to communities, in Montana uh, New Mexico uh *und* Hamburg, like this. I play this game before, lot of times. It's uh, good game, *gutt, ver gutt*?'

Look at her, six foot tall with hands and voice like a

man's. Lentil-eating bore, they love rules and giving people tasks. Think the world would be a better place if everyone put their tea bags in the compost – humourless, pedantic, pure. Stop it.

Then it's the men, for some reason they are seated together in a clump of three. Next, next, next. Your mother did this three hundred times, and each time it was her turn, she said the bare minimum. Do it like her. When it is your turn tell them what they want to hear.

'Hi, my name is Johann, I am from Hamburg.' Tall, balding, fiddling with his hands, with his wedding ring. 'I am married with two beautiful children. I am not so sure of my future. I have been getting into Buddhism and . . .'

A Zen adulterer. His chinos, posture, corporate keep-fit torso. Banker. Wanker. Sneaks into the empty conference suite to meditate alone.

'. . . And also I am reading Plato and Socrates and feel the love of man, of mankind, is good, not bad. I come in here, sorry, is more than one sentence. I come here to find love, uh, without body.'

And you were right. Repressed gay, midlife crisis. Sad, your first dad was openly bisexual, your mother never had a problem with that.

Tamara says, 'Our pasts are full of conflict. Just say your name and share it with us, together, as each person realises how little there is in a name.'

'Sorry, yes,' he says. 'Sorry. My name is Johann and these are my friends Marianne and Jules and Heidi and Tamara.'

When you plugged the mobile into the lighter socket it might have started draining the car battery. Best to go for a drive while you charge. Stop it. Focus. Your mother taught you how to do this. How hard to make a child focus. Sasa's attention span is worrying. Josh has been fretting about this for two months now. He reads the list of developmental stages to you. She should be able to focus on her toys for twenty or so minutes. Why is it that every time he buys her a new toy she's more interested in the packaging? She's not even touched the Teletubbies interactive garden. Why does she only want to play with your hairbrush?

'Hi, my name is Tom.'

The ponytailed American. A shared intake of breath in the room, before his next word. Oblivious, he's laughing to himself.

'Jeez, where do I start?' He exhales loudly. 'I'm OK, I'm OK,' he says. 'Just gimme a minute.'

His minute is five seconds.

'Morgan Stanley. Oh Jeez, no, that's not my name, Jeez, sorry, no, fuck that, I just need a second.'

His second takes a minute then two. Tamara delicately interrupts, telling you all that you have as much time as you need. 'God, yeah, I so understand,' and he starts again then stops then starts, laughing to and at himself again.

'You know, this guy I knew, he like told me once that life was like a "Lie" without an "f" and like how "f", it was, it was like "if". Like, you know . . . like "if only".'

Tom is a stereotype. He must know this too, maybe that is his problem. Tamara shifts her feet. The Italian is gripping your hand tighter. She wants you to look up and share her smiling hatred of the American. But your hatred is bigger and older than hers. Your little secret.

'Sorry, it's just so good to be here and . . . yeah, and to share, really share. God! I so look forward to uh, sharing with you all, all of you. Yeah.'

You look to Tamara because you don't want to face the Italian. They all look to Tamara because sharing is a lie, there always has to be a leader.

'Right, right, sorry, the name is Tom and these are my friends, Johann and . . . You're from Sweden, yeah, yah. We were talking before and . . . Mary-Anne and Jules and

110

Heidi and . . .' He pauses like there should be applause. '. . . Tamara.'

And so it goes on. Hi, my name is Glenna. Hi, my name is Lo-Mi. Hi, my name is Sylvie. Overweight, from the north of England, looks like someone's mother. She says she's been sick and she's got into holistic things now, cos Western medicine has no answers – and these are my friends. Breast cancer is your bet. It goes round the circle. Four more to go till you. You can't close your eyes or focus on the candle in the middle of the room. Hi, my name is Istvan – Rotterdam – another midlife crisis. Close your eyes, just get through this.

What will you say? Only one body away from you now and coming towards you. Hi, my name is Rowan I have come here to search for my mother.

Eyes closed. Work it out. Stop gripping the Italian's hand.

My name is Rowan, I have come here because I was born here and I am tired. And you are all liars and hypocrites and cowards. Concentrate. You are smarter than these people, tell them what they need to hear so you can pass.

She speaks beside you. 'My name is Mia. I come from Roma but live now in Berlin. I love very much the free expression. I work in a sauna and do reiki massage.'

What will you say? My name is Rowan and I deserted my baby.

'I love very much the nature and the beautiful land of Scotland. I feel already I will find myself here. My name is Mia and these are my friends – Lo-Mi, Istvan, Sylvie, Glenna, Alex . . .' and she stops. '. . . And Morgan Stanley,' she says.

Everyone laughs, even the American. 'Please don't ever call me that! The name's Tom!' he says.

'OK, Tom and Johann, Marianne, Jules, Heidi and Tamara.'

Tom claps his hands and shouts 'Wahey, all right!'

Silence. You look up. The Focus Leader is looking at

you, waiting. Mia is squeezing your hand.

'My name is.' What is your name, the one on the credit card or the one you were given?

'My name is Rowan. I come from London. I am married with a child and I drove here.'

Silence. Absurd.

'Sorry, that's all, sorry . . . and these are my friends Mia, Lo-Mi, Istvan, Sylvie, Glenna, Alex, Tom, Johann, Marianne, Jules, Heidi and Tamara.'

'Thank you. Thank you, Rowan. Thank you, each and all. You all did so well. Really this group is quite something. You really must all be so excited, I can just feel it in the room. This energy that is bigger than the sum of each of your energies.'

Tamara asks you all to close your eyes or focus on the candle if that is more comfortable, to keep on holding hands. You close your eyes.

'Let us just take this time, this special time, together, to hold and feel each other. To know that we are friends together now and not strangers. To know that who we were before has no meaning in this place, that we are together, in the now. Feel your breath in the room, know that you breathe the same air as your new friends, that you are one in that next breath, that we are here together and we are one. And pause and just say that. Let us just say this together now. We are together, we are one.'

This is what it has come to now. The radical commune. A Wall Street trader, a corporate clone, an anorexic, a cancer victim, two midlife crises, two career crises and an actress. You open your eyes and stare at the candle in the middle of the room. Burning smokeless. You repeat the words of the woman whose name sounds like tomorrow.

'We are together, we are one.'

*

112

There were words we had to learn to fit in at school.

Grass is gress. You is ye. Like is lek. What is fit. With is wey. A girl is a laskie. Crying is greetin'.

Fit ye doin' on 'e gress greetin' lek a laskie?

Every day when the school bell rang they would chase us onto the football pitch and pin Jono down, punching him, kicking him, making him say things so they could laugh at his English accent, at his growing stutter.

'Say – am a wee laskie.'

'Fu . . . fu . . . fuck off!'

Four of them pinning him down with fists, with knees, laughing, spitting in his face.

'Say – ah'm a smelly tinker.'

Their names were Splinter, Jim, Tommy and Debbie. Splinter was bigger, they'd kept him back a year. Debbie was a tomboy but the prettiest in the class. Her Adidas Kicks were worn down at the heel. Her parents must have been poor. She was the worst of them all. Debbie Mackay. They only tortured us, I think, to show off to her.

There was this one girl, Suzanne, she was in the top year, she must have felt sorry for Jono. They sometimes left him alone when she was around because she said her mither wis a teacher at 'e skool. She used to run after us sometimes, after they'd given Jono a doing, to try to teach him.

'Naw, ye dinny say garden, it's gerdeen. And a boy is a biy.'

He hated her more than anyone. And she wasn't there that day. The day they made Jono eat mud.

We needed 'Ad . . . Adidas Ki . . . Kicks', Jono said. It was the wellies that were the problem. It was hard to run in wellies but we had to wear them because of the mud in Ithaca and because our parents couldn't afford trainers, not even for school. It was a long walk up the dirt track once we got off the bus. No one ever got round to fixing the track, never had the money. It was hard to drive down too because they didn't believe in filling in the potholes, because they didn't believe in cars. So the wellies. We had to do sports at school in our bare feet, and they used to laugh at our dirty toenails. They called us tinks – gyppos – hippies – darkies – white settlers – poshies – and Englishers. Jono said they were stupid. How could we be posh and gypsies at the same time? They called him a poof and he told me what it meant in his long stuttering sentences.

Sorry, school, the local primary school was in Wyster. It had been a big Victorian fishing port but then it got over-fished. It was typical of man's greed and stupidity, Eva said. Most people there worked at the nuclear power station or the American Army base on the coast. The jets flew over us three or four times a day. The locals worked there doing shit jobs, capitalist slaves, Pete said, but a lot of them didn't work at all. It was a rough town, the kids hardened by poverty. Sorry, the mud, that was what I wanted to say. That day Jono and I tried to run but couldn't because of the wellies and how they made him be a cow.

'Mek him eat gress,' Debbie laughed.

'Ye wanta eat some gress, tinky boy, is at it? Ye wanta sum gress, like a coo? Say moo, lek a coo.'

They held me back, made me watch. Splinter would kick Jono in the face, till he did what they said.

'Muh . . . muh . . .'

And they copied his stutter, chanting, 'Muh, muh.'

'Fit wis at?'

'Belt him wan.'

'Say moo lek a coo.'

'Muh . . . muh . . .'

'He wants his mammy. Aw, wee baby greetin' for his mammy . . .'

Splinter pulled Jono's hair, got a handful of grass and mud and stuffed it into Jono's mouth. Debbie held his nose so he couldn't breathe and his mouth so he had to swallow.

114

He choked it back and started crying. The kids laughed, but Debbie was disgusted. She shouted, 'Fuckin' wee poof,' and kicked him in the mouth.

On the bus he told me to stop crying but his face was covered in mud and blood. I spat on my rolled-up sleeve and tried to wipe it off and said we should tell Tessa, but he said, ' Stu . . . stupid . . . hih . . . hih . . . hippie . . .' The last time Tessa had turned up at school to complain they had stripped him naked after and whipped him with branches. If I ever told again, he would run away and never come back, he said. He made me swear on my mother's life.

We got off the bus and he paced on ahead up the dirt track, found a stick and started bashing things: the stacks of peat, the pile of car seats, the old shell of Angus's abandoned Beetle.

There was no one around as we passed the new caravans. Jono stopped outside Tessa's croft and tried to get the words out. I knew what he meant – I was to make sure that she wasn't there. I checked and told him the coast was clear. 'Ty . . . ty . . . typical,' he said, 'fu . . . fuggin . . . sluh . . . slut.' Pete never told him off for swearing, he said it was the subconscious revolt of the proletariat. Tessa said Jono was turning into a little fascist, which was maybe why she ran off so often.

Jono went inside to get cleaned up; I could hear him cranking the water pump as I sat on Tessa's big bed, and gazed up at the cloud patterns. There was only half a roof at Tessa's, an old tarpaulin hung between the rafters to catch the rain. Pete had had a plan to fill a water tank for everyone to use. We still didn't have piped water.

I lay there, staring and touching Tessa's things: the oriental silks, the tie-dyed rugs and skirts, the frozen cascades of candle wax, the American flag with its graffittied peace sign, the reefers and empty bottles, the bed covered in blankets and rugs, the spooky pictures she'd

115

drawn of writhing naked nymphs. Tessa had stopped sleeping with Pete by then and other men had come to fill her bed. Jono had walked in on her more than a few times at night and seen things he didn't have words for. My mother got us all to sleep with her in the caravan then. 'It'll be like going on holiday, every night,' she said.

Jono slouched in, moaning that he was bored. He was always bored. He wanted a telly, the kids at school all talked about *The Six Million Dollar Man* and *Charlie's Angels*. He got Pete's penknife and ran out, swiping at the air.

I followed him, past the goats and chickens. Tessa had bought them but soon lost interest. There were meetings about whether we should sell them or eat them. Tessa, Eva and Pete were vegetarian. My mother said that all of us kids needed more protein but she couldn't bring herself to kill anything.

Past the sheds, Jono found a metal rod and hit one of the goats with it. 'Smelly fucking tinks.' He didn't stutter as much when he shouted. I told him to stop being violent. He told me to shut up. 'Puh . . . puh . . . puh . . . posh fuckin' hippie.'

I caught up with him in the vegetable garden. He was swiping at the seedlings. I begged him to stop, Jenna had slaved all summer at them, but he laughed, his rod smashing the leaves. 'Duh . . . duh . . . duh . . . dead already.'

He ran past the A-frame house that the new people had started building. They were going to have a real toilet, not holes and buckets like the rest of us. Jono said they were poshy Englishers, but they had Yankee voices. My mother said things would be better now because there would be serious people and more money in the communal pot, but I sensed she was wary of them. One of them said he'd heard Eva's voice in a dream and that he was the great-great-great-great-grandson of Mary Queen of Scots. They were Eva's people. Religious.

116

'Cuh . . . cuh . . . mon, stinky fuckin' tink!' Jono shouted. I ran to catch up. Past our croft, our caravan, past my naming tree, past Angus's abandoned kiln, and the rusted fridges he'd salvaged from the tip and tried to fix up. Past the third croft; music inside. It had been Mike's place but Mike had been growing weed and selling it on the streets, bringing outsiders, druggies, into Ithaca. Eva had banished him and my mother had wept. Mike had been the M in JAM.

Jono raced me across the mud. The noise started up, choking and spluttering. The generator. Jono tried to stick his metal rod in it but I told him No, what would happen if he broke it?! It had caused so much strife, that damned generator. The ones like Tessa who despised its noise and bad karma, and Pete who was against petrochemical corporations. But still they moaned and fought when the lights cut out. They'd had no idea, my mother said, that there would only be seven hours of daylight in winter.

There was this huge roar. I thought Jono had broken the generator, but it came from the sky. I ducked and covered my ears, Jono threw his stick at it. The jump jets from RAF Delta always flew so low. Pete said they did it as a deliberate form of intimidation. To quash the rebellion.

My ears were still ringing as I raced after Jono, past Eva's, the last place before his secret place. There were voices inside. Not arguing. It was no song, there were no words. My mother said if they didn't waste so much time on chanting then maybe something would actually get done for a change like maybe some proper electricity or a real bath. Jono ducked down as he passed the window. 'Cuh . . . cuh . . . come on,' he said, 'eh . . . eh . . . enemy inside.'

We waded across the stream, through the nettles, to Jono's secret place in the ruin. No one said we shouldn't play there. It was just a shell, really. Scary-looking, like in the horror films Jono told me about from school. Jono threw a brick at what little was left of the windows. His stuttering words were about David and Goliath and Splinter. He gathered sticks, so I copied him.

When you went in the floorboards were missing and you had to balance on the beams and jump. His secret place was on the first floor. We always got skelfs from the broken wood and he used to cut them out of my hand with the penknife. He never stuttered when he put on his spy voice in his secret place.

It was just this old room really, with half a roof and a window frame that looked out over Ithaca. Quiet. There was old wallpaper peeling off and nails in the floor that could catch your feet so we never took our wellies off. He had a secret box in a hole in the wall. He hid Mars bars and crisps and comics and porn in it, which he'd stolen from the shop near the school. Pete was against chocolate.

We sat down and he gave me the little half of his Mars bar, then he started sharpening the sticks with the knife. 'Splinter,' he kept saying. The pointing to the pointed end. 'Spuh . . . speeh,' he said. 'Wuh . . . wuh, then we'll . . . muh . . . ki . . . kiik . . .'

My mum told me never to interrupt or finish his sentences for him even if I knew what he was going to say. But it was so hard watching him fighting for breath, his eyeballs rolling upwards as his tongue went into spasm, like a disgusting thing, a fish gasping on land. I didn't say a thing. Even though I knew what he meant.

Splinter, he was making a spear to kill Splinter.

*

You are running through the car park. The car door, the mobile in your hand. Get inside and sit, prepare yourself, close your eyes, ten breaths more, then disconnect it from the charger. Turn it on, don't be afraid. But you know what you'll find – the message box will be full, there will be voice messages from him too. Breathe. Turn it on.

It has charged but there's no signal. Admit it. The first feeling is relief. But then it comes to you. Everything is a sign for you now. You have no network. It means so much more. No network of friends to call. You are off the scale. When you left, all your friends became like Charlie. All their petty prejudices. Lisa, Joan will be whispering about you in the play park.

You have to call him, to say, just please let me say what I have to say, just please, a few more days then I'll explain. Tell him to stop panicking, be practical. Remind him of your vows, in sickness and in health. It's twelve now and she should be having her first nap. Routine is very important. She should be waking at six and sleeping for an hour in the middle of the day. Don't let her sleep longer. Wake her no matter how much she protests. Stimulate her with games and funny faces.

Key, ignition. Drive to higher ground to get a signal. You're not running away again. You'll only be fifteen minutes till you hear his messages, then back. Reverse out of the car park. That's it. Focus. Watch for oncoming traffic.

She has to go to the play park. Tell him that. If she doesn't she has excess energy. It's like people in prison. She gets angry because she has this surplus. Tell him it's not in the books. You've learned this from her. She sleeps better after two hours in the play park. If she's stuck at home all day she is just angry, like anyone would be.

There are no hills for miles, you know this, only the ones south. You are at the crossroads. The town of Wyster or Thryster? The place the kids beat you or the one where they pulled your mother from the razor wire.

And how important it is to liquidise the soup, the scoosher thing is under the sink, he must rinse it after

119

he uses it, put it in the bowl first, then turn it on. Otherwise he'll splash himself and everything when he turns it on. The bananas in the yogurt. She'll scream for it if he doesn't. She says bab a babab. This means banana, though it might just be a sound. Everything is baba, but if you give her a banana, she quietens. She'll be in her high chair chanting Bababababababa. You have to tell him. The baba shouldn't be mashed or scooshed, she can take them as they are but chopped up. Just a little bit of sugar on top. You know, you know, he doesn't know and he wouldn't agree but the bananas from Sainsbury's are never ripe, then as soon as you open the packets they go off. From Waitrose or the local market, not Sainsbury's, and just a bit of sugar, she hasn't got teeth yet. What harm can it do?

The thing starts beeping. For some reason in the middle of the moorland on the single-track road, a signal. The message box is full. The voice message box the same. Park in the lay-by. Stop putting it off. Click OK. It's dialling up voicemail, it takes twenty seconds. You know this. Breathe. A jet roars overhead, breaking the silence.

Fuck, Thursday, 3.30. It's so important that he must call Sally, her name is in your little black notebook by the PC. Sorry sorry sorry, tell him to say sorry to Sally for you. Ask him, please, just to deal and not question, could he please just apologise to Sally for not RSVPing. He doesn't know Sally, Sally is the mother of your daughter's little boyfriend. Tell him that. Jude, Sally is Jude's mother. Call Sally, the number is in the little black book. Turn down the birthday party tomorrow. And please check the direct debits with BT, the gas and electric. And has he got enough Pampers, size three, she's really only size two but they're easier to put on even though there's a bit of leakage, and don't forget the organic milk feed to supplement what's left in the fridge and tell Sasa you love her.

Beep. His voice, put it to your ear. Breathe.

Emma, if you don't call me back I don't know what I'm going to do. For fuck's sake. God, just tell me you're OK.

Beep. *I've called the police, OK. You've made me do this. I don't even know what. Is this my fault or . . . Jesus, just call me, for Christ's sake.*

Beep. *You are so up your own arse. I just fucking knew you'd do this at some point. I hope you can sleep at night. God, I fucking hate you.*

Beep. *I'm sorry. God, I'm sorry. I was drunk. Baby, please, ignore the last message. I was up late. Can you just come back, please, baby, then we can talk?*

Beep. *I spoke to Dr Foster. He tells me you were doing so well. You're doing fine. You're just tired, he agrees with me. You need to get back into the routine, he says. I'll help you with that. I can take ten days off. I'm sorry, I should have done this sooner. I spoke to the HR guy today and he says . . .*

Beep. *Darling. Please pick up. Lisa thinks you might be clinically depressed. I'm sorry I didn't see it, babe. Please call me, I don't know what to do here. Dr Foster says maybe this is a negative reaction to your antidepressants. Did you come off them and not tell me? He says they have to be phased out slowly. I know you were worried about them passing into your milk. He's booked you in for an appointment in two days. That's Saturday. Twelve forty-five. Please call me. Tell me where you are.*

Beep. *OK, you are officially a missing person. I'm proceeding with legal matters. Just thought I should let you know. Sasa is with my mother. If you won't talk to me then . . .*

Beep. *I never knew you, did I? Let's face it. How could you fucking do this? OK, you want me to be honest. I married you because. Because. Fuck . . .*

Beep. *Can you hear that? Lemme turn it up. Wait, sorry.*

I'm back. You hear that. This is our song. I know I can't sing. It was playing on our first date, right. You don't like it. It's boring. I know I know. I'm boring. Boring, boring, boring. Baby, please. You hear that. It's so beautiful, you're so beautiful. God, listen to that. Like the way. What is that? The black guy singing. Sorry, sorry, sorry, sorry. Fuck it. I loved you I fucking did, I fucking love you. Sorry, that was just me. I just knocked it over there. Hello. Sorry, I'm a bit pissed, can't you . . .

Beep. *The police have you on file now. I gave them pictures. Mother wants you to know that there will be legal repercussions. She's having to pay for a nanny.*

Beep. *Baby, baby, please. I'm sorry if I pushed you into having a baby. I'm so fucking sorry. Why won't you pick up your phone? God, please.*

Beep. *They're going to fire you. I'm serious. Just tell me what you want to do about work. OK? They've been emailing you. They want you back Monday.*

Beep. *Baby, please pick up the phone. I've been sorting through our things and I found your Plath book and all your notes. It's so fucked up, so fucking sad. I really need you to call me and explain. I can listen, I can do that. Please, baby, just call me, so I know you're OK.*

The phone rings in your hand. The screen says HOME.

*

In a normal family the kids would be protected from parental arguments and fights. By the time they woke from their slumbers the broken pieces of crockery would have been cleared away, and artificial smiles stretched across faces. But in the year that followed the failure of the second festival, the year in which Jono could no longer hide his many cuts and bruises from the grown-ups, everything was uncovered and cross-examined in the new after-dinner

122

confessionals. And we, the children, had to witness it all. 'Living in a glass house,' they called it.

Pete called an emergency meeting. He'd been hauled in front of the school council as there had been complaints about 'the hippie children'. On the way out two local mothers hurled abuse at him: 'Hippies go home!' Tessa laughed as Pete confessed his worries. 'Fuck it, stupid plastic bastards, fuck them!' 'No, there's been more than enough fucking going on,' Pete yelled. 'When I said reach out to the masses, I didn't mean spread your fucking legs for every local Tom, Dick and Harry! No wonder the kids are getting abused!' My mother stroked my hair over my ears but I heard it all. 'Which local farmer are you fucking today, you stupid slut?' Pete yelled as he shook her. 'Oh, listen to the impotent intellectual,' Tessa laughed. 'Maybe I wouldn't have to if you weren't such a drunken limp dick!' She slapped his face.

Angus forced himself between them. 'Jesus, people, nobody owns anybody, we're all free, that's why were here.' Pete and Angus, sprawling on the floor, grabbing fistfuls of each other's hair. Eva screaming for silence, getting everyone to hold hands round the table, saying that all this openness was a positive step in making the communal bond stronger. My mother and her silence, holding me and Jono tight to her breast.

Jono woke me one morning in a panic. 'Kkkk . . . eeera's guh . . . guh . . .' My mother found her note. Angus announced he was off to find Tessa and bring her back. He promised he'd only be a few days and didn't say goodbye. My mother moved Jono's things in with us. 'Hey, you can be a proper brother and sister now,' she said, 'and Saphie can be your proper baby.' Saphie couldn't sleep so my mother sang her lullabies over and over.

123

Can ye no hush yer weepin'?
A' the wee lambs are sleepin'

I didn't like her singing it, because it had been my lullaby, my song about my dad.

Birdies are nestlin', nestlin' the gither
Dream Angus is hirplin' oer the heather

We never found out if Angus found Tessa, because neither of them returned.

*

'"It", two volunteers will be "It". They have to chase and touch other people to make them It then they are no longer It. If you're being chased then please be careful not to bump into other runners.'

You are together in a circle in the big pine-floored exercise hall called Fuchsia. The seats have been pushed back for the game. Everyone is so excited, Tamara is raising and lowering her hands in that way you are all learning means Be still. She talks through her smile.

'There are two safe havens. Trees. Those who for one reason or another don't feel like running can stand still and be trees. If you touch a tree then you're safe and no one can touch you. Runners – you can only hold a tree for thirty seconds and then you have to run again.'

You choose not to run. To be a tree.

'Ready, steady, GO.'

Adults running like children around you. The corporate German, hiccuping with laughter as his big feet pound the floor. Heidi the Swede bouncing and flouncing in her catch-me-if-you-can way. The Its chase the not-Its. Laughing more than children would.

124

His voice on the phone. Drunk. He never gets drunk.

They run to you, they hold you, then run shrieking from you. Because you are a tree.

Morgan Stanley grips your shoulders.

'Can't catch me,' he shouts to the others. 'I'm safe.'

What does '*legal repercussions*' mean? Is he already suing for divorce? Morgan Stanley lets you go and runs, laughing.

The picture high on the wall by the window.

A wide open green field. The sun throwing halos around golden hair. A little girl, three, picking buttercups, rosy complexion, white dress glowing, a little oriental boy behind her hands in the air, to the left a little coloured girl in a floral dress running with her arms open to no one. This painting you are staring at, as they run and giggle around you.

You work out how the painting was made. Three children from different photos, countries, brought together in pigment. The little girl must have been running to someone, her mummy. The mummy has been removed, where the mummy should be is a huge beaming yellow sun. The child is running arms open as if for the joy of just running as if embracing the field, the sun itself.

Feet from you the big Dutch grabs Morgan Stanley shouting 'It', her man-like laughter booming through the room. He's protesting then chasing the screaming laughter and limbs.

He won't sue for divorce. It was just a threat. He'll put you through marriage guidance counselling. There will be more self-help books.

You look around. The other tree, with her hands spread wide like Christ and his cross, is Mia. Tree-hugger. God, you hate her. The way she smiles over at you, her fellow tree, as they cling to her.

The police have you on file now. I gave them pictures.

125

'OK, OK, people,' Tamara shouts. 'That was great. Wow, I can feel the energy in the room. You were great. Let's just all form the circle again. We're all here. Jeezs, I thought I lost a few of you there. Wasn't that wonderful? OK, you're all breathing hard. Just take that breath and focus it towards the room, this big beautiful room where we all ran and played together. And just close your eyes and hold hands and say the words to yourself – We. Room. Together. We are in our room together.

'We are in our room together.'

'And breathe. Good. Now stay on your feet, in a minute we're going to do free-expression dance.'

Oh Jesus.

'And trees,' she says addressing you, 'this time we want to see you really move.'

The music, she explains, is authentic Tibetan drumming. You each have to find your own spot and let go to the rhythm. As it starts you hear the drone of synthesisers.

Within seconds Mia is leaping into perfect toe-pointed ballet jumps, four feet in the air, trailing Isadora Duncan's imaginary scarf. Morgan Stanley is standing with his feet wide apart throwing his head backwards and forwards and snapping his fingers, lips pouted as if in some seventies disco. Jules, the Londoner, is moshing as if to hardcore, throwing her arms around in big aggressive arcs, almost knocking Marianne from her classic handbag dance without a handbag. Johann the corporate man is wiggling his hips and pumping the air with his fists, a cross between Bronski Beat and Jane Fonda's workout. Lo-Mi is doing some kind of t'ai chi thing with soft fluid moves, eyes closed, oblivious to the beat. Glenna seems to be in the gym on the treadmill. Tamara is clapping her hands and skipping in circles around everyone, like an elf in the forest. Making signs to come on loosen up! Tom is shouting, 'Yeah!' He starts doing some-thing that could only be moonwalking.

126

And you. Your feet together, your hands glued to your sides, face to the floor.

You are officially a missing person.

'C'mon,' Tamara's eyes say, 'c'mon.'

You can't move. You can't.

'C'mon, people!'

Tom is doing air guitar now and there is no guitar on the track. Mia cartwheels past to whoops and claps from the others.

I found your Plath book and all your notes, it's so sad. If he's read them, he might guess that you are here, you are running out of time.

Enough. Turn a foot towards the door. But you can't. You have to pretend to be one of them till you find out the truth. So then you're trying to make it look like the step to the door was part of a dance routine. You're taking steps backwards and forwards, backwards and forwards, stiff-legged, like a robot. God, make it end.

'OK, OK, people,' Tamara shouts as she turns off the CD. 'Let's get back into our circle and share how that made us feel.'

Living on Light – a workshop with Simone Iray. £175 for 2 days. Lesser Hall. Starts Monday.

You went back to the start. The Information Centre and eco shop where Pete and Tessa's place use to be. Searching the noticeboard for clues.

Spiritual Eco-nomics – workshop with Iris Pender and Robert Gelfin. We have experience with a wide range of clients ranging from charities such as Friends of the Earth to corporations such as United Petroleum and Pharmacon. £775 for 3 days.

Crazy to think you'd see your mother's name here. You should maybe ask inside the eco-shop. Go then.

Gluten-free breakfast cereal, ecological washing-up liquid, Spirulina powder, Fairtrade, organic, decaf coffee. Nothing you couldn't get in the organic section at Sainsbury's. Handmade rainbow candles the same as the ones in tourist shops, essential oils, the prices higher than the Body Shop. It makes sense, it's just another shop. The only difference is that no one talks. Maybe four others in there with you, but silence. Apart from the ching of the cash register.

In the place where Tessa's bedroom used to be is a small books section. You walk in, trying to feel something. The past is not a place. Apart from the bare brick walls all is gone. Eva's face smiles down from the book covers. Pictures of mountains and skies. *The Voyage to Virtue. The Global Garden. The Path to Peace.* Alliteration.

You should eat. You skipped dinner, couldn't face the communal dining room. Halva, hummus, a selection of macrobiotic cheeses from indigenous Highland eco-farms. Ridiculously overpriced. And the woman at the counter. Knitting. Forty-something, she won't take her eyes off you, as if you're a potential shoplifter. She hasn't seen your face before. It's her task to monitor strangers. If you leave without buying anything you will only draw attention to yourself. If you ask about your mother she will tell everyone. You'll be thrown from the premises.

In the car park you pass another sign. *Please don't use your car after 9 p.m. Respect the need for silence. Thank you. The car park angel.*

The road splits into two. A circle, remember, the place is built on a circle, joining up the four crofts. The spaces between now filled with houses, caravans. To your right a row of ten or so A-frames.

If she was here she would have earned some kind of permanent place by now, a large caravan at least. You shouldn't but you do. Peering through windows, peeking, sneaking. An elbow, hands cooking, the back of a head, hair braided, a middle-aged man reading, a Habitat paper lampshade. No music, no noises. Terrible silence without wind. There should always be wind here. You remember that, how it unsettled you as a child when the wind stopped. It was what connected you to the land. You breathe the same air that sways the trees. Your eyes wet in the wind. You feel the place inside. The dust in your eye. When it is gone you see. Don't feel. You feel the need to feel, not see.

Rubber boots and clogs outside carvans. A spade. Letter boxes on wooden stands like American suburbs. A little hedgerow. The window people are too young, too many packed in. An old woman could not share.

There is nothing here that speaks of her presence.

This used to be your croft. The lights are off inside. To the back was Angus's kiln. Close your eyes and you will see it. The windows are bigger now. On the shelves female forms writhe up the sides of pots, bowls in the shape of flowers, free-form thrown clay abstract sculptures with rainbow glazes. *Express yourself Ceramic Workshop with Tobe Caro. £12.50 for afternoon session. £22.50 for whole day.*

You walk the path. The edges mosaicked with tiny multicoloured ceramic fragments. A dove in white clay pieces in the middle of the concrete. The path winds. You remember this. They didn't believe in straight lines. Organic forms, everything had to be curved, anti-linear. Men build straight roads, empires, destroy. The Angel of the Garden Path shows you her ways. Let her guide you.

You freeze. The vegetable hut, where you saw the old woman. She is there again now, or someone else, taller, maybe. It's dark. Hard to make out. A certain movement of the hand seems familiar. Now you pray that it is not her, the time isn't right. You duck behind a caravan and peer round. She moves slowly, painfully refastening the

129

lock with arthritic fingers, her hair is long, grey, covering her face.

It's the story you told yourself. She came back in '82. She lives on one bowl of soup a day.

'Are you lost?'

A voice behind you. Female. Posh London accent. Turn. She is thirty or so, denims, wellie boots and a smile that asks you who you are.

'No, I'm fine, just . . . wandering. Sorry, I'm here for Sharing Week.'

'Ah,' she says. 'Did it six years ago. I'm still here, I guess.'

The old woman has vanished.

She tells you her name is Jolanda, she's on her way to the Greater Hall. There's a talk tonight on Spiritual Psychology. She'll show you the way if you want to come. She's not saying it, but she's telling you you can't wander. You tell her OK, you'll come. You decide to ask her questions before she has the chance to question you. She is open, friendly, points things out on the way. The eco-windmills in the distance. Enough energy for half the community. Some people are opposed to them because they disrupt the local birds. She laughs, tells you that it's always hard to get consensus here, everything is so slow, the old people mostly are against any kind of change. You see an opening. Ask her if she's heard of Jenna. No, wait.

You pass five huge wooden houses. A sign says Eco-Village. Bay windows, lights on, no one in sight, three storeys high. An entire roof of solar panels. Driveways, an SUV. 'Yeah, the yuppies,' she says and gives you the whole story. A couple of years ago the institute was in financial trouble so they sold some land to private investors. Sure there were rules about eco-living and what have you, but basically these yuppies moved in, built these monstrous mansions, with big contractors and equipment from down

130

south. The houses didn't fit in with the rest of the place, and they didn't really mix. Terrible, she said, most of the folk that worked for the institute were still on waiting lists to get out of the caravans and then these rich folk just come in and . . . well, she calls it Ego-Village. 'Sorry, I'm being negative,' she says, and laughs.

You have only a few hundred yards. Ask her now.

'I was wondering if you'd heard of an old woman here, she would be about sixty-something now. Jenna. Jenna Mathews.'

She shakes her head. 'There's a Joan.'

'She would be about five nine. Dark eyes, long hair, maybe . . .'

You dry up. Everything you can recall is thirty years out of date.

'Is she German, and on the steering committee?' she asks.

You shake your head and say thanks, never mind, just an old friend of the family. You stop where you are. 'I'll just stay here for a bit,' you say, 'catch up later. Was really nice talking to you. Thanks.'

She walks on, waving goodbye, then you are alone with the windmill silhouettes and the sky. She didn't ask your name. There were three original children. Your mother loved Jono and Saphie, maybe more than their own mother. The blades of the static windmills make you shiver. It is more than the wind that is missing. More than noise and music and laughter. Since you arrived you have not seen a child. A single child. The three windmills tower above you like crucifixes.

*

They came from afar and weren't like the ones before, they didn't bring guitars or sing or even talk to us much. They came for Eva's lectures and workshops on Spiritual Awareness

131

and Communal Living. Eva called it phase two. They paid good money, my mother said, and she was put in charge of the kitchen. She had to feed maybe forty every day, and since Tessa had gone and Eva was so busy, she worked alone or with whoever else volunteered, but no one really did. I recall an argument she had with Eva. 'They've eaten every damn thing in the garden, we're going to have to go to the supermarket from now on! What the hell happened to self-sufficiency?' Eva replied quietly, 'Let's focus on the positive side of having new energy and ideas among us.'

One night I woke cold, no adults in the bed to keep me warm. I finally found her in the kitchen, the whole place stinking of burned food and sweat, piles of dirty plates stacked high around her. She was scouring a huge pot by candlelight. Suddenly, she broke into song, her voice booming round the room, full lung.

Oh, whit'll we do wae the herrin's heid?

She stopped as suddenly as she'd started. It scared me and I ran.

One morning she got us up really early and told us we were having a secret day off and we had to get dressed quickly, quietly. Just me and her and Jono and Saphie and Pete and we'd all have to budge up in the Beetle because there were big bags too, and it would be fun and cosy, an adventure. 'I might even let you hear *Octopus's Garden*, if you're good,' she said.

She and Pete talked in quiet voices in the front and we weren't to interrupt because they were making plans, she said. We were heading south into the mountains. We had to stop on a slope somewhere because steam started hissing out of the back. She showed us a blueberry bush and taught us how to pick them and not prick ourselves. She got one of her scarves and made a bag out of it and we were to collect them but mostly we just ate them straight from the bush while Pete swore at the engine. We sat down

132

in some field to eat the rest and Jono sat in some poo. Then Pete was joking that poo wasn't so bad. 'One man's shit is another man's gold,' he said. Then he showed us how it was dry and you could pick it up and not get your hands dirty. How if you found a really big dry one it could be like a Frisbee. He tried to show us, but it crumbled in his hand as he tried to throw it and then he was jumping around shouting, 'Shit, shit.' Then we were all running around the field grabbing cowshit, throwing it at each other, laughing, even my mother, for the first time in a long time, fingers and clothes covered in it, till Saphie got hit in the face and had to be cleaned and cuddled and the farmer came and swore at us and threatened us with the police.

Then we were just parked there and they wouldn't put the music on and we weren't going anywhere and they kept telling us to be quiet in the back and eat the blueberries. Pete said, 'Ten miles is all I can get out of it,' and she said, 'So, I guess that's it, we're going back then.' Then they had to push it to get it started and it jumped and shuddered, and we were going the way we came with them both silent in the front. *Octopus's Garden* came on but nobody sang.

When we got to Ithaca Eva's people were queuing outside the kitchen. There was smoke and things smashing inside. My mother put us in the caravan and read us *The Hobbit* and tucked us in even though it was still light. As soon as she was outside I could hear her and Eva shouting. She said she never signed up to be a domestic slave. And how the hell could they preach self-sufficiency when the garden was empty and left to rot. Eva, for once, conceded that she had been wrong, the garden was the heart of the community.

That was when my mother was appointed Crop Leader and the manual came out – *The Complete Book of Self-Sufficiency*. The rotational year planner. What to grow in every season.

I used to love the pictures. The details. Pen and ink. How you could flick from one page to the next and it would be the same picture of the same garden but the lines on the page had grown. The plants. She told us if we all worked hard enough it would be just like the pictures.

Cauliflower, plant in January, harvest in September. Beetroot, plant in February, replant in March, then harvest in October. Spring, summer and winter cabbage. Reading it together so slowly. Making butter and cream, baking bread. Rotating your cabbages with your carrots. Thinning your leeks. She told us all about crop rotation. How some plants took things from the soil and others put things back. How it was a bit like people, how some took and others gave but that in time it found its natural equilibrium.

I wanted to grow artichokes because they looked funny but she said first things first. There were no pictures of children in the book.

We went back to the field with the cowshit, me and Jono and Pete and her, we brought bags and spent a day picking it all up and filling them for the garden. Pete held my mother's hand as they lugged the stinking bags. I told myself 'Jenna and Pete'. It didn't sound like Jenna and Angus but she said Angus would never come back and she wouldn't sing *Dream Angus* any more. We put the shit round the carrots and Pete told us that revolution would grow from the crap of capitalism.

There were nights when we were all tucked up in the same bed when she'd use the manual to teach me and Jono how to read; she said he was making great progress with his stutter. Much more than her carrots were.

'Go on, tell us what to do!' she said.

'Carrots need a fine seed bed just like turnips, and not too much fresh muck, it makes them fork.'

She slapped herself on the head, 'Damit! No more shit. Go on, lazybones, next page!'

'Carrots will not thrive on acid soils, so you will have to add lime.'

She got up suddenly and said, 'Right then, so that's that!' She was off to see Eva.

Then suddenly, the next week, there was lime. Bags of it. She said we had to be careful because it would burn you if you got it on your hands or in your eyes or mouth and we were not to throw it around like it was snow. And then there were bags of organic compost from down south and poles for the beans, and new hoes and rakes and spades and a special hut for the goats. And we got new clothes, me and Jono and Saphie. She took us to the shops in Wyster and had our feet measured for trainers and boots and she didn't just buy cheap ones like before. She bought Adidas Kicks like the kids in the gang had. And Jono got a pair of brogues. He told me they would be good for kicking.

I remember asking her where all the money had come from. She said it was grown-up stuff and not to worry.

When Eva came to the garden it would not be to work. She'd come with the new people, showing them around, explaining to them the spiritual significance of the garden, the pelvic chakra. Whenever that happened, my mother would stop what she was doing – putting on the sand or the salt around the leeks to kill the slugs – and look up at Eva, then take a deep breath, then start digging faster. Me and Jono used to copy her. A big sigh then dig like crazy.

One morning we came and there was one of Eva's people with a shaved head and suntan sitting in the middle of the leeks, crushing three or four of them under his arse, mouthing sounds to himself.

Aaaaaa, Eeeeee, Iiiiiiii, Oooooo, Uuuuuu.

Jono picked up a stone to throw at him and I had to stop him.

Aaaaaa, Eeeeee, Iiiiiiii, Oooooo, Uuuuuu.

One night I heard my mother whisper similar sounds to Pete, something about an IOU with Eva.

My mother had put down all of her share in the formerly co-owned land as part collateral on a massive loan from Eva. A loan for the garden.

*

You passed it earlier and sensed a presence within. The library, just at the top of the stairs across from the Sharing Room. Something about your mother is hiding in there. The light is off now and the other sharers are at the mediation class.

Go on, step in. No one will know. Turn on the light, close the door behind you. Don't panic. It's just a typical small room with a strip light and the smell of dust, the wood bent slightly beneath the weight of books left there, no doubt since the seventies, by visitors, guests, fellow travellers from fraternal communes. And they will make you laugh, the titles. There is of course an immense self-help section, and you recognise the ones you've read. *Finding Yourself. The Road to Me. Living and Forgiving.* Then there's the small but tightly packed Other Worlds section with all the titles in silver lettering on the black spines. *Planetary Consciousness. We Are Not Alone. Abduction and Rebirth. The Alien Within.* You are only laughing because you glanced at some of the older books. This is denial laughter. Like laughter at a funeral. They were on the shelf behind you, in an old glass-walled cabinet you half noticed when you came in.

Turn. Even if you close your eyes you'll see the titles. You saw them so many times, lying around on tables, in people's hands, your mother's, the others'. There will be something in there from her. A photo, a letter. Between the pages. You hear footsteps getting nearer. You freeze. They can't read your mind, they don't know you're in here. You prepare an excuse, 'Sorry, I was just looking for . . .'

The feet pause. A shadow of a woman on the glass of the door. You hold your breath. It walks on. You breathe.

Quick now. Take the cabinet handle in your hand. It seems to be locked. Pull a little harder. The sudden smell of dust and must as it gives.

They're all here, like old family. Wilhelm Reich and R. D. Laing and the *Art of Loving* by Erich Fromm and *Sexual Relations and the Class Struggle* by Alexandra Kollontai and everything by Bakunin and Marx. And *Small is Beautiful* by E. F. Schumacher and the *Atom of Delight* by Neil M. Gunn. You stop. Can't face it. There, staring back at you. Laid across the top of the others. You tell yourself that it doesn't mean anything. It wasn't like it was waiting for you. It is just an outsized book. Too big to fit with the others vertically. The spine curls at both sides. The lettering worn almost off. Only four letters and a hyphen are still legible . . . . *elf-S* . . . But you know what it is. The one you read together on her lap. Pick it up. *The Complete Book of Self-Sufficiency* by John Seymour. The book that told her how to make the garden.

You can't.

On a new shelving unit are four new paperback copies of *The History of Ithaca* by Eva. You lift one, feel its weight. Open it up, check the index at the back for your mother's name. Your eyes flitting. A chapter on the early years. Beneath is a stack of newspapers. A pair of scissors in a plastic sheath, a Pritt-Stick, a huge lever arch folder. Open it. Clippings, three hundred or more each in plastic sleeves, they seem to cover many years.

Not here, they will find you, find somewhere. Steal.

*

Then they came. 'The rains,' Eva called them. She said they were biblical. Not forty days and nights but three weeks solid.

137

A wet wall of it that pushed us back inside, that hit our faces like a slap. My mother's eyes at the window, as the potato furrows turned to rivers, as the garden became a lake. My face at the window watching her soaked to the skin, pulling up the black rotted stalks, trying to save the drowning crop.

Pete started drinking then. He'd sleep late and be too sick to work. He was always making his excuses, he was off to hunt for Jono, he would say. Jono had been playing truant, because of the bullying. Pete would come staggering back home, stinking of whisky, without his son, hugging us all.

After the rains, the man came. The farming specialist, and he cost more money. They told her it wasn't possible. Not with this soil. He did tests. Acid, he said. Peat. No amount of lime or manure, he said. Scrub and lichen, that's all it's fit for. The basic science of it all.

One night, she was sitting alone in the kitchen and she showed me a blighted potato. Small and black and wet. She sang to me, the old song, but it felt weird because I was too old then for hugs and songs.

Oh, whit'll we do wae the herrin's bellie.

The song was Scottish and she was English, she said, maybe that was why the potatoes had died. Maybe we had no place being here. I remember feeling weird about how it was that I was stroking her head and telling her, 'Shh,' like she told us all before, 'everything's going to be OK.'

She didn't believe in God, she said, but if I wanted, because I was just a child, I could pray for the garden with Eva and her people. And that confused me because she'd said God was just like Santa Claus and the tooth fairy and all the other fibs they taught us at school. But one night I saw her through the window, on her knees in the mud, her long hair streaked with rain, her body shaking, her hands clasped together, aiming at the sky.

*

138

You have wandered the entire house looking for a secret place to read the things hidden under your coat. You have found yourself, either by choice or by the end of choice, sitting on the back stairs between floor one and two, by the laundry. If you read in your room then Mia will interrupt, want to see and share and touch.

You tear through the pages. You have to see her name in print. Yours beside it.

The 'Before Years'. You skip the introduction and head to that chapter. Page after page then a word catches your eye. London.

I saw it on their faces, it was not just me. The bosses who seemed so burdened by their roles, who tried to joke it off, the co-workers who would distract themselves with gossip, chat, talk of anything, office flirtations, drink, the weather, the news, the latest album, anything, who got drunk and who kissed who in whatever department, anything other than face the reality of their day ahead which was identical to every other. I saw their eyes say what I felt – If only I could leave it all – I have been so false – I have never belonged – Every day is a pretence which saps my will to live – I can barely endure it. But still I could not communicate with them. And then I saw the horror of those who were perfectly happy to chat about the weather, the news, the office intrigues, the latest story about government corruption and what song from the hit parade, what film star was in and who was out. And, oh, I felt it. It came to me like a voice. I was woken by it every day whispering to me, to leave the world of noisy clamour, to find others like me and no longer be alone. To just hold another and know that we are alive and true to that voice and the joy I had glimpsed within it. That voice that spoke to me of silence shared.

You hadn't bargained for this. That you coud be moved by Eva's words as your mother once was.

Go to the index, look for Jenna – J. Jainism, Joy, Judaism, Jung.

Mathews. Could be under her second name. Jenna Mathews.

Maharishi, Mankind United, Marriage, Maternal Bond (see Bowlby), Matriarchy, Meditation, Methodist (see Bakunin, Kropotkin, anarchist critique of), Modern School, Mormon (Book of).

You check founding members. Under F you find Fecundity, Feuerbach (see Marx), Fraternity (problem with concept of, see French Revolution), Freedom, Freud, Friendship Societies.

Your mother is not in the book. You could spend days combing it but Eva talks only of herself. There are people called the others, 'the others at the start'.

The seventies were a period of great turmoil both in the outside world and within the community, with as many as two hundred individuals staying for periods of anything between one month and many years. It was only as the seventies came to a close that I overcame what had been the greatest obstacle in the way of sustaining a growing community. That obstacle I discovered was myself.

Your mother was just one of the earlier others and there were hundreds. Page after page tells you this.

Someone passes on the stairs. You have to go to your room.

You pretend to be asleep. You wait till Mia and Marianne come in and wait while they chat in their excited whispers. Finally when they are down, you wait half an hour more, then turn on your little light and quietly open the big folder.

You skim the titles of articles on conferences, on eco-living, on recycling, on the windmill generator – the first in Scotland – reports on organic gardening, on sustainability, on planetary consciousness, poems about personal awakenings, reviews of workshops, of Sharing Week, columns by journalists who went undercover, articles in *Psychology Today* and *New World* on Eva's philosophy, comparisons to Gurdjieff, to the Rosicrucians, to communities in New Mexico, Alaska. An exposé by some woman who claimed to have been brainwashed. A piece about financial inaccuracies in accounting, articles on proposed plans to create a global centre for ecological studies. A tabloid diatribe against cults in Scotland.

Two pages, years apart, jump at you.

You read and reread, checking the details. Hacking through the hype and journalese. The thing which gives you no rest, which has you turning, is – you have thought these stories before, as if imagining them made them happen.

Newswire, 20 October 1998

WILDERNESS DEATH WOMAN WAS 'LIVE-ON-LIGHT FOLLOWER'

A woman found dead by her tent in a remote part of Scotland was a follower of a New Age movement which promotes fasting and 'living on light'.

The woman, aged about 50, had been practising some kind of 'cult ritual' and fasting could have contributed to her death, according to police who found her body on the west coast of Sutherland.

She is thought to have been a follower of a New Age guru known as Jasmuheen who advocates not eating. Jasmuheen, an Australian woman whose real name is Ellen Greve, claims to have been living on herbal tea, juice and the occasional biscuit since 1993 after being told to change her life by her spiritual mentor St Germain.

Her philosophy was based on 'breatharianism',

141

which promotes the idea of 'living on light' and almost entirely without food or liquids.

It is understood the woman found in Sutherland was also a member of the Ithaca Institute, Caithness, an educational and spiritual establishment which is unconnected with the Jasmuheen movement.

A spokesman for the Northern Constabulary said he was unable to confirm the identity of the woman, whose body was found last week and in an advanced state of decomposition. Relatives had still to be informed.

Joshua Bennings, manager of the Ithaca Institute, confirmed that the dead woman had been a member, but would not disclose her name.

He said: 'She was a well-respected and much-loved member of our community and we miss her greatly. We are in a period of coming to terms with the shock of her death.'

He said the Ithaca Institute was an educational and spiritual establishment with around 110 members which was founded in 1971.

The Northern Constabulary said a diary found among the woman's belongings suggested she had been taking part in a cult ritual.

A spokesman said: 'She was found on the west coast in Sutherland near a tent which she had pitched. It is quite a remote area and it seemed as if she was following some sort of long-term ritual as part of a cult organisation.'

The exact cause of death has yet to be determined. The investigation continues.

Press and Journal, 25 August 1987
HIGHLAND BOMBER DIES IN BLAST

A Ministry of Defence (MoD) spokesman today confirmed that, on the morning of Thursday the 22nd, a Volkswagen Beetle, registered to Mr Sandy McAlpine of Caithness, exploded by the perimeter fence of a remote area of land near East Tulloch owned by the MoD. The driver died in the explosion and is believed to have been a middle-aged woman. The Northern Constabulary (NC) have not yet issued details about the identity of the driver. No witnesses have come forward.

McAlpine is a member of the Ithaca Institute, a New Age community on the coast of Caithness. The institute has issued a statement distancing itself from the incident and claiming that McAlpine had reported the vehicle lost or stolen two weeks beforehand.

In the last thirty-six hours several organisations have claimed responsibility for the incident.

The Angry Brigade issued a statement to Reuters News Agency a day after the bombing. A similar statement was received by the *Scotsman* a day later from the Scottish Revolutionary League (SRL), a breakaway faction of the Scottish National Liberation Army (SNLA). The SNLA condemned the action and SRL were unavailable for comment. The Campaign for Nuclear Disarmament (CND) today issued a statement distancing themselves from the action and condemning all acts of violence, while opposing what they claim to be the secret subterranean nuclear weapons facility at East Tulloch. In the last twelve hours the NC has received further claims of responsibility, but these are suspected to have been hoax calls.

A full scale forensic investigation is under way to establish the identity of the bomber. According to the *Talloch Times*, the explosives were home-made and an unverifiable government source has suggested that this was an isolated incident and that the bomber acted alone.

A full public inquiry is expected to take place over the next eighteen months.

The words blur before your eyes. You are sure that neither is your mother, and yet both are. You stare at the folder in your lap. The archive of clippings, so carefully cut out, the name and date of the newspaper written so neatly in exactly the same kind of pen at the top of each page. What kind of mind would do this? Obsessively cataloguing all the sucessses and failures. The stack of newspapers in the library, the scissors lying on top in their protective plastic sheath. What kind of mind would scour the world's news to find validation, when everyone else here had turned inwards? What kind of person? When do the clippings start? Go back to the start.

October 1981.

It is not the draught from the window, not the sound of the other women's sleeping breath that makes you shiver. Her copy of the self-sufficiency manual was on the bookshelf.

The shadow, pausing by the library window. Knowing you were there, but not entering. The shadow of an old woman on the frosted glass. Footsteps silent. Tiptoeing away. Letting you read, letting you steal.

There was a copy of *Ariel* by Sylvia Plath.

Your mother is the librarian.

*

If I told anyone, he said, he would kill himself with a knife or run away for good. Jono was skipping school all the time, and I had to cover for him while enduring the hatred of the local kids alone. While they taunted me, Jono roamed wild, running around the moorlands, stealing from corner shops.

In his secret place he stashed Mars bars and Smarties and Embassy Regal and *Mayfair* and *Playboy*. He told me more secrets, about fucking and sucking, and he showed me the pictures. He said I was too young still, but that I was getting tits. That Debbie at school gave line-ups and gang bangs. He said I'll show you mine if you show me yours. He laughed when I did and said I had to have hair before we could fuck. He made me cry. His stutter had become so bad he couldn't say a single word, it made him shake all over, violent. He scared me.

He'd practise throwing punches at me and would demonstrate how to get someone down and kick them in the face, by doing it to me. Then he'd stutter his sorries. On the days when the truant officers caught him and forced him to go to school, they would gather round him taking turns punching 'the spaz'. They even held him down so younger kids could 'practise'. One time they made him stand in the bike shed, back to the wall – 'Don't fuckin' move, tinky boy' – and took turns spitting in his mouth from ten feet away, calling out 'Bullseye!' until he puked, his face dripping with their yellow spit. His stutter only made them laugh all the more. 'Go on, poofy boy, run, run, ye too scared, eh, fuckin' English poofter.' They held me and said, if I ran, I was next.

He stopped running from them then. After the bell rang he would wait by the school gates, close his eyes with fists clenched, as I screamed, 'Run, run!'

One day Splinter dragged him to an abandoned building and they all gathered round chanting, 'Fight, fight, Splinter, Splinter.' Splinter kicked Jono in the guts and face, while the others twisted my arm up my back. Jono was bleeding, taking the blows, till Splinter got bored and started to walk away. 'Fuckin' tinky spazzy poof.'

Jono leapt then, screaming like a fit, fists flying, and Splinter's head hit the wall. For a second Splinter was dazed and Jono yanked his hair. You never forget a noise like that. A sight like that. It makes your skin freeze, thinking how thin skin is.

145

Harling, they called it. It was this chipped white stone they stuck on walls to make it look better. A lot of the buildings in Wyster were harled.

Jono forced Splinter's head onto the wall, the traces of blood left on the little white stones, as the head was ground into them, then worse, a splash, a spray of blood after the face was forced again across the wall, then again, then again, the sound. Like shredding, the shredding of cabbage, this almost silent sound of ripping, so many small tears over and over again. After that, the stone grinding against bone. The sight as Jono finally let him free and he fell to the ground, of bits, of face, stuck there on the wall. The way everyone went quiet and then Jono whimpering and Splinter wailing and everyone standing, then running when a grown-up came.

The Social Services banged on the door that week and my mother had to pretend to be Jono's mum and she told me after that the government would take him away if it was just him and his dad. So she was officially his mother then, signing for adoption. 'It'll be so cool,' she said.

Splinter was kept off school for three weeks after that, but I had to go. All the kids, even the tiniest ones, said the same thing to me. Jono was a dead man. But I couldn't tell my mother because Jono said he would stab himself if I did.

*

She woke you from sleep, her hand on your shoulder, her voice so close to your ear telling you the time. Mia. They moved round the room, quietly so as not to wake you. Marianne whispered about Eva, she may visit the workshop today. She rarely does, she's been ill, they say. Mia hushing herself, to not be so excited, in Italian and English. The sounds of papers and zip fasteners and clothes being pulled on while you pretended to sleep. When the door was closed quietly behind them and you were alone you opened your eyes.

146

You couldn't face breakfast. You couldn't face the corridor, the dining room. Everywhere, every second, you feared you would see her. You walked swiftly past the library, flinched every time an old woman passed.

You are standing in the doorway of the dining room. You scan the tables preparing yourself for the sight of her. Some things must be the same. Her eyes. The hair would be thin now. By the window is a table of old people. You could go from table to table, face to face, but you can sense it – she is hiding, waiting for you to come to her. The library. She has waited this long, she can wait longer.

Mia and Marianne and Tom and Istvan and Lo-Mi are seated together. Mia waves ciao. Everyone eating in silence, hospital-like. Muesli, prunes, yogurt. You won't be able to eat or sit with them. The sight of the huge brown handmade ceramic serving bowls, the faint smell of the goat's milk. The acid rises in your throat.

Speak to your husband, ask him what to do. There's not time to get to the car, to get a signal. The cyberroom then, you saw a sign for it. The workshop starts in fifteen minutes. Go then.

You pass the noticeboard, the sick yukka with the sign, follow the signs to an extension, where nothing was before. Run over what you must email him. Don't apologise, don't tell him about your mother. Tell him everything will be resolved tonight. Tomorrow you will drive home. Tell him you love him, you will explain later, everything. You'll be back the day after tomorrow.

The door is ajar. You push it open. Step back. Her back to you, the long white hair, face hidden, looking at the computer. She turns to you.

It's OK. Just the woman from reception.

'Sorry, just be a minute. You can book time online if you want, there's a schedule.'

She motions towards the folder on the wooden table,

nothing else in the room. Two tables, one computer, one folder, no windows. A prison cell. A room they don't want to admit exists. And cold, that's why you're shivering.

She gets to her feet.

'OK, I can sense that it's urgent. On you go.'

'Thanks, really, thanks.'

He has sent you twenty-seven messages, five more are from Charlie. Titles – 'Call your husband now!' 'Where are you?' His titles like his voice messages – 'Police', 'Sasa is upset', 'Sorry', 'Pick up the phone', 'I have changed the locks'. There is no time to read them all. There is one that your eyes won't leave alone. It has an attachment. The file is called 'Solicitor's Letter'. Click open.

Your recent erratic behaviour and communication failure has been a source of upset and trauma for Sasa and myself. Such a situation, ongoing as it seems, is simply not acceptable. In the absense of communication I can only anticipate the worst and so my solicitor has drafted a separation agreement. Enclosed.

Money has also become an issue. I am informed that you recently withdrew six hundred pounds from our joint accounts without my consent. These are now frozen. On your return I ask that we arrange to visit the bank to shut down the joint accounts. Please print out the solicitor's agreement, sign it and return it at your earliest possible convenience.

It is not the cold legal language, or the talk of money above all else, or the fact that he has already so quickly prepared his plan of action which you have no say in. It is not the fact that, actually, he is right, that if he had done to you what you have to him, you would have written something even colder. It is none of these things that suddenly makes the buzz from the computer fill your head, your skin tingle, that makes you check over your shoulder as if you were touched by an icy hand. It is the names. The lack of names.

He has not written Josh. Has not written Emma or Rowan. Already he has erased the names. He calls you only 'you'.

You must speak, he must hear your voice and deal with it. Even if you cry when you try, even if you can't speak, he must listen to your silence.

Click on 'Compose'. Type his name.

Josh, I have received your letter. Let's speak today to discuss. What time is convenient?

Delete all.

Darling, I'm sorry about —

Delete all.

Josh. I need to call you today. Please don't ask me where I am and don't discuss legal matters. This is not for ever, I need such a small amount of time, can you just —

Delete all.

Josh. I am going to call later today. I would like to talk to Sasa. What time is OK? Emma.

You hit send. It is done. The effort it will take to call later saps you even as you think of it. Keeps you in your seat a second longer, another. A minute staring at the screen, before the strength comes back. You have to get to the workshop.

An American voice. AOL. *You have mail.* Of course, he'd be child-minding with the computer on, his face glued to the screen.

Call at 1.00, during Sasa's nap time. When you call, please do not request to speak to her as hearing your voice will only upset her more.

Where the hell are you?

*

149

Jono was dead, I felt it in my bones. I ran to her and she took my hand. 'Don't worry, he'll be at Eva's,' she said – everyone was round at Eva's all the time in the those days. Eva had started developing the old laird's house, with diggers and scaffolds; they had installed electricity.

She thought I was overreacting, as I still hadn't told her the truth about what had been going on at school.

When we got there Eva kissed her, and led her into the circle around the big central fire. Eva said she was so sorry to hear about the garden and announced to everyone that Jenna was here to sing for us all and how she had the most beautiful voice in the world. In spite of my pleas, my mother sat and said, 'Give me ten, OK, babes, just chill.'

But then she was toking and smiling at the cats. And every time they asked her to sing, she'd say, 'Soon, soon, sometime soon.' And Eva, in her big canvas smock, nodding at her from across the fire. That strange mix of adoration and envy that Eva had for my mother's voice, as if Jenna could touch levels of soul while singing that Eva could only talk about.

I hauled at her sleeve. 'But, Mum, we have to go and find Jono.' I had these images of him lying in some gutter, or hunted down by Splinter's gang and Splinter stabbing him with his own knife.

She just sucked on the blow and passed it on. 'Soon,' she said, 'soon.' It was all my fault for not telling her sooner. The longer I'd left it, the more it had grown from a secret to a lie.

I looked around for help. There were two teenagers there, Astrid and Moon, but they'd only been with us a few weeks.

This guy, this long-hair with tattoos and naked belly, touched my mother on the shoulder and leaned to kiss. And she accepted, the kiss not stopping. She whispered something to him, he pulled back, and looked at me with a big smile. 'Man,' he said, 'no way, wow,' he said. 'Shake,' he said. 'Incredible, no way, you're like a family.' I gave him the look Jono taught me. 'Hey, hey, it's cool,' he said, whispering again in her ear, her raising her shoulder, smiling as his beard touched her neck. She nodded to him not to me. 'OK,' she said, 'now, I'm ready.' She got up to her feet.

I thought we were going, but she got up to sing. 'But, Mum, we have to find Jono!' 'Go and ask Eva,' she said. 'Be cool,' the guy said, as she took his hand, to the centre of the circle. Everyone chanting her name.

'This is a song about immigrant workers,' she called out. 'It's by Joan Baez.'

'What key is it in?' some guy shouted across the fire.

'All of them!' she shouted back and they laughed.

I ran. I ran from the pause of reverence before she started, from her lowered head and her pause before her first intake of breath, from the first strum of guitar and her first perfect note. I ran till her voice was stripped away to echo by the speeding branches. Along the river through the mud to Jono's secret place. I called up to him – sometimes he'd be in there and pretend he wasn't. My bare feet sought out the rusted nails to jump. 'Jono!' The empty feeling grew inside and above me before my eyes showed me.

I wasn't allowed to be in there when he wasn't. I'd sworn. I thought breaking the rules might summon him. I wanted to provoke all the forbiddens. To see his *Lord of the Rings*, his penknife and stash of Embassy Regal, his box of stolen matches. Pete gave him a screaming for smoking, weeks before, but then one night Pete had a reefer and gave Jono a puff.

I took out the Regals and lit up. It caught in my throat but I told myself that smoking Jono's fags might bring him closer. I tried it with his secret porno stash. I turned the pages and found he'd burned their eyes out with fags, torn tits off.

I looked out the window at where the sun went down over the dirt track. Blood-red peach in puddles. No lights on in the caravans. No lights in the barn, no one in the kitchen. Past the barn where his mother's goats were. He hated them, struck them with branches, fed them plastic bags, trying to kill them. Every time with their teats in my hand I thought about his porno pictures. He said spunk looked like milk; I didn't believe him till he showed me.

I looked in the outdoor toilet, over the flooded garden, the dead black stalks. My mother's song beyond, drifting.

I tore the pages of the porno mag, scattering limbs. I stubbed the fag out on a sexy face. He said he was looking for Tessa in the pages, because she was a sell-out and a whore. And all those vistitors that came before who were our 'friends', well, she'd slept with them all, and sleeping didn't mean sleeping. Everything grown-ups say with a smile is a lie, he said.

I tried to do a little ritual like Eva did, to bring the spirits to the garden. I said his name over and over. Chant for what you wish and it will come true.

I took his knife out of his cubbyhole and chanted his name. Jono, Jono, John oh John oh John.

I put the blade to my arm, and pushed till the blood came.

I remember forgetting about Jono. I remember trying to forget other things that I could not: Eva holding my mother in the kitchen after a fight, days before, then kissing her forehead, her mouth. The way the kiss lingered. My mother reaching for Eva when Eva walked away.

I remember waking from the forgetting. I climbed back down and ran through the mud, screaming his name to drown out my mother's song. Jono, Jon-oh, Jon Jo!

I ran past Tessa's old place to our croft and found little Saphie, all alone, half naked, crying and reaching for me.

I picked her up and a wailing came, louder than hers,

152

over and over in flashing light. I looked for its source and
shadows ran past our door. Between the flashes I saw Jono's
face in the window of their car.

The police.

*

'Now, form two circles. This half from you, Glenna – from
Glenna to Johann in the outer circle. Then the inner from
Mia to Tom. That's right, two circles, holding hands. One
inside the other. The inside circle should face the outside.
Tom, Johann, you got that?'

Giggles as they get it wrong, change direction, take
hands again. Johann the corporate man's grip is sweaty in
yours. Little Lo-Mi's hand is tight, muscular. You made sure
you were standing as far away from Mia as possible. She
had been shooting you concerned glances since you entered.

'OK, now close your eyes. Now, the inside circle move
three steps to your right. 'That's right, now both circles take
one step to your left, so you're going in opposite directions.
Then four to your right. Don't open your eyes. OK, now you
are facing someone else in the other circle. Someone you
may not know yet.'

Childish. Look at a child, Eva said. We must learn how
to be children again.

'Now reach out slowly, keep your eyes shut and reach
out to touch the hands of the person facing you. Don't ask
who they are.'

A hand reaches for yours. A man possibly. Your mind
runs through the names. Tom, Alex, Istvan. Marianne has
hands like a man. It doesn't matter, get it done.

'You're feeling their fingertips now. Explore the fingers.
Take them in yours. The nails, the knuckles, the palms and
wrists. Try not to think about who the person may be, just
concentrate on the feeling of exploring and sharing.'

153

The workshop finishes at twelve. That gives you an hour before the call. You will have to go to the library then. No, speak to him first, you have to be OK when you call. He has to let you speak to Sasa.

He, she, is pulling your fingers, stroking the back of your hand.

'As you touch you may find your mind drifting back to past memories, try to focus on the present, let the past go and really feel the hand in yours in the living moment.'

You are wide awake now and last night seems silly. You were tired, emotional. Reading things into things again. The woman in the library can't be your mother. The important thing is the call. You have to work out your words to him.

'That's right, take time to appreciate the warmth of touch. Be gentle, try to ask questions with your fingers. How are you? Are you happy? Try to feel the answers through the fingers.'

You are not responding to the hands. Feel in some way guilty. The skin is rough, the hands are slightly bigger than yours. The nails bitten down to stumps. You can hear her breathing, smell her, faint trace of lavender and sweat, deep breaths. Her fingers strong.

'OK, now feel the energy in the hands. The tension trapped there, feel it. The power in each other's fingers. No peeking now.'

You must not tell him about the past. You must talk only of now, not the future, not plans, not legalities. He must listen for once. Her thumb and forefinger knead your knuckles. A pain shoots up your arm. If he wants you back tell him you will leave tomorrow, no sooner. You will meet the library woman, you will ask Eva, then it will be done. One way or another.

Her touch digs deep. She must be one of the women who do massage. The big Dutch? If you could just look.

You were never allowed to look. When you were eight, ten, the big grown-up hands holding you. You always used to say, Mum do I have to? And Jenna with her eyes hard, teeth gritted, mouthing the words, close your eyes, Rowan. And even when you did you knew she was still looking at you, because she couldn't close her eyes either, ever.

It's Mia. It must be. The neediness in the hand, the lavender.

'OK, now feel anger in your hands. Try to feel anger.'

Open your eyes, no one will know. But now the fingers are twisting yours, pulling, pushing, hurting. So it happens. You grip tight into fists and you don't give, don't share. You raise them up and she is trying to slip hers into yours but still you won't open, her fingers prising into your clenched fists like a fuck-forced dick into your hole and now you are angry because this stranger has no right and then you're angry at him and his fucking at-your-earliest-possible-convenience and how touch with him was always artificial like his fucking language.

'Let go of your anger, push it, force it out. Don't be afraid to let go.'

And now you're slapping her hands hard and she's trying to restrain you and he has no right not to let you speak to Sasa. Even to hear her breathe down the phone. He has no fucking right. She's gripping your wrists and your nails find the flesh of her wrist and you're digging in and you can hear her breathe, the hurt, you're hurting her and it feels better.

'OK, OK, so now be nurturing, take care of the hands in yours.'

Her fingers leave you and you hover empty, purpose-less. You have scared her, this stupid smiling hippie. And then there is a touch so gentle. So gentle you could laugh. Yes, she is an actor. Not a bad actor at all. This is the way it works here. They tell you to feel something and you feel

155

it. You say the words over and over again. I am at peace. I feel love. And you repeat them until you do feel love, until you do feel peace, or the words at least are all that remain of the feelings. Like your marriage vows. It's their fault, the fucking hippies, they emptied your words of meaning long ago.

Keep your eyes closed, Rowan.

Her hands cradle yours in hers, her fingers gently stroking the backs of your knuckles. Like she knows you lost it there for a second, like she is telling you she cares. Stroke, gentle stroke. You are supposed to be showing her nurturing too. Tell her to stop. A cynical exercise in caring for the care-less. Mia comes to these workshops to try to feel. She is so like you, that's why you can't let her.

The woman in the library is not your mother. You can't go there.

Her hands leave yours and you are alone and can't stand it and you're reaching for her. Millimetres, centimetres, alone you feel their warmth before you find them and when you touch there is a surge because you are not alone in this dark. And her skin is so warm and her fingers so soft. Then it happens. Sasa's tiny hand in yours. And you hate this. Stop it. Her tiny hand as she drifts off to sleep. When it gripped you automatically in the first few months, fist clenched round your one finger, then those months when she couldn't grip and had to learn to, again.

Then it starts. The hand gentle in yours, cradled inside yours. Surging inside you and you have to do what they say, be in the present because that will be the only thing that will save you. Sasa.

'Now take those hands and feel love through the fingers.'

If only you could tell her. You will one day. If only you had told him the many years you spent with the touch of strangers. After your mother left. You were the tart, the school slut. Sexual abuse they would have called it. You welcomed it, it was power. Twelve when you first let them inside you.

Ten more seconds of this, then open your eyes, nine, eight.

Your hands are exhausted. You are a taker. You took from them when they closed their eyes and moaned.

Five, four, three. Fight it. Fight it. Tears welling up like vomit. Remind yourself, you are Rowan, you despise all this. Enough. Open your eyes.

It's Morgan Stanley. Tom. Not Mia, not a woman. He opens his eyes and he is just like you: eyes wet, red. He inhales deeply and squeezes your hands. You sense he wants to speak but cannot. Tamara must have seen that you'd stopped.

'OK, everyone, so take a few more seconds to absorb what you've experienced, take a deep breath, then in your own time open your eyes.'

You can't help it, it bursts from you and sets him off. You are both laughing like idiots, like Eva said you should, like children, idiot children.

*

The Social Services took Jono and little Saphie. My mother blamed herself, she'd never filed the paperwork, had adopted them only in her heart. Eva said it was evidence of the rot at the heart of the state. Pete shouted at her, 'Well, we'll have to change the fucking state then, won't we?' He left to fight the cops and the courts. He moved to the town and only ever came back to borrow money.

My mother was silent through it all. Her garden was taken over by the guests who worked shifts as part of their 'inner work tasks'. It still didn't produce enough to feed us, and with all the new people they had to buy sacks of rice and greens from down south. That was the beginning of her

157

quiet time. She became the Focus Leader in the communal kitchen, which had been redeveloped to accommodate all the hundred or so that came that year to learn about Eva's 'living haven'. My mother kept herself focused on her many cooking tasks, working sometimes from before I woke till long after I went to bed. I said she should stand up to her boss like Pete always said the masses should but she said Eva wasn't her boss, she had freely chosen this for herself. The way she spoke then, as if speech itself was a burden. I was lonely too as there was no one left to play with, only the goats and the bugs.

There were new rituals. Before the twenty sat down to eat Eva blessed the food and afterwards she led the confessions. I would sit there, the only kid at the table, beside my mother, and wonder why she accepted it all. Before, she would have protested, stood up and told everyone she was an atheist and fucking proud of it. But she sat silent, as the others poured out their souls, nodding to herself, her food half eaten before her, staring into space. I was angry that she had so little time for me. Worried that she'd lost much more than the weight that'd fallen from her face, making her eyes sink into her skull; the anger that I once feared, gone, but then missed.

At night in the croft that seemed so large for once after my brother, sister and fathers had gone, she would explain how strenuous daily labour was an important part of breaking down the ego and healing. 'Digging a hole takes you deeper.' I remember the words exactly because they seemed strange coming from her mouth. She repeated them many times, as if the words themselves were a hole she was digging.

She seemed content only when she was slaving in the kitchen. On weekends I would help for a bit. It would start at six thirty. The group, which was never the same, would assemble round the big wooden table and hold hands and focus on the tasks. My mother would lead.

'Close your eyes and think of the day ahead. Of the purposeful work we are doing here. The importance of healthy food.' Or, 'Know that what you are doing will nourish many people and feed your inner self.' Things like that. Always the same. 'Then open your eyes. Take a minute to feel your feet on the ground and breathe. Then slowly, one by one, tell us your name and where you are from,' and then she would smile but it wasn't her old smile, it didn't come through her eyes.

'Tell us what vegetable you are today.' Or 'what colour' or 'what animal'. They never did minerals because it was too hard for the foreigners.

'My name is Ivan, I am from Germany and today I feel like a cat. Full of energy with big open eyes wide.'

Then she would say thank you like Eva taught us and the others would join in saying thank you and then she would nod to the next.

'My name is Holly, I'm from California and today I feel like a cow. Looking around at the field, yeah, just quietly munching on grass. Yeah, I feel very positive about today.' They nearly always picked vegetarian animals. She would squeeze my hand hard under the table when I smirked or tutted.

'Thank you, Holly.'

She was an eagle, a shark, she saw red, she craved a fight, but she always just nodded and said thank you. I noticed she used to repeat the same things, with each new batch of folk. They never stayed for long, so no one would have noticed. She always said green, or grass, or chicken or anything at all that was small and quiet and needed no explanation, and had no anger or humour in it.

'I am a cabbage today.' 'I am a sparrow.'

She was a liar and it was fucking boring all of it and I just wanted to run away to town, and pinch magazines and tapes and make-up from Woolies. I thought maybe if I

159

could get caught like Jono then we'd end up in the same place. But I stayed, for her sake.

They didn't believe in rules or leaders, so it was hard for her to run the kitchen efficiently. Every daily decision had to be arrived at by 'unanimous consent'. One day five people volunteered to make the salad dressing but no one wanted to scrape the mud off the carrots. So she had to go round the table again and again, three times, reminding them all that not every task was equally glamorous, but every task was of equal value to the communal whole. That was how it worked, or didn't. Nothing got done till everyone agreed or those who didn't were made to agree.

No one ever wanted to take out the bins or cut the onions, so she usually ended up doing them all herself, on top of making the soup and baking the bread. She hid it well, but I sensed she hated them all as much as I did. Hippie fucks, Jono would have said. But they didn't even look like hippies any more, they looked straight, like Christians.

Then it would start. The big new gas stoves turned on and the vegetable stock from the day before heated and then she would turn on the old tape machine. I would help her scraping the carrots because she didn't trust me with chopping or sharp knives. I would scrape away at the damn things, hundreds of them, but mostly I'd be chilling with Janis and Joni.

Something happened then that made it all make sense. Ten strangers from all over the world, focused only on their own tasks, somehow shifted past each other with razor-sharp knives, with heavy ceramic bowls of shredded cabbage, with arms full of leeks and huge boiling pans of soup, balancing on one foot as they turned off the gas with one hand, while holding vats of home-made mayonnaise with the other – not one clash or slip, no arguments or accidents, everyone absorbed in an intricate choreography in time with the music.

160

Impossible, it would seem now, for ten strangers to act in unison. The kitchen was the only place this ever happened in the commune. What made it happen was her voice.

She'd be cutting the onions, wiping her eyes, turning down the heat, scrubbing the potatoes, stirring a vegan cheese sauce, supervising but never forcing her will on others while turning it all into a song with Janis, Joan, Bob and the Beatles, oblivious to the fact that she was singing at all. A bowl of boring fruit salad turned into *Strawberry Fields Forever.*

Then every day, just when we were having fun, without warning, she'd turn the music off and shout Shh! at me, because it was the twelve o'clock news on Radio 4.

Thatcher and NATO and the new deal to site US Pershing II ground-launched cruise missiles in remote parts of the UK.

She wouldn't stop work, just kept on cutting with the sharp knives.

'*Possible sites include Greenham Common, RAF Molesworth, Faslane and Forse.*'

'Shh, shh!' she would hiss if anything about Delta or Dounreay came on the news. They were just five miles away.

Then she would sigh, so loud you could hear it across the kitchen, but still say nothing, just cut harder, harder. Like she did every time one of the jump jets passed over-head. There would be no music after that. Just the sounds of taps, knives, gas. Her only words spoken – turn it down, take it out, lift it off, more salt, less cheese, we have to conserve. She would start fussing, bossing, dinner was at one, why did no one care, we were running out of time.

There was this one woman, Agnes, about forty, from Sweden, skinny and severe. She always hid her eyes and had a big badge that said 'I am silent today' and this slow way about her that freaked me out. I'd try to speak to her but she'd just point at her badge and nod. My mum said she was bereaved and studying Zen and I shouldn't bother her. Whenever Agnes was in the kitchen things went at snail's pace. My mum never shouted at her, just cut the carrots for her instead. Freak.

I usually got the hell out of there and snuck to my bunker. I'd steal a few more cans of beans from the big new fridge and hide them to make sure we were ready for what she told me we should never tell anyone else. Promise. Our little secret. Soon, she said. It would just be me and her in there, prepared. Very soon, it was going to fall. The bomb.

It may have been weeks later. I don't know. The daily routine of food and confession. The newcomers always confessed first. Eva always left my mother to last.

'I was doing the potatoes,' they'd say, 'and I couldn't stop thinking about Gertrude and the abortion and where she is now and I couldn't focus on the potatoes.' Things like that.

Always straight to Eva, all of them, this community, looking to her. They would often break down and Eva would say quietly, calmly, 'Thank you,' and then the person's name, then nod to the next.

'I have had trouble today. I was thinking about pollution. All those people out there with bloody cars and hairsprays, spewing into the atmosphere and the dead fish on the beach . . . I just hate them all, I'm sorry, I'm so . . . so angry.'

And Eva would nod and then say, 'Perhaps you need to be angry.'

Always, she would take the last thing someone said and turn it round to make it a question with a 'perhaps' at the start. She said she was a mirror not a leader. If they hadn't been crying already then they would at that point, then Eva would smile with her big eyes, and pause and speak.

'We still hold onto our anger because it was so much a part of who we thought we were before. We blame the outside world but really it is the self we had that makes us angry. Your ego is furious now, because you are becoming one with us and it feels itself slipping away. Let the ego die. It will pass.'

And they would nod and my mother would sometimes touch my knee or hand, beneath the table.

And Eva would say, 'Negativity is always to blame. It is always about "them", out there. But there is no outside world, only what you have taken here with you. The world is no alibi, no excuse.'

And my mother would concentrate on her breathing.

'People squander their lives, by looking outwards. They waste their energies trying to *change the world*, when the only real change we can make is within ourselves. Only once we have cleansed ourselves, can we shape the outside. And teach by our living example. We achieve more here today by meditation and gardening than two hundred years of revolutionaries. Any rebel that screams for change without first inwardly transforming herself has death on her tongue.'

Often they cried openly at her words and my mother would pull her hand from mine to clutch her fist to her face.

I recall that one time, the hanging silence before Eva concluded and blessed us all. A certain agitation in the room. My mother tense in her shoulders, sensing it.

'Has anyone got any worries?' Eva asked. 'Anything that we could do to make things easier here for us all.' The silence as no one ever said anything negative. Agnes cleared her throat, pointed to her badge.

'There is one thing that has been brought to my attention,' Eva said, and my mother held her breath.

'The radio,' Eva said. 'In the kitchen.'

Impossible to forget that look she gave Eva.

'Jenna,' Eva said, 'people have been finding it hard to focus when there is music. Both in the kitchen and outside. They can hear you in the garden. The singing.'

163

My mother squeezed my hand.

'I think we all agree.' And Eva looked round the table and there were nods, embarrassed. 'It's a distraction, it interferes with the inner work, this noise, when what we need is inner quiet.'

Her nails digging into my skin. Her eyes with that look that came whenever someone metioned Jono.

Eva took her time. 'Music has its place: the inner-voice workshop every Friday. You should come along, Jenna.'

My mother nodded. The last time she took me there everyone stopped when she started singing.

'It's more than that,' Eva said. 'It is the radio. The news.'

My mother and Eva stared each other down. I felt it as I saw it. Eva lowered her eyes first. She did. It was only then that my mother released her hold of me.

'It's just the news,' she said. 'Not going to bloody well kill us, is it?' And she laughed. No one laughed with her.

'Perhaps you feel you still need to listen to the news,' Eva said.

'Perhaps we should all listen to the news,' my mother said, 'so we can learn what's happening.'

'Perhaps you should stop using the words "we" and "we all",' Eva said. 'Do you claim to speak for everyone?'

She shook her head.

'When you say "we", when you say "we all", what are you denying?'

A long time it took her to say it. The small word, the smallest.

'I,' my mother said. 'I am denying "I".'

'Yes, perhaps what you are trying to say is "I need to listen to the news", not "we", not all of us.'

'Of course.'

'And why do you still need to listen to the news, Jenna?'

'I just . . . I . . . I . . .'

I don't know how it happened. Something to do with

the many eyes staring at her, perhaps. Suddenly she started to cry.

Eva was on her feet then, round at my mother's back, hand on her shoulders, telling everyone that no one in the community worked harder than Jenna and what they were seeing here was *the awakening*, so far from them now but a goal to aspire to. Her fingers kneading my mother's shoulders, my mother collapsing under her pressure. Eva saying that in a moment of courage, Jenna had confronted the terror of doubt and now we could expel that fear, together. 'Let us join our hands.'

My mother, her face hidden behind her hair, reached for my hand. I stepped back, and Eva took my place. My mother did not call after me as I turned and ran.

The last words I heard Eva say were, 'We are together, and we are one. We can all learn from Jenna.' She didn't say 'I'. She said 'we', and no one else was allowed to say we.

*

'I feel love in this touch game like I've not felt before. This energy in the room, I feel it, between us. This beautiful peace in this beautiful place. This is all I want to say, thank you.'

'Thank you, Glenna.'

You are all seated cross-legged in a circle. Tamara has reminded you all to talk only of yourself and what you felt, to be in the shared now. But you are not in the now, you are at home in a few days' time, you are in the library in half an hour, you are back in 1979 sat round the table while your mother confessed. While Eva said, Thank you.

'Thank you, Alex.'

You are thinking about your mortgage, the lawyer you will have to hire, as you stare up again at the picture of the three children playing in the field, alone in their photo-montaged heaven.

'The holding hands, it made me drift away. I was in a garden and I was touching the leaves, the trees, the bark and every blade of grass. It took me back to . . . childhood maybe. It was a very beautiful experience. Thank you.'

'Thank you, Marianne.'

You are thinking about how cynical it was of you to marry a man who had money, about the self-help books and the jargon you repeat every day just to get through the next twenty-four hours.

'I felt we were all holding hands round the world. That if all people could do this, there would be peace. I feel, already, in some way changed. Thank you.'

'Thank you, Lo-Mi.'

You *did* feel something. And now they do this, they repeat these clichés that Tamara said yesterday; that Tamara once learned from Eva. When you call him you must say, 'Actually, I'm fucking angry at you! It has not all been my fault.' He never held your hands like Tom did in that exercise, he never.

'Rowan?'

'What?'

'Would you like to share with us?'

You could tell them what they want to hear or spit in their faces.

'It's OK, take your time, we could pass and give someone else the chance to speak, then come back to you.'

You'd like to share that your mother was destroyed by this place, that she starved to death in a tent, that she blew herself up with home-made explosives, that she is upstairs in the library.

'No, it's OK, I'm ready now. I have something to say.'

The faces – Mia, Marianne, Tom, Lo-Mi, Glenna, Istvan, Johann, Tamara – waiting open, smiling.

166

Shake your head and laugh to yourself. Look up. Go from face to face as you say it. Say it with a smile.

'Honestly, I think you're all full of shit.'

Their faces, faced with you. You are in the moment and the moment is anger.

'The way you speak, all this jargon, copying each other. Like after – what is it? – one day, and you've all already achieved spontaneous enlightenment. Really, I mean, c'mon, who are you fucking kidding?'

Tamara's face, as if slapped. The same way that Eva's was, the day your mother broke her coercive control.

'Actually, I felt something rather beautiful. With Tom, when he touched my hands. But I can't tell any of you because I don't trust you. Any of you. You're all lying or pretending. This is a steaming pile of shit.'

Let the silence hang. Lower your eyes to the floor, then say it.

'Thank you.'

'Thank you, Rowan.' Tamara says, her smile stretched taut across her face.

It was a mistake to get up and walk out. To leave them there to whisper about you. My God! someone said as you made it through the door. One started crying.

You will have to leave today. Time has run out and you have blown your cover. You storm down the corridor to the library. If the woman is your mother, then you will give her the anger. You did not come here to make peace, you are thankful for realising that now.

The door is open and she is not inside. Pull the door behind you. They won't find you here. Breathe, calm down. Feet are approaching. Hold your breath. Voices beyond.

'Who does she thinks she is?'

'Outrageous.'

'I dunno, she seemed very sincere.'

They pass and leave you staring at the pile of old newspapers, scissors on top, the pen, the glue. At the bookshelf. *Ariel* by Plath. Sit down, just think. If your mother is here you would have seen her at breakfast, somewhere, surely. You see. You do this, you get in a panic, you get delusional. You were sure it was her because of the self-sufficiency manual, because of the Plath. But you already have her copy of *Ariel* back at home in that box. Everyone her age had one, and the manual, it's not hers, look at it, take it down. Go on. There won't be her name on the inside cover.

The phone call. You have to try to ask him for help. Can he just put everything on hold, all the legals, can he just get you Dr Foster, can he just give you time? You're going home, ten minutes then you'll start the drive. Maybe he can meet you halfway, or get an ambulance. He was right, you did come off the antidepresssants too quickly; you can become psychotic from withdrawal.

Reach for the copy of the self-sufficiency manual. Prove it's not hers. Even if it is it doesn't prove a thing; she left it here that's all.

It must have been your pause, the silence that grew, almost as if you were asking to be found so you wouldn't have to touch it. It happens in slow motion as your hand reaches for it. The shadow crawls again across the frosted glass of the door and the book falls. The long-haired silent silhouette, face lowered, hiding behind hair. The door handle is turning. The creaking of the hinge.

Close your eyes. Her footsteps, her breath. She is standing in front of you. Open your eyes.

Her eyes through the grey hair are blue not dark. Breathe again. It is the old witch from the vegetable shed.

'Sorry,' you say, 'I was just . . .'

She stares at the old book lying face down on the floor, pages splayed. How stupid you are, not understanding that

168

she was waiting for you to pick it up. For not noticing her brightly coloured flowery badge fastened to her grey garments that reads in small letters 'I am silent today'. She lowers herself and reaches for the book and you're fumbling, silly, embarrassed talking, talking.

'Sorry, I know, I mean, I think I read somewhere, in the info pack, about the hours, and how it's open certain times but I, I'm sorry.' The book is in her hand. She points to her badge, slowly, soundlessly mouthing the word, 'S . . . O . . . R.'

You're laughing. You look at her and you too silently mouth the word, 'S . . . O . . . R . . . R . . . Y.'

Then she's laughing and her laugh makes you laugh even more, even though she's the librarian and you shouldn't be there, and everyone should always be quiet in a library. There is something about her laugh that wakens a sense. The traces of blonde in her grey.

She was only ever happy when she was running, kissing, screaming with laughter. When she danced round the fire bare-chested and stoned and the eyes of the men burned for her.

She doesn't see in your face what you see in hers. The eyes, the cheekbones, a certain way of brushing her long hair from her face.

Tessa.

If you say it she will break her vow to ask, 'Do I know you?' She will mouth your name, and every syllable of that memory might cause her pain. You see now why she is here – where else, after the decade-long party had ended? The youth in her limbs that became a fading echo with every anonymous fuck. The ageing exhaustion of hope and vanity, the long road that brought her back. To this. This library of dust and must and this vow of silence. That made her watch over the words, protecting them as if they were the children she had lost. To be the guardian of words and never speak.

Tessa, you could say, and you could touch. But there is no recognition in her eyes. 'The past is pain,' Eva said.

Before you, you see an old woman with arthritic knuckles who groans as she reaches up to put the book back in its rightful place. You spare her and leave the library, without a word, placing your hand gently on her shoulder, squeezing a little, so as not hurt her, as you go.

Her eyes did not name you. As in his email, your name has been erased.

*

Tessa and Pete had named the goats Rosa and Woolly, after Rosa Luxemburg and Mary Wollstonecraft, Pete said. 'Bollocks,' Tessa said, it was Rose after her favourite wine and Woolly, cos Woolly was more woolly than Rosa.

Rosa had become sick since Tessa left. She'd been eating too much, looking bloated, just lying in the mud and sleeping. One night she made these weird scary noises that woke us through the gaps between the old stone walls. My mother thought it was maybe tapeworm. She got the self-sufficiency manual out and even grabbed Pete's copy of the *Home Doctor* for humans to see if there was anything comparable.

The barn was a cold wet horrible place with damp and fungus on the stones and walls as old and dead as the Jacobites. She cornered me in there and asked if I'd been feeding Rosa anything for humans, she'd heard months back that Jono had been giving Rosa Mars bars and plastic bottles. Had I done anything like that? I told her no, never, cross my heart and hope to die.

She put her hand under Rosa's belly. 'My God, I felt a kick. She's bloody pregnant!' But how could she be? Woolly was female too. Pete staggered in, half drunk, and

170

started joking about the miraculous conception. My mother sent him off to look for help. 'Don't worry,' she said and kissed my head. 'We'll take care of her, all by ourselves, if we have to.'

She tore through the self-sufficiency manual. 'Shit, there's no chapter on goats, only sheep! Shit, shit!' Rosa was bleeding, bleating, making a noise like my mum and Pete made sometimes at night. We stood there stupid, watching the blood spasms, and I remember thinking Angus would have known what to do, he'd have been on his knees in the mud shouting: We need water, we need bandages, we need rope . . .

She said she couldn't see the small print in the dark, what did it say? What did she need? Read. I told her that it said warm oil. Why? she asked. I dunno, it just says that, I said.

She ran off, came back with the gas lamp and a torch and a pot full of warm vegetable oil. She put her hands in the oil and pulled them out, dripping, looking confused. 'Shit. *Read*,' she shouted to me. 'I can't touch the pages now. OK, what now? Just shout it out.' I kept staring at pictures of sheep in the book, then at Rosa the goat. 'Read, Rowan! NOW!'

I remember it all. Every word. I can even smell it.

The pictures of a little lamb's feet coming out of a lump of fur with human hands attached, the picture of the little baby lamb like something dead wrapped in some kind of wet cloth. 'Don't be scared,' she said. 'Am I supposed to see a head or feet? Please, Rowan, it's just a story, tell me the story or put the book down beside me so I can at least see what to do, please.'

I read like she taught me and Jono, tackling the big grown-up words, one bit at a time, repeating them, not wanting to see the stuff like soup that splashed on my mum's arms, focusing on the page, reading for the first time all by myself.

'Intro . . . introdu . . .' Stuttering like Jono.

'Introduction? Introduce?'

'Introduce your hand.'

'Good, great, more.'

'. . . your hand carefully, but only while the ewe is not straining.'

Trying not to look as she put her hand inside Rosa's gash. 'God, I can feel the feet!' she shouted, laughing. 'The feet, is that the right way round? Rowan, please!' Her voice like a shriek, like Rosa's. My eyes on the letters, struggling them out, turning them into words, her guessing when I couldn't get them right.

'What do I do?'

'Grab the feet, between contra . . .'

'Between contractions. Good. Thank God, thanks, Rowan, keep on going.'

'Pull more strongly while the ewe is straining. Don't pull when she isn't. As the lamb's body appears, support it with your arm. When she is half out twist a half-turn to relieve pressure.'

I remember all of this, the words.

I closed my eyes, heard the groan, the gush, my mother laughing and shouting and swearing. 'Fuck, yeah, yeah. Jesus fuck.'

'Make sure the lamb's nostrils are clear of mucus and leave her for her mother to lick.'

When I opened my eyes it was just like the picture even though it was a goat. Rosa with the little thing alive, and my mother, reaching for me. Her hands all covered in goat slime. She stopped, rubbed some straw on her arms.

'Come here, baby,' she said, crying as she put her arms round me. 'Look,' she said. 'A whole new life, and all thanks to you. What d'you want to call her?'

I thought for a bit and said, 'Jono.'

'How about a new name?' she said.

I named her Lamb because of the book. It didn't matter anyway, because a month later Eva's new people announced that they couldn't stand the sight of animals suffering in an enclosure, they were vegans and wouldn't drink goat's milk. So one day they were gone and that was when my mother's new silence began.

*

They stand there at the end of the corridor, whispering about you. Tamara and Mia and Lo-Mi and Jules. They fall silent as you backtrack up the stairs, along the first floor then down the back steps to the fire exit.

Only thirty minutes till you speak to Josh. Draw up your list.

– Tell him you are not scared by his threats.

– You need more space. A more equal share of childcare.

– He needs to stop pressuring you on many things. Work, sex. He loads too much on to you.

– Tell him to stop pretending to be nice to you.

– Tell him to call the office. Fuck them – you're going to look for freelance work elsewhere, in PR, HR, copywriting.

– Reassure him this is temporary. Ask for three more days. What day is it? Check date.

– Tell him you've had a nervous breakdown. It runs in your family. You have withheld this from him. There have been periods of euphoria then depression, like your mother had. They repeat every six years or so. You've always come out of them. Say sorry, you thought they were over.

– Tell him Sasa likes the brown bear best.

– Tell him, when she's crying, do the face game. Hide your face behind your hands then say happy face, and pull your hands back, like a jack-in-the-box face. Then hide your face again. Then say sad face, then grumpy face, then angry face, then . . . Her favourite one is the surprised face. It always surprises her when she sees your face again. She wants this again and again. She likes things to be repeated. It can get boring but she loves it. Don't do it before sleepy time, though, or she'll get too excited to go down.

Where on earth will you get a signal for the call? You are staring now, out the window at the car in the car park. Imagine yourself, driving round with one eye on the road and the other on the mobile screen. Stupid. Deadly.

You're running back down the corridor and up to the top floor. To the place that was Jono's secret place. A sign says 'Sanctuary'. Go to the sanctuary, then.

The door is locked and a sign says *Please do not enter when the green light is on.* You locate the light and it is green. There are five pairs of shoes outside. *If your meditation requires chanting or meditation please book in advance at reception.* Turn then, find a corner, a place by a window, a toilet with a lock. Behind you, the sanctuary door opens and there are voices, hands reaching for shoes. Another grey-haired woman. Speak, Rowan.

'Excuse me, is the sanctuary free now?'

'Sorry?'

'There's not a booking next or . . . ?'

'I don't think so.'

'D'you mind if I . . . ?'

They file out and you squeeze in. Close the door. Check. Yes, there's still a signal. The room seems so small, smaller than you recall. All is white. Eight kneeling rugs round a table with a shrine: a Buddha, a crucifix and some oranges. Above on the wall is another copy of the Eva portrait. How can you do this with her smiling down at you? How do you lock the door, turn on the green light?

He will have many questions. When you go back you

174

will be answering them and apologising for many years. Twelve minutes.

You have to decide whether to let him separate from you or not. You have the power to sway him, you know you do.

The signal fluctuates as you move. Where to sit? How does anyone do this? Sitting not pacing. Take a chair and put it by the window.

No, the view is wrong. A group are out in the garden holding hands. You won't be able to watch them while you hear his voice, the mismatch, the clash. Sit at the low table then, get some cushions for the floor, make yourself comfortable.

Around the table is a circle of what look like playing cards. They have a graphic of pair of wings on the back. Face up they each have little line drawings of angels with a single word underneath. Sobriety – Tolerance – Tranquillity – Confidence – Creativity. Another game. They must give you a card each, your card for the day, the week, life. Nine minutes.

If he's going to proceed legally then the fight for access starts now. He has no right to deny you access to her over the phone.

Josh. I can't tell you where I am but you should know that I'm safe.

No.

Stop fidgeting. The signal is strong and stable. Tell him:

Josh, hello, darling. I would like you to just listen for a minute then you can speak. OK, we have to have a way of doing this without getting upset.

No, be stronger.

Josh, before we talk I'd like you to put Sasa on the phone.

Seven minutes. Look at you, working yourself up into a state. Do something, anything.

175

Shuffle them. Pick a card, any card.

Forgiveness. The angel has her hands wide open at her sides.

Idiots. They think they can make you forgive just by saying the word 'forgive', like they think they can make you laugh with week-long laughter-as-healing workshops. Humourless.

Sasa's first big laugh. That time she tried to crawl all by herself. Then fell down. Bump, you said, so she wouldn't cry and she didn't, she laughed. Then she did it again, pushing herself up on her hands to make herself fall down again. Bump, bump. Giggling, gurgling, doing it again, again, till she fell on her chin and wailed and it was your fault.

Five minutes. Pick a card, any card.

Openness. Stupid. Another.

Communication. An angel reaching outwards.

He must not prop her up in front of the TV at half six in the morning. The adverts. They have it sussed. The plastic people. These adults that work so hard, so late. You've seen it. Plonk their kids down in front of the telly. Becca, Lucy's four-year-old. Shaking her hips, running her fingers through her hair. Shooting the grown-ups come-hither glances she's copied from MTV.

Three minutes.

Sa. Tell him. 'When she says that Suh noise that sounds like Sah, she's not trying to say her name.' It makes her cross when you say, yes, that's right, Sasa. She means, 'What's that?' like 'Wassa?' He should tell her the names of the things. She'll be pointing at them. Sometimes it's hard to guess.

Don't assume she doesn't know what things are called. If he gets the wrong thing she'll get frustrated. Tell him to just touch everything near where she's pointing then ask her, this or this? And when it's the right thing she'll say Sa. Then tell her. It's a TV, it's a dog, it's a fireplace. She's remembering all the names, she just can't say them yet. She's storing them in there.

Two minutes twenty-five seconds. Turn a card. Grace. An angel with hands crossed over her chest.

To age gracefully. One day she will ask you how old you are. If you are a hundred. If you were alive in the olden times. When there were cowboys and horses. And you will tell her, yes, there were horses, and goats, but that really you grew up in the time of cars. She will toddle around the room and ask, Were there lights when you were a girl, Mummy? Yes. Were there tellies? Sort of, but my mummy didn't have one. Wow. Were there telephones? Yes. And windows? Yes. And cookers? Yes. She'll be running around then pointing at everything – and laptops? No, darling. And she will ask you if she will be the same age as you one day? And you will tell her that, yes, she will be and how you are the same age that your mummy once was too. A three and a nine. All her fingers is ten and all her toes is another ten and if we put all of our fingers and toes together, you and her, then that's about how old you are. Wow. And her eyes will open. Will I have big hands like you one day, Mummy?

One minute fifty.

Yes, of course. And she'll ask to put her hand out against yours and giggle, It's tickly. And you'll say, Look, see how much your fingers will grow. Wow, she'll say. Wow, Mummy.

One minute ten. Go back to your list. Pick one thing to say.

Will I have a baby too, Mummy? If you want to, yes of course, although the world might not be good for babies in the future. It's silly not to have a baby when you're a lady, isn't that right, Mummy? I want to have lots, and lots and then she'll hold up her fingers again and try to count. Struggling to hold some fingers down, concentrating so hard,

177

then she'll put her two hands in your face – that many babies. Seven, eight babies, really, you'll be a very busy mummy. Yes, she'll say, very proud of herself with her serious face on.

Fifty-five seconds. Call him now, be strong, tell him it's over between you and all that matters now is what's best for Sasa. You will stay with him for her sake and in time . . .

But then the confusion starts. She is still counting her fingers and seems anxious. Will I live in the olden times too, Mummy? No, no, they're gone, they don't come back. Like your mummy? And then her lips starts to tremble – I'm never going to die, am I, Mummy? And you will try to tell her that everyone dies some day. Will you die, Mummy? Yes, but it's a long, long time away. And then she will cry and you'll hold her and scold yourself because you have crossed the line, because children have to be protected, even from the truth. Because childhood is, and must always be, the time when nothing dies.

He was timing the contractions with the digital stopwatch he'd bought specially for the occasion. You'd planned it together, down to the last second, the last dilated centimetre and breathe. You'd wanted it so much to be a natural birth, for you to really feel it. To be reborn as you gave birth, as they said in *The Real Mother*. '*This overwhelming experience of oneness with your newborn and your partner.*'

'Count through it,' he said, leading you to Ward 3B. 'Breathe – one, two, three, four, five, six. Let's go for a walk. Can you walk? *Walking can accelerate the dilation process,*' he said. 'Your contractions are only every four minutes or so, we're doing just fine.'

Through the birthing ward. The place looked like a Victorian prison, painted magnolia, or a dole office. Twenty women there. One staggered by in an old terry-towelling dressing gown, a teenager with tattoos over her neck, a vast black bloodied ladder of Caesarean stitches across her punctured gut. The fear then of what your body would become. The torn muscles, stretch marks, loss of bladder control. You'd avoided that chapter in the manual. The shivering started, the spasm.

Jesus fucking shit and piss.

'OK. Three minutes fifty seconds,' he said when it had passed, clicking stop on the watch. He sat you down in the corridor away from all the other mothers. 'You're not dilated enough,' he said, 'and the birthing tank's not free just yet. I'll check with the midwives again in a min, they seem to have it well under control.' Emotions, all of them, rushing inside you, as if trying to squeeze in before the next contraction. Fucking useless bourgeois cunt cunt cunt – you were chanting the word. He couldn't hear you and that scared him. 'Darling,' you said, 'hold my hand.' Your weight on his arm, pacing the corridor, tiny screaming footstep after footstep. *The pelvis is separating with each contraction,*' he said, '*the cartilege and muscles are stretching as the baby lowers itself into position.*' His voice seemed to come from the floor. The Stalinist magnolia lino, sounds of screaming from the birthing rooms. 'They're coming every three minutes thirty-nine seconds now,' he said. 'Good strong contractions. It's OK that you're digging your nails into my skin,' he said, 'it's fine you swearing at me.' *It's important for your partner to share every moment with you in the labour process.* He was telling you that you were being so brave and so good. *Give your partner verbal encouragement.*

You drifted further from him each time it came. Alone, terribly alone. God fucking Jesus. The swearing a protest at that.

'We're doing brilliantly.'

'We' he said. *Say 'we' to your partner.* Page 178. You tried to focus on anything other than the nausea panic that

179

the man who was your husband was reading lines from a book you gave him and wanting acknowledgement for how word-perfect he was. Idiot. You told him you loved him.

'Your eyes are bright, that's an indicator,' he said. 'Are you nauseous or do you feel like burping? Are you feeling hot then cold then hot again? That's another sign,' he said. 'Your legs seem to be shaking. One of the surest signs is that you feel like you have a large grapefruit pushing down on your anus. Do you feel like that, darling?'

He was running around then, trying to get a signal on his phone just in case they called, the midwives upstairs and his mother. He was worried over the sign that said no mobile phones, running back to you, agitated. Maybe if he was to just nip outside for a second or two to get a signal. *Stay in constant physical contact with your partner through the experience. She must feel that you are an integral part of the process. This can be of great help if she later suffers from post-natal depression.* Maybe if he just went to the nurses' desk. It's only a min away, he'll be straight back.

He left you alone then. You tried to be positive, ran over your list. He is so considerate taking time off from the big PR job he's working on. He's taken care of everything. Made a special compilation CD for you on his PC, taking out the angry tracks specially. The birth plan, laid out just like the book recommended. Scented aromatherapy candles and lavender face wipes. He had them in his pre-prepared bag, along with the nappies, the Rescue Remedy and *The Best Start in Life*.

A girl. Plastic seats at the end. Fifteen at most, massive. Alone. You watched her, breathing. Holding her gut. No one there for her. A chav, a ned in a shell suit. Your fear of the urban poor that ran all the way back to childhood. How somehow along the way it had turned into hatred. You pay your taxes so people like her can have a life for free. Never worked, easy way out. Will not breastfeed, will stick her kid on formula day one, Coca-Cola, fucking Michael Jackson Pepsi. Never read a birthing manual, probably can't even read. Hasn't drawn up a birth plan. Never heard of the birthing tank. Hasn't specified if she wants her favourite album playing during labour. Probably rave music like the others. Christina Agui-fucking-lera. Same shit she was listening to in the toilets of some shit dive nightclub when she was fucked by a stranger. Going to name her kid after some celebrity. Keanu Macdonald. Uma Sutherland, Jordan, fucking Jordan Jordache. Her mum probably did the same. She'll be called Sheryl or Kylie. Kylie definitely. Smoked all the way through her pregnancy. Drank through it. Drugs too and no father who'll own up to it. Her mother too drunk or stoned to turn up. The way she looked into you in her sweat-stained sweatshirt that read BABE, as if she had the right. How could he leave you alone with this?

You caught the surge of pain flashing in her eyes just as, mirroring her, it tore through you. Ten yards away, she was panting, grinding her teeth, one hand on the plastic seat, the other holding her back, legs shaking, all alone. You stared at each other through the spasms, counting breaths together. Across the gap, you saw her face slacken and felt your muscles subside and you were smiling at each other and you wanted to laugh, to run to her and hold her because you were in this together.

As his hand touched you, you pissed yourself. 'I couldn't help it,' you said, then he was jumping around. His hand wet with it, recoiling at the stench, and it still just dripping out of you. *'In the final stage the waters may break anything up to twenty minutes before labour starts,'* he said.

Christ fucking crunching. A brick, a dry brick, no waters to make it soft, pushing through you, tearing. The sound of someone panicking, someone panting, chanting.

Him screaming. Holding one hand and trying to reach

out as far as he could to shout into the reception area. 'Nurse, PLEASE. FOR GOD'S SAKE. There's no one here! I'm sorry, love, we're fine, doing just fine. Your eyes,' he said. 'Come back, I'm here, grab my hand, that's it, squeeze it tight. We have to walk now, darling. Please. WHY THE FUCK IS NO ONE HERE? NURSE! NURSE! You're on your feet now, let me take your weight, we're doing so well.'

You think that was when it started. You had this sense that she was really close to you, singing, you thought maybe it was Kylie. He walked you past Kylie but her mouth was closed. The voice pissing from you. 'We are experiencing something beautiful,' he said, 'you are so beautiful.'

They rushed round you then. 'We've booked the birthing room,' he shouted. 'She's in labour. Is it free? But we booked it. Can I speak to the administrator? We had this all planned. I have a CD and a list.'

You tried to talk, but could not. It was that other woman following you, talking to you. Shouting and singing. *You take the high road, and I'll take the low road, and I'll be in Scotland before ye.*

'Don't be disturbed, sir,' the nurse said. 'Women sometimes sing like this. If you'd like to take a seat in the waiting room.'

He was shouting as they lifted you to the birthing chair, spreading your legs, putting a pillow under your back to get the angle right.

'Posterior!' one of them shouted. Those things over their mouths.

'Please, sir, you're going to have to leave.'

'We need a blood sample now. IV drip, MD.'

'Is that drugs?' he said, his voice like an echo. 'We're not taking any drugs at all. Not even oxygen. Is there still time to make it to the birthing tank? I couldn't help but notice there were other people who hadn't signed up who seemed to skip the queue.'

Voices. 'Pulse a hundred and twenty-five. I need adrenaline and atrophine. Page Dr Johnstone. Now.'

A hand in yours. 'Close your eyes,' he tells you, and his voice is that of a woman, *For me and my true love will never meet again . . .*

'Why is she singing?' he said. 'Is she OK?'

'Haemorrhage. Umbilicus oxygen deficit.'

. . . on the bonny, bonny banks of Loch Lomond.

You tried to look up at him. There was a drip and a monitor and cables and wires in the way of his face. You heard screaming.

'We need to operate now, sir, your wife is losing too much blood.'

He was shouting that he bloody well knew they were forcing more Caesareans to cut back on the waiting lists, that he would file complaints, he had contacts. A hand gripped yours. Long black hair over your face.

'Twas there that we parted in yon shady glen.

Needle in arm. Such a nice colour of red. Twenty milligrams morphine. Done. Adrenaline ninety milligrams. Done. Sir, we must ask you to leave the room. The plastic mask on your face. Breathe, the voice says, don't push down. Your eyes closed and going darker and darker. Warm rush. Scalpel. Little machines beeping.

Little boxes on the hillside, little boxes made of ticky tacky. The songs accelerating and changing, like a disco mix.

Hush me my dearie and sleep without fear.

He seemed to be crying. 'I'm sorry. Can you just come back? We're so close.' Running his hands over your arms, chest, hips. 'My legs have gone,' you told him. 'I can't feel my toes.' No legs me, leggy me. What lovely legs he used to tell you. All gone.

For aw all the fish that swim in the sea the herrin is the fish for me.

'Shh,' you tell him, 'we mustn't upset her, someone's

having a baby and she's been singing songs, all the best ones. Shh, you're spoiling it,' you tell him. 'Don't you know the words?'

Nurse, nurse, he's screaming.

A long single note playing.

Sing fa la la li-do, fa la la li-do, fa la la li-do li-day.

You opened your eyes and tried to move your arms but there were tubes in your skin. The room was wrong. In your gut you felt it. She was gone and so was he. Something told you to roll over to see. Keep your eyes open. You made yourself roll. Your head spun when you moved. You tried to focus but were woozy.

She looked like an old lady, all scrunched up and grumpy-looking. Your mother's chin and nose, her hair, raven black. You reached out to touch her little perfect face. Your fingers hit a wall. Invisible plastic. She was in some kind of container. Chest rising, falling. You heard a radio, somewhere distant. Some pop tune, some girl, singing, some song about love. You closed your eyes.

The phone rings in your hand. *Home.* You are not ready, you have prepared nothing.

'Josh?'

'Yes.'

'Sorry, I thought I was going to call you and I was just waiting to. Is everything OK?'

Silence.

'Sorry, I . . .'

A crackling noise, a rustling.

'Hello, sorry, what was that? I think you're breaking up, what's that noise?'

'Crisps, I'm eating crisps.'

'Is Sasa . . .? Are you feeding her crisps?'

'For God's sake.'

184

'But is she there? Have you been liquidising her soup, like I showed you?'

'Emma.'

'You have to leave some lumps in, not liquidise it till it's smooth, she likes the lumps, she's learning how to eat bigger things.'

'Emma, please.'

'Sorry, Josh . . . I'm sorry . . . I . . .'

Silence then.

'I spoke to Charlotte.'

'Aha, yes?'

'Jesus. I can't believe you. She said Emma's not even your real name. Any more secrets you'd like to get out of the way?'

'Darling, I'm sorry. Please, is Sasa there?'

'That's all I have to say.'

'She's crying, I can hear her. Josh, please, can I speak to her?'

'You got my email?'

'Josh, you can't, it's not, it's not even legal, you can't not let me.'

'You read the email? I suggest you read it.'

'My God, she's crying. At least pick her up. For Christ's sake, please.'

The phone is set down, footsteps, her crying stops.

'Josh, you there? Josh?'

He picks up again. He's shushing her. Calling her baby, shh, baby.

'Please, put her on, she needs to hear my voice, it's calming for her.'

'You are so selfish, you know that?'

'Please, Josh, let her hear my voice. For God's sake.'

Breath down the phone. Her breath. He must be holding her in one arm, the phone tucked against his neck.

'Baby, are you there? Hiya, Sas, it's Mummy.'

Her breath down the phone. A hiccup.

'Sasa, Mummy's here. Hiya, Sasa, you being a good girl? Mummy's coming home soon, baby.'

Just her breath.

'Can you say hello to Mumma? Mumma. Can you say Mumma for me?'

You are stupid, asking her to speak, to forgive. You say sorry.

Something distant that sounds like sorry.

A click and the line is dead.

*

'Breathe in. You are in your white room. Your perfect place. Nothing from outside can enter without you wishing it to be here and no one can harm you. And breathe out. And open your eyes.'

You are seated in the circle. Glenna and Johann are holding your hands. Tamara is telling you that she has some good news. Eva will be visiting the group in two hours' time, and we should be grateful as it's very rarely that Eva blesses Sharing Week with her presence. First she would like us to explore and share some of what occurred during the intimate hand-touch exercise.

'I know that some very strong opinions and . . . emotions were released and I feel it would be good to share those feelings with each other.'

The hands leave yours. Open your eyes. Everyone is staring at the floor.

'We'll start with Jules.'

Jules looks up. Nods politely, fold her arms, and returns her gaze to the carpet.

'Feel free to take your time.'

Jules looks up at you. Bites her lip. She shakes her head.

186

'I'll pass.'

'OK, sure, good, we'll come back to you in your own time.'

Look around. The others are folding their arms, hugging their knees, curled in on themselves.

'Tom?'

Tom takes a deep breath. Stretches his arms over his head, looks to his left to Johann. Johann stares at his palms. Tom looks to his right. Mia is biting her nails. His breath whistles through his teeth. He shoots you a glance. 'Sorry, I . . . uh, I'll pass.'

'OK, OK, fine. Well, this has never happened before, but uh . . . I think, or rather I feel this energy in the room. It's not entirely positive but . . . as Eva says . . . all energy must be welcomed.'

Tamara staring at you. The others slowly raise their gazes.

'I believe . . . I feel it would do the whole group some good to hear some of the things repeated that some of you shared privately, and in confidence, with me earlier. Any volunteers? Mia?'

Mia shakes her head immediately. Her eyes flash to you. Don't let her touch you with her need. Close your eyes.

'Anyone? OK. Well, maybe it would be good to hear from the person who . . . inititated this . . . situation.'

Sasa's breath down the phone.

'Rowan?'

Keep your eyes closed. How can you face anyone? What you've done.

'Rowan, could you help us here?'

A sharp intake of breath, to your left, from across the room.

'I think it would do us all a lot of good to hear from you.'

Nod. Tell them you're sorry. Your story. Tell them about Sasa, about Jono, about Eva.

'It's fine. Take your time.'

Your face is tingling, your palms sweating, no one is breathing. They are moving away, vanishing, further. You can't breathe, you are going to be sick, your seat is spinning. My God, what is this? A voice from far away. A baby is crying. A baby is crying. Where is my baby? The crying getting louder. Her wailing coming from your mouth. It will not stop. You open your eyes but it keeps coming. Your mouth wide open, this animal noise, choking. You can't be alone like this, animal mother without child.

'I . . . I . . .'

Tears echo from across the room. Chairs are pushed back and someone is on their feet. The sound of a man breaking down. A hand gropes for you, gripping you tight. Arms around your head, your chest, enfolding you. Shh, shh. Lips in your hair.

'I . . . I'm so, so sorry . . . I . . .'

Their many voices, all as yours, reaching for words.

You stand on the gravel by the door. Tamara said it would be good to take a breather after the intensity of the session. Half an hour. Clear the air in the room before we meet Eva.

It all connected when you cried but now in the aftermath you feel foolish. You hate this about yourself. That something could feel like the end of the world and then it passes and you feel nothing at all. Laughable. You drag others into your melodramatic mire then leave them stranded. Your therapists had a name for this.

You are wandering deeper into the dark, wondering why it happened again, following the scent of rosemary bushes. You could lie on the grass, and feel the whole circumference of the earth moving beneath you. You could try. There is no one around to see you. Hug the earth, bite the grass, fill your mouth with it, say sorry.

188

Idiot, the voice says, fucking hippie. Laugh at yourself. No one has ever understood your laughter, have they, Rowan? They don't know that it's just walls that you've built in every direction to keep yourself safe, but which now look a lot like a prison.

A sound behind you, feet on gravel. You turn. A shadow of a man against the door light, coming towards you. Don't be scared. 'Hi,' he says. His accent. Morgan Stanley.

'Sorry, you having a private time or . . .'

He puts his thumbs into his chino pockets.

'. . . you mind if I sit beside you? Is that OK? Don't want you thinking I'm invading your personal space or . . .'

'It's OK,' you say. 'I was kind of tired of sitting here anyway. I'm so shit at nature.'

He's not laughing. He sits down on the stone furthest away from you.

'Is it OK if I talk, you know, about what happened?'

'Hit me.'

It was stupid to say that, your defensive knee-jerk Anti-Americanisms.

'Sorry,' you say. He does too, you both do, overlapping.

Now he laughs. A choking laugh afraid of itself. You try not to look at him. Look at the trees. The trees laughing at you and your pathetic attempts at relating to another human. You should probably give him a hug and leave him here. Tree-huggers.

'You . . .' he says, 'you were so, when you cried. I couldn't, they were all around you and I wanted to join in but I couldn't.'

'I shouldn't have done that. Sorry.'

'No, no,' he says, and you can feel him looking at you hard, in the dark. His hand tightening round yours.

'No, seriously. Please, you were absolutely right, it was all bullshit . . . and I'm such a friggin' phoney . . . you called us on it . . . but I didn't stand up for you or anything

189

. . . cos after this thing we'd been through, with our hands, me and you . . . It just made me so . . .' He clears his throat. 'So angry,' he says. 'Angry,' he says again, and squeezes your hand. 'With myself. Cos when you were touching me, she . . . she came back to me. Sally. Sorry, she's my . . . she's my . . . sorry.'

His sorries take you out of yourself and you want to know who Sally is. So you ask.

'. . . my daughter. Seven. Looks like Sheila, her mum. We've been divorced for a year.'

'OK.'

'I thought I was coping OK, you know, routine, my own place, no alcohol. Sorry, they said we're not supposed to do this, therapy sessions . . . you sure you're OK with this?'

'It's OK.'

'Sheila lets me see her twice a week, I babysit . . . There was this time Sally was sick with flu, and I had to take care of her at my place, she had a temperature and couldn't sleep and I had to run her back and forth to the toilet to get her to pee, cos of all the water I got her to drink and she kept asking me for her mommy. But I didn't want her to go back to her mommy. So I gave her some Calpol and tucked her in and read her some *Miffy* and she dozed off clutching my finger. Every time I tried to take my finger away she would wake, so I lay down beside her. Just looking at her. She has my . . . she has my eyes.'

Shh, shh. He has not finished, there is more to come out.

'And it makes me so mad cos I cheated on her mum. I fucked up. One drunken one-night stand and I fucked it. I've been trying to make myself OK, coming to these spiritual courses, you know, saying the words . . . but you were right. It's all bullshit. I fucked up, nothing's gonna fix that.'

He takes both your hands in his and holds them.

190

'You're so special,' he says. 'You're the only one I can trust. Could you do something for me? Could you forgive me?'

'Sorry?'

'Could you just say, I know the words sound crazy, but could you just say them? Say, I forgive you, Tom.'

Wow, the stupid ironic voice in your head says, this is really something. You hate this about yourself.

'OK. I forgive you, Tom.'

'Thank you. Thank you so much.'

He kisses your hands, gets to his feet, and walks away, saying thank you, thank you, before you can tell him that his hands were Sasa's. That she held your finger too in sleep, as you would stand there beside her cot, hour after hour, watching her tiny chest rise and fall, struggling to believe that it was not your will that was keeping it rising, falling; that her breath would not stop if you left the room. As Tom's shadow disappears, you can hear him whispering to himself, thank you, thank you.

Fifteen minutes till you meet Eva. On the way back inside there is a silhouette against the conservatory windows. Waiting. The security light clicks on and there is a face. Jules. The air seems to get colder, you wrap your arms round your chest.

'Hi,' you say. 'We should really go in – Eva's coming soon.'

She bites her lip, shakes her head.

'Look, I'm sorry,' you say. 'I didn't mean to upset anyone or accuse or . . . it was all a bit melodramatic.'

'Can we walk?' she says. She seems to have dropped her phoney accent.

'Just a minute then.'

She walks back in the direction you came from, across the gravel.

'I've been to a lot of these courses,' she says, 'looking for

191

some kind of experience, out of the body or what have you, and to be honest, they've always been a bit of let-down.'

She stops. The security light goes off.

'But you have it,' she beams. 'Before you cried, I felt it. The others did too! I couldn't breathe, my hands were sticky, I was sweating, this power just filled the room. Like electricity. I was frozen to the spot. Just before you cried the candle blew out.'

You have to say something. 'Maybe there was a draught, or—'

'No, no, you see, you might not know it, not yet – they usually don't – but I've studied it. You went into a kind of trance. You took everyone's different-coloured energy and channelled it into a white explosion. I've spoken to them all, they all felt it too. You have the power. You're a medium.'

'Well, I certainly did upset a lot of people if that's what you mean.'

The door light clicks off, just like you really have special powers. You must be out of range of the motion detector. Be gracious.

'Look, Jules, I'm tired, you must be too. I'm sorry—'

'Of course you are, that's normal. It must be so exhausting. Some psychics pass out afterwards.'

'Can we go inside now?'

You turn to go. The security light clicks back on again.

'I just wanted to thank you. For giving me faith.'

'I'm going now.'

'Just tell me . . . I don't trust any of those other buggers. Just tell me . . . what should I do?'

'About what?'

'Well . . . my life.'

'Well, first things first, you should probably come inside or you'll be late.'

'OK. Thanks, Rowan.'

She calls after you. 'Oh, Rowan!'

You stop. What now?

'Could you let me touch you?'

Why not? You permit her to hug you and she beams with joy, thanking you over and over. As you look over her shoulder, you see Tamara pacing about inside the conservatory, waiting for you. Jules runs back inside.

'Rowan, a word please. If that's OK.'

This is becoming ridiculous. You have the force, you are the warm glowing epicentre of universal love. You stand before her among the yuccas and cactuses with their little signs with names and instructions. It's a speech, she's prepared a speech.

'I just want to say that I may have misjudged you. I don't know if you sensed it, but when you arrived I sensed you were maybe . . . problematic. I'm sorry about that because now I see that you're really a very honest, open, caring person with a lot of generosity of spirit and . . .'

They've had an emergency meeting maybe. The Sharing leaders trying to work out your eviction plan. All of this, it's just distracting you from why you are here.

'Any negative feelings you have, we're more than happy to hear about them. I just want to know if you're OK. OK with being here?'

So she wants you to leave voluntarily. No fuss, no police. You have unsettled the authority she has but would never admit to. She hates you for that, for making her feel hatred again when it was the thing she wanted more than anything to escape. The same hatred Eva had for your mother.

'I'm fine. Shouldn't we go in? Eva will be . . .'

'Well, that was the other thing. Before we meet Eva, could you . . . ?'

'I'll be a good little girl. OK.'

Her eyes are confused. You have the power and she desires power.

193

'I was joking, Tamara. I'll be fine. I've finished my little cry so everything'll be hunky-dory. OK?'

'OK, great, great. Well, I'll see you in there. I'm sure it's going to be a wonderful session.'

She walks off and leaves you alone with the plants.

The sign on the cactus plant before you reads: *My name is Desert Wind and I have travelled many lands to be here. I welcome all the peoples of the world to our safe haven.*

And you smile. You smile with that inner power that could burn this place to the ground or perhaps save it from itself.

*

'Close your eyes and imagine yourself on an empty road,' Eva would say.

I never walked that road, I ran it. Since Jono had been put into care there was no one to stick up for me at school. I ran down Eva's road every day with my eyes wide open.

The school bell would ring and I would tear over the football fields, over the fences, through the alleyway, to the river. In my hiding place among the briar bushes I would wait and watch the kids running past searching for me, shouting their obscene names, their ugly threats.

I had missed the school bus and it would be an hour till the next one. I had to wait till the coast was clear. I'd crouch in the mud and thorns, trying not to breathe too loud, closing my eyes and ears to make the voices go away. Eva said that to start the reawakening you had to escape out of time. I'd push my eyeballs with my thumbs till the sparks came, then the flash.

I run as quickly as I can to the bridge.

Two old women stand by the bus stop with their shopping bags, their hands covering their mouths, their mouths black bleeding holes. They talk about how under the weather

194

so-and-so is. 'Oh, I know, I know.' And who is having an affair and who is pregnant. 'That Jeannie should never have married into the Gunns.' 'Oh, I know, I know.' I watch them as the grey dust falls and they think it will snow, they complain about the weather.

I walk on, watching my footsteps in the grey.

Then three single mothers with their little buggies parked outside the ruins of what used to be Boots the chemist, their babies so quiet in their prams, flies eating their eyes. A young man passes and one of the girls passes her hand through her hair, and it falls out in clumps with leaves of skin. They go inside and I watch them, picking up hair-care products and hair dyes and colours for going out at the weekend.

And I walk on, invisible.

The five unemployed teenagers who always stand against the wall of the Bank of Scotland are still there. One blind, one with third-degree burns, and one shivering and pissing himself, joking like they always do about the football and the fight last night and who's the hardest guy in town and who's shagging who. I watch them turn their heads as two teenage girls stagger past them; one holding the other up. 'Too much to drink, eh, lassies?' shouts one of the lads. They don't see the weeping scabs burning their way to the bone, through the stockings that have become welded to the skin. 'Fuckin, shag that one, eh?' 'Aye.' 'Lost a bit of weight, eh?' 'Aye, no bad now, eh?'

I walk past them, and they do not hear my steps.

I am inside Woolworths, it has been plundered, dogs have torn away what little they could find to eat. Now they stand there, thirty or more, with shopping baskets, in the chocolate and magazine aisle, their bare feet bleeding on the shattered glass. The pages are dust, sparkles of it fly in the air. One woman tries to force down a Milky Way bar and vomits it back up with thin yellow bile. Her eyes blood red from the spasms. Her friend whispers that she was sure she saw an article in *Marie Claire* with diet tips on how to regain your body after a baby and get back into a size ten and win back your partner's affection. 'Oh, I can't even watch the news. It's dreadful, isn't it, how no one seems to care about their appearance these days.'

They let me pass. Their eyes are white, scorched by my flash.

The children walk the empty aisles, the security man lies on the floor in a pool of dark brown, his arm round a fallen mannequin.

I see the school crushed like a doll's house, the statue in the main street like all the windows in all the houses, melted.

And the man trying to revive his friend who lies on the street. 'Get up, ya drunken bugger.' He cannot see the hundred scattered others like dropped dolls which cover the entire street.

I reach to touch him but he cannot feel me.

The people out there are blind, Eva said, pity them, it's too late to save them. We have to build a wall between us and them. They're dead to us already.

My mother could not accept that, she wanted to save everyone.

But I saw the beauty in Eva's words. I could feel the white cleansing light of the coming apocalypse growing within me.

*

In a few minutes Eva will be with you. You are not going to panic. Listen to the rasp and wheeze of your lungs amplified behind closed eyes. Try to concentrate on the lecture.

'. . . in nineteen seventy-four Eva started to receive signs from the land telling her how to transform Ithaca into the spiritual haven we now know.'

Breathe. You expect lies, accept, respect them. When Eva enters every word she says will be an absolute lie. This is not a panic attack, listen to the voice of your Sharing Leader. Your glorious Leader.

'The signs told Eva to plant trees and people would come. She planted trees and they survived and thrived and people came.'

The pregnant pauses Tamara makes.

'. . . and the wonderful mansion you are now sitting in was renovated with local indigenous labour and the hands of the many who came to learn . . .'

The synthesised ambient music playing in the background.

'. . . with the help of generous donations from like-minded progressive spiritual followers from all over the world . . .'

Your mother drove here that night. Eva sat with her in the circle of others and said she must erase the darkness within, go into the wilderness and live in the light.

'Eva rarely ventures out to meet people so we are privileged today to have her visit . . .'

The voice says that interviews with Eva have been printed in eight languages. That Eva has found profound peace after a period of illness. That the community would ask that you don't treat this like a celebrity interview or therapy session, that you will all no doubt have many questions for the spiritual leader but it would be preferred if this was just a quiet sharing time with her in our midst. That Eva believes that sharing does not require words. That we are to take hands now and breathe together, because Eva will be here in just a few moments, keep our eyes closed and focus on all the positive things we'd like to communicate to Eva, without words.

The hands reach for yours again. Glenna and Jules. You have not seen Eva since you were ten. You have forgotten how to breathe. Now you are. You are scared.

You hear the door creak open. You peek. The first thing you see is the wheelchair. Two helpers steering her into the empty space between two chairs. Then her smile. Not like the pictures. Half of her face seems as if frozen.

When she looks up she'll recognise you. It was stupid to do it like this. She'll have you thrown out. You should have stuck to the first plan.

Breathe. Run over plan two. When Sharing Time is done, you will follow her and her helpers back to her home.

One helper puts the safety brake on. You glimpse Tom and Mia sneaking glances.

'You can open your eyes now.'

A crescendo in the music, as if they have timed and rehearsed this event.

But the way her right hand hangs lifeless and she cradles it in her other, the palm and fingers facing upwards as she is helped to sit upright. They haven't said it but you can see. The signs of a stroke. A sigh of reverence through the room as she heavily exhales, as she looks up to face you all. The expression on her face, not a whole face, a half expression. The old smile on the right-hand side; the left side dropping, drooling. Half smile. Half Eva. Energy surges through the circle into your hand. One person to your left may already be sobbing. Lo-Mi, you think. Travelled eight thousand miles, for this. They don't see Eva, this Eva, they see her from the pictures and now the picture is alive for them. Half alive.

'Welcome,' says Tamara.

'Welcome,' everyone says at the same time. Eva says nothing.

She has not recognised you yet. Her eyes seem at once focused on everyone and nothing.

Everything you planned. How could you? Look at her. Her floor-length cotton tunic with stains from food or urine, her varicose-veined feet falling out of her sandals, her long thin grey hair yellow at the ends, what looks like a tube for a catheter.

Her head moves so slowly. The helpers stare at the side of her face with awe, as if the turning of the head was a miraculous event. It must have been a bad stroke. Her one good eye looking round the circle, face to face, smiling, nodding, her eyes coming closer to you. Past Tom, Glenna, Jules.

She may not recognise you but recognises the fear. Her eyes move past Jules, a nod, then you. Straight at you. A smile, a nod. Nothing, and then she moves on. You are one of thousands over the years. Her eyes move past you to Lo-Mi.

Why does this upset you? Maybe you came here just to be seen, for her to say Rowan, for her to tell you what to do.

Her eyes complete the slow circle. She rests, closes her eyes, smiles, opens her eyes again. Her half mouth moves.

'Love,' she says. 'Love . . . ly.'

She struggles with the next word, she raises her one good hand into a fist, grips it tight, releases.

'To . . .' she says. 'To . . . geh . . .'

'Together,' the helper says, holding her dead hand. Eva closes her eyes. Her skin yellow, waxy, silken, semi-transparent, stretched over arthritic knuckles, blue lumpen veins. She breathes. Half a minute now since her last word. Everyone waiting, holding their breath.

This must be how it happens. All her life she preached positivity. Reject the negative. Do not question – accept. An answer for everything or silence to every question. This must be what happens. The left and right side of the brain. Live with only answers and the questions die. Half a person. Half life. Nuclear. And she would tell your mother to ignore the jets and the bomb, block them out. This must be what happens. Twenty years of denying doubt and half of you dies.

Two minutes now, like waiting for Jono to speak. The helper closes her eyes, squeezes Eva's hand tighter. The others in the circle waiting. Tamara discreetly exits.

'Words,' Eva says, pauses. Everyone waiting. 'I am,' she says. Marianne nods beside you. Exhales. Mouths the word 'Yah'. Mia smiles, repeats 'I am' in a whisper.

They think this haiku, divinely inspired. This poor old woman who can only splutter the clichés of her youth. Peace. Love. Lovely. This poor old woman who was maybe trying to say, 'I am sorry.'

Still she struggles on, eyes closed. Forehead furrowed, her one good hand clenched fist-like by her face. A surge of concentration through her good side, her shoulder tensed. The eyes of the room willing her to speak. Like a séance, the word from beyond. Jules digging her nails into the back of her hand. Johann grinding his teeth. Tom mimicking Eva, his fist by his face. Suddenly it passes, her fist falls to her side, her eyes open.

'Bis . . .' she says. 'Biscuits.'

There is some confusion. Twelve bodies become restless. How could it be 'I am biscuits'? Faces anxious with incomprehension. The helper gets to her feet. 'Time for tea and biscuits,' she shouts with a smile, and suddenly, as if the angels had intervened, two new helpers enter with trays and cups and plates while Eva sits, smiles to herself, nodding.

'Pee,' she says. 'Pee.'

'Peace,' the helper says to us all.

'Peace,' people reply, confused as they are caught between the banality of biscuits and the power of this word.

Many get to their feet. Some hesitate as they pass her on the way to the tea table. They must feel the need to do something after such a cryptic anticlimax. Many eyes and hands betray their need to touch her as they hover. You sit there still and it's only you and Eva. Six empty seats between you.

There is some satisfaction. Watching her attempt to stand by herself, failing, almost falling, having to wait for help from her helper who is too busy with the tea. You see now, clearly, the incontinence bag.

She has still not noticed you. Ironic, that a woman who all her life preached living in the now is stuck in an eternal present of biscuits and tea and the need to pee. You do not laugh. You must do something, now.

You get up from your seat and in the ten paces you cross the thirty years between you. You stand before her and offer to wheel her to the biscuits or toilet. The eyes of the others are upon you as she reaches out and grips your arm. You release the brake with your foot.

The helper rushes over.

'Sorry, but Eva insists that I'm the only one who—'

Eva spits out a noise – 'Nuh', maybe 'No'. The helper is embarrassed. In all those years you never heard Eva say 'No'. Eva's eyelids flicker, eyes coming to rest somewhere near your shoulder.

'I think she needs to pee,' you whisper. You feel Eva trying to move forward.

The helper hisses at you, 'We have a system, we can't just . . . I'm a trained geriatric nurse and Eva . . .' The helper pushes your hands away from the handles. Eva starts shaking her head, 'Nuh, nuh!' striking the girl's hand. People have started staring. Someone beyond asks why there isn't any soy milk and the helper is thrown into confusion. 'Yvonne,' she calls out, but the first helper has gone. 'God, Yvonne's on catheter duty and I have to do the scones!' she mutters under her breath. Eva is motioning towards the door, almost shouting, 'Puh . . . Pee!'

You take the handles and push. 'We'll be fine,' you whisper with a smile that is so gentle, so caring. 'It's OK, I've been here before.'

The helper whispers, 'Look, I have to get some soy

201

milk, could you take Eva to the lift? Yvonne'll be on the ground floor. OK, the lift is—'

'I know where to go, thanks,' you say, as Eva grunts 'Pee' again.

The helper announces to all assembled that Eva will now be leaving, and the group stand there, embarrassed and confused with their plates stacked with biscuits.

'Let us all say thanks to Eva.'

'Thank you, Eva,' they all incant.

'Thanks,' the helper whispers. 'Just get her to the lift and Yvonne'll take over. God, I knew this'd happen. I'll be down in just a few minutes, thanks so much.'

Your smile carries you the few feet to the door, and through into the hallway. You don't know where the lift is or why you are doing this. Her weight seems to lead you forward. All that matters, step by step, is the weight of her body. Her need for your help.

You close the door behind you and you are alone with her at the head of the stairs. It would be so easy to release your grip, to watch her tumble, her neck breaking as the weight of the chair pushed her over and over.

You take the lift then. You stare at the back of her head, this woman who destroyed your mother, counting seconds as you descend, preparing your question.

The doors open. Others eye you with suspicion as you wheel her out. You give them the smile, and wheel her on. Eva mutters the word 'Pee' again. You pass by reception. Thankfully it is closed and there is no Yvonne or anyone to question your actions. Eva throws her hand out, gesturing to the door, the garden. Ten feet, the difficulty with the step.

You are outside and amazed that no one has come to stop you. All the possibilities amass before you, but the wheels in the gravel are so slow. Each jolt seems to cause her pain. In the slow measured paces it rushes at you again. You have her now, it would be so easy to lead her away, to

202

take her to your tree, your stream, to let her fall. To force it from her, names, dates.

But she is the same age your mother would be. You woke beside her many times. She was the one that held you when your mother wasn't there. She taught you the words for *Yellow Submarine*.

You feel her weight push against your arms. Where are you going? Your mental map is all wrong. You still see things as they were. All you know now is where the car park is. You could drive her away. She is tired of this place now. Take her south to your home. Perhaps she has recognised your face after all and this is why she does not resist.

Take her to your tree by the stream. Complete the symbolic order. Just minutes away, the little bridge she built with Josh and Pete and Tessa and your mother. The sound of the water, you can smell it. The one time there that you told Eva she was your favourite mummy.

You look over your shoulder and no one is following. It's absurd the reverence they pay her and now this neglect. The place was never good at caring for the weak. They must be searching for her on the ground floor. Another few steps and the security light clicks off and suddenly you are in darkness together. She keeps motioning forward, as if she knows.

Your tree. Your stream. You park her by the black water's edge, listening to its whisper. You take her one good hand in yours and run over what to say. I am Rowan, d'you remember? Rowan. Over there is my tree. My mother was Jenna, you remember Jenna? What will you say?

'Nuh,' she says. 'Nice.'

'Yes,' you say. 'Nice, the water. Isn't it?'

She once bathed you here. She told you you could catch a trout by tickling its tummy. Guddling, she called it. If you ever caught one you should put it back because it was bad to eat them. You never saw a fish. Bubbles were all you saw, on the surface. You used to sit there with her

203

waiting for the bubbles and she told you about Jonah and the Whale. She told you that the old stories were the best but they were mostly about men, that the future would be yours, that one day you would be a woman and women would lead the world away from its destructive course. She kissed your head by the stream.

'Bubbles,' you say, 'where the fish are. You can see the bubbles sometimes.'

'Bub,' she says.

So easy to let the brake off. To let her roll forward. Hold her head under. To scream at her – Tell me, where is she? Her one good hand splashing the water, as you hold her face under.

You will watch till there are no more bubbles then release your hold. You will tell them there has been a horrible accident.

'Rowan,' you say, 'remember. You planted the tree when I was born.'

'Trrr,' she says as if you are teaching her the word for the first time. 'Tree . . . tree.'

Your anger fades as you stare at her mouth. It is clear now, so clear. Your mother cannot be in this place. Your mother was anger, you would feel it if she was here. This is a place with no past. Where people come when they leave the world, to learn again the meaning of words as if they were children. Eva is one year old.

'Tree,' you say, 'trees.'

You can only see the good side of her face in the dark and that smile looks as it used to, long before she turned it into an image of a smile. Your mother is gone. She lived in the half of Eva's head that has died.

'OK, let me take you home,' you say.

The helpers came in a fluster and panic and you were reprimanded by Tamara. You watched silently as they

204

wheeled her away. In the refocusing dark you saw little bubbles in tiny whirlpools in the stream, perfect circles, forming and unforming. The more you looked the more they became constellations, stars, planets orbiting.

There was nothing you could do with it. This feeling. Like a first breath of air after surfacing. You came all this way to find your daughter in an old woman's body. Circles in water. Bad poetry.

To laugh out loud. To run blind through the dark. You will never know what happened to your mother. Maybe it is better this way. Say goodbye to her now. Laugh. Laugh at yourself. Put your toes in the stupid bad-poetry water.

It is so simple. You will fight for custody and win, then you will return here with Sasa to start again. Pick up where your mother left off. This place has never left you. How can anyone ever escape from a childhood that was an experiment in change? And all the cynicism that you lived with before, what was it but anger at how the dream never worked out. But it could, in a simple stupid way, here, so far away from the world. One word at a time, you could make yourself believe again.

Slip off your shoe, hippie child. Feel the water. It tickles your toes, cold, it feels good.

It's so clear. The old energy is dying with Eva, they are just mouthing her words from twenty years ago. The place has been taken over by the mediocre, by clones and copyists. They need new words. You have energy, they say. You will teach them the new words. You will bring Sasa here and start with the first word on the first day.

Your feet are warming in the water. Of course, this is why you were called here.

The place needs children. You will start a school, something like Montessori, but inclusive, free. The local children will come too. There will no longer be the divide. You will take the knowledge you have of advertising and promote this place, bring in money, succeed where your mother failed. Sasa will grow up with music festivals and wind power and brothers and sisters and conferences on spreading the word. You will find engineers and scientists and sponsors. They will come from everywhere to discover the secret and spread your methods, and even Josh will feel the pull of the place and become a convert. You will dig clay from the earth together and make pots, you will plant the food you eat. You will reconcile the dark and the light. Eva's ideals and your mother's anger. You will have them sit round you while you preach the new gospel. There will be no more of this penance. No more struggling each day with impotent rage, punishing themselves, meditating, going back to their empty rooms to pray forgiveness for their doubts. All that energy, you will take and give direction. Release through action. The children will grow with hope and conviction and you will teach them how to make weapons. You will hijack the fighter planes. Breach the security walls. Shut down the roads. You will stop killing yourselves slowly and kill others with a single blow. Die for the cause. Kill the Angels. Overthrow the American voices, set fire to the meditation room. March naked to the airbase. Destroy. This is why you came here. The voice has known all along. It wasn't her, it was destiny.

A noise behind you, heard through your laughter. Mia. She lowers herself quietly beside you, puts her finger to her lips, Shh, touches her heart, then your mouth. How can you not speak when you have everything worked out? Everything's going to be fine, Mia – I have the plan!

You watch her as she gracefully removes her sandals, tests the water with her foot, nods to herself, then slips out of her jeans. You have to laugh – how can you not? – the water so cold. Then her top. You are giggling. She puts her finger to her lips. She pulls off her top and her small breasts bounce free. A scar runs across her chest. You see now the silver lines that trace her wrists. Suicide strokes. She stands before you in her panties and smiles. 'I see you long time,' she says. 'I know you. Shh, come.' She steps into the water, a little unsteady at first on the rocks, then slowly wades in, a gasp escaping from her. Insane. She motions for you to join her. She looks back at the house. 'No one,' she says and extends a hand. 'Come, is nice.'

Look at you, the voice says – stupid hippie shit – nymphs in a woodland glade – fucking Woodstock – and you are so tired of that world-weary voice but you cannot get beyond it. You cannot undress as she has done. She is paddling now, shivering with the cold, smiling at you, gesturing for you to come in.

Do something for once, don't judge. Jump.

She opens her arms for you. Her fingers find yours. You hesitate, you look over your shoulder at the house. She pulls you into the splash and you are yelping, laughing, stumbling, dripping in your soaking clothes.

Then you are chasing her through the water, falling, splashing her. You want to catch her, kiss her.

The lights come on in the house and you hear footsteps and voices.

'Shh, they find us,' she says, pulling you into her arms. 'Shh, you are most beautiful.' She kisses your head. And you are both giggling, laughing to and at and with the sky.

*

Tambourine Man. Her teaching me how to whistle. The sounds of them singing as we slept six kids to a bed. Driving with Pete and Jono around town hunting for things to recycle – the old sofa, the fridge, the clothes in bin bags that still had years of wear in them. *The Times They Are a-Changin'.* A picture of the first man on the moon in the *LIFE* magazines we found in a bin and the moon through the hole in the roof. The Great Bear, the North Star. *Lucy in the Sky with Diamonds*. Puppets made of old socks on the little theatre me and Jono made from the shell of an old TV. *Nowhere Man*. Jeans patched and patched again till they were more patches than jeans. Ponytails and pigtails held with ribbons of torn cloth. No mirrors to see how pretty we looked. The smell of peat smoke, hashish, boiled vegetables. *Copper Kettle*. Angus bare-chested, covered in grease, roll-up in his mouth singing with his head under the bonnet of the Beetle. *The Fool on the Hill*. Frozen feet in hot water. Her breath steam in the air, cupping my hands between hers, blowing on my fingertips to make them warm. Glowing warm after an hour walking through a thunderstorm. *Blowin' in the Wind*. The dark of the road then the eyes of the goats glowing in the headlights, which meant we were home. Throwing stones at the low flying jets. *Back in the USSR*. Catching my mother pretending to be the tooth fairy. Her crying when John Lennon was shot. *Give Peace a Chance*. Rainbows that filled the sky and rainbow-coloured tie-dyed T-shirts. How to find a dock leaf and crush it till the juice came and rub it on the sore bit where the nettle rash stung. *Rocky Raccoon*. Skimming stones with Jono in the stagnant pool at the quarry. The faeries in the flames of the old range. *White Rabbit*. Standing on a seat at the range, stirring the big pot of soup all by myself and stoking the fire. *Norwegian Wood*. Her licking my cuts, licking my eyeball to get the grit out, biting out the splinters of wood, kissing my cuts. The bitter taste of home-grown kale. *It Ain't Easy*. Making a race out of pulling up potatoes. Running as fast as the boys. Bare feet in the morning dew. The old metal bucket full of blueberries. *Parsley, Sage, Rosemary and Thyme*. Making men out of the warm wax from the candles on the range. Digging up clay, making monsters from them and waiting for them in the kiln, our faces burning, Dresses made from curtains. *Eleanor Rigby*. Milking the goats. The sickly sweet smell of them drying on our skin. Dandelion clocks. Blowing the seeds. One o'clock, two o'clock, three o'clock. Stories told by candlelight. *I Pity the Poor Immigrant.* Running naked with strangers. *Ciao. Bonjour. Auf wiedersehen.* Staying up late while the grown-ups sang. Saving Simone the stray cat that had been run over. Running across the moors trying to catch a red admiral. Feeling it feather in cupped hands. Crying as its wings turned to dust as I tried to pin it to my dress. *Here Comes the Sun.* The bog cotton, the pretty white flowers that you should never try to pick because they only ever grew where the marshes would pull you under. The ancient marsh kings lost beneath the ground. *Where Have All the Flowers Gone?* Riding bareback on Jocky, the tinkers' Shetland pony. Finding myself alone one morning and seeing her so far away on the moors, being unable to scream to her. *The Sound of Silence.* The night the tarpaulin roof blew away. Four adults and three children huddled under the covers, the snow falling on us. Stomping our feet and swearing to keep warm. *Dream Angus.* Angus with a hammer and a ladder and ropes in the storm. Helping build the roofs with old slates saved from abandoned crofts. Angus and Tessa and Jono and Saphie and Pete and Petra and Storm and Sean and Eva singing along, always, through everything. Singing along to her songs.

*

From nowhere it starts, on this fine day, when you have been woken early by the sun, while the others in your shared room slept on. When you looked at Marianne and Mia's closed eyes and were overcome with something so simple, without judgement, as you waited for them to wake, so you could tell them of the joy you felt rushing from nowhere on this fine morning. Of this phrase you woke with. Whispering in your head.

'It is what it is.'

On this fine day when you sat in bed watching the light coming up and forgave Eva and the garden and said for the first time in so long 'I'. 'I am here.' 'It is what it is.' 'Everything is.' You stretched your arms and found a place for them to rest, where it felt right, a couple of inches beyond your face. What the hell were you doing? Feeling the limits of your aura? You would have scorned at even thinking it, but still it made you smile. 'It is what it is,' you whispered again, and then, as the words started so too did the tears. Out of nowhere. You were not thinking of where you were, what you had done. It is what it is. The beauty of that single simple sentence.

Then at the breakfast at which you helped yourself to a second bowl of muesli and yogurt and sat back with the smiling faces at your table who you now call your friends, whose smiles touch you because they ask nothing of you more than just that. And slowly you felt it was coming back from somewhere, long repressed. That smile without reason or excuse.

There was a muffin sitting on a plate. A wholegrain blueberry muffin and you found yourself staring at it. You weren't thinking about the hands that made it, the devotion which is baking, or how it was an American invention or about global capitalism and the Americanisation of everything. You were staring at the muffin and told yourself, 'It is simply what it is. Accept it.' You had to get to your feet, excuse yourself because you were going to cry.

Then you were in the kitchen, where your task for the day was to be performed. Looking at it all. The sheet-metal cutting surfaces and tables. The magnetic rack of knives. The rows of pots and pans laid out in progressive order of size. The vast industrial ovens. The twenty gas hobs. The hose attachment as big as a shower unit. The walk-in refrigerator. The immense vacuum air extractor like something from a ship. You said the word 'Kitchen' to yourself, silently.

210

The words, 'Our kitchen.' 'It is our kitchen,' and this, too, moved you. Why? What is this feeling?

It is what it is.

A woman was there, she welcomed you inside. Short white hair, in a smock, her arms strong. Her smile seemed in some way pained. She would be about the same age as your mother. But your mother was gone. It is what it is. Everything is. Just is.

I am. Here.

You were seated round the table. This time it was you who reached for the others first and then you closed your eyes waiting for Tamara to lead you with her words for the day. You welcomed them, repeated them silently to yourself after she said them.

'*We thank the garden for the wonder of its many gifts. Let us focus on our day ahead, and the meals we will make that will nourish and feed us physically and spiritually.*'

Tom's hand in yours, firm and needy. You did not mention his tears of last night. He smiled at you silently, not out of embarrassment. Marianne's big fingers through yours. You accepted her and did not judge.

'*And open your eyes and look at each other.*'

The smiles no longer seem fake. The uncertainty on their faces is what it is, like need in the hand, reaching, real.

'*Let's just start by telling each other our names and saying what vegetable we feel like today. I'll start. My name is Tamara and today I feel like a cabbage. With many outer leaves. I feel a little vulnerable today, but as I work on my task I want to try to get down to the heart.*'

This stupid vegetable game — today you accepted it, without irony or scorn. Tamara eyed you with suspicion. You tried to tell your eyes to tell her not to worry.

'*My name is Tom and today I feel like a globe artichoke, because today I'm thinking about the world outside.*'

He laughs. You love his nervous laugh.

'*Sorry, I know that sounds like such a corny American thing to say.*'

Glenna and Marianne and Tom are all looking at you now, as if waiting your derision. Tamara averts her eyes. You feel it before you speak. The intake of breath in the room. You must tell them that they have nothing to fear. You are just you. Make a joke.

'*Hello, my name is Rowan and today I feel like an onion, because I'm a bit tearful but in a nice way.*'

They exhale and their eyes thank you.

So it progresses. Marianne is a potato because it's simple and humble and she would like to be like that. And then it is the old woman.

'*My name is Sophie and I am a turnip because I feel hard today because I am fighting a lot of physical pain, but I hope that through the day, I will get warmer and more soft until I am ready to be eaten.*'

She is still looking at you. You look up and smile. She could have been your mother. Where your mother is now is of no importance because you are here.

Tamara tells you all that there are four main meals today, two soups and five salads. She lists the tasks and says that of course no one likes cutting a hundred onions but . . .

'I'll do the onions,' you say, 'so I can learn how to stop being so weepy.'

There is laughter and Tom squeezes your hand. Then it is. Just as she said it would be. Everyone, as if some secret force was guiding them, selects their role and there is no argument, every job is covered.

There are seventy onions to be diced. The old woman got them for you from the organic storeroom and you found a bench in the corner. She helped you select a knife and an apron and explained how the skins go in the green bin for the compost heap. The procedure seemed to focus you both away from the smile you felt between you, unpsoken. Then

212

she was on to the next person and you were alone with the stack of onions.

The first few slip from your grasp. You are too slow at taking off the skins. You cut too deep in removing the top layers. You worry that you are wasting too much. You are no cook, he always does the cooking. You look around. Tom is peeling carrots. Marianne is shredding cabbage. Jules is on salad dressing. There is talk but only of practical things. And you and the onions. It is taking for ever and still you have only done five. Everything is wrong. There are too many different procedures. There's no rhythm to it. Whenever you did this before it was only ever one onion, for a pasta sauce. You'd always be thinking about something else. But now you have to focus. You have sixty-five more to do, getting frustrated with yourself. You make the mistake of rubbing your eye, then it is the onion juice stinging into you. You drop your knife.

She is there beside you then. Holding your shoulders. Old Sophie. Her voice gentle and guiding. She shows you how to leave the ends on before slicing because they hold the onion together. How to get into a rhythm. She turns on the water in the sink beside you and explains that it takes the sting away, she laughs that she doesn't know why. She takes your knife and cuts one for you, fast.

'When I do it. I hum to myself,' she says. 'It helps.'

And she is humming so quietly, as she shows you. Then she is away again, helping Tom with the carrots. He's panicking over scraping or skinning.

It works. You feel the rhythm, you hear the song, a kiddies' song, the slicing is the strum of a guitar, the knife hitting the board is the drum.

And ten green bottles will accidentaly fall and you are thinking about Sasa.

You stop. You look around and you feel it. That Tom and Marianne and Tamara and Jules are all alone in their tasks and all fighting feelings like you.

213

Sophie is smiling over at you. She knows. She is the mother of the kitchen. She must once have been beautiful. She has the eyes of a mother. She has lost a child and now you are all her children.

You want to hold her. It is hard to contain this sudden rush.

A minute has passed and you have done nothing. Cut the onions. Have you done enough? Will it all be ready in time? Are you holding things up, spoiling it for everyone?

Sophie's hand is on your shoulder again. You can't speak. Her smile says she knows, that this happens here. That there is no escape from these moments.

'Am I . . . too slow, am I? What time has the soup got to . . . ?

'You're doing fine.'

'You sure? I thought . . .'

'You're cutting them very artistically,' she says. 'Maybe you could cut them bigger, like this.'

She takes the blade and shows you. Her hand lingers a second and squeezes yours. She knows why you are here. Who you are. She accepts you as you are and leaves you to it.

Take the skin from the next onion. It is what it is. Focus on it. You must stop rushing, destroying the subtle things because of your urgency. There is time. Twenty-five more onions, a day or two till you go home, forty more years to live. You could be happy here. No more ambition, frustration, anger. To strive no more, to just live simply. To live here. To concentrate and feel the unique needs of each vegetable, to wonder at and learn the craft of the knife and the . . .

You have cut your finger.

You stare at the blood dripping onto the board and Sophie is already there with a Band-Aid. She leads you to the sink, she washes your hand in hers. She puts the plaster on. Then she is telling you that you've done more than enough for today and what a good job you've done.

You want to hold her. You have to do something. Standing there watching her put your onions in the soup pan. You love her.

And Tom, with his frustration with the carrots and his American need to apologise for being an American. You love him too.

And Marianne, shredding her cabbage like a machine. You love Marianne. And Jules with her salad dressing. And Tamara with her need for control. They are what they are. Everything is.

You will stay here, even if he doesn't let you see Sasa. You could survive anything here. Even the loss of your child. You will live and breathe and find peace here, alone.

You really just said that to yourself.

It is like the sound has been turned off. Like your movements are in slow motion. The feeling before you faint. As if the room has just become infinitely large. As if you were speaking words and none could be heard.

Out of nowhere, the words start drifting away from the objects, all connections pulling apart. There is olive oil, salt, seasoning. A spatula made of wood. Say the words, make it all make sense. Beside you Marianne is telling Jules that they have the same name for coleslaw in Sweden. Tom offers you a carrot, it is a thing that grows in the ground, grows in shit. God, what is this? The echo of a pin drop in an empty room. A solitary raindrop in an ocean.

Tamara, Tom, Jules, Marianne, Sophie. They are what they are. They are each alone.

The knife on the work surface. Look at the knife. Bring the words together again, knife, wood, skin. Plunge the knife through the back of your hand.

You take off your apron and walk past them all, out into the dining area. Tables and chairs. Windows and walls. A certain choice of wallpaper, of furnishings at a certain time. The seventies, eighties. Carpet because the climate is

215

cold, because it absorbs sound and heat. The empty dining room is wrong. People eat to survive, a certain amount of calories per day. Vegetables grow in the ground, some are boiled, some steamed and some fried, some come from Spain, some Israel. They are sometimes put together on the same plate. Plates are made from clay, which is mud. It is fired in kilns which are ovens, knives and forks are made of steel, which was invented during the Industrial Revolution. Spices come from India and China, herbs from Europe; they were brought together by the British Empire, by battleships and genocide. You are staring at the salt and pepper and the world is collapsing around you.

Out into the garden. Say the names. Lodgepole pine, Alpine spruce, Sitka spruce, the pine trees, the stream, the crofts, the caravans, the sky, the clouds, cirrostratus, altocumulus. Your mother taught you all the names of the trees and Eva the clouds. How did this happen? How have you come so far in so short a period of time. London is a universe away.

How can you say again, 'I am a mother'?

Only Sasa will make the words come back. All last night and all of today, you had not one thought for your daughter. How can you feel like this? This self-satisfied nothing.

In the car park. Shivering in the sun. Cars run on petrol which is made from oil which is millions of sea creatures, millions of years old. They build drills that cut through half a mile and ten millennia of stone. They fight wars in which thousands die so that a spark can make an explosion in a piece of metal and wheels can turn. They build roads for cars, economies on cars. Everything is as it is. Everything could have been otherwise, your mother said. If oil had never been found. If it were all still horses and carts. If there were no planes. Silence screaming in your ears.

God, please help me. God is dead, Rowan.

*

We were weeding in the garden when the shock came. A rush of wind where none should be, electrostatic in the air. Black shadow lightning. Silence as the thing like a vast metal bird shot above.

Then it hit. Ears exploding, breath ripped from lungs, her mouth open, the scream stolen. The wall of sound, knocking us to the ground. 'I can't hear, I can't hear.' Sound with no object. The loudest ever, then all silent. Heartbeat in ears. I scream to try to make it sync up. My mouth is open, my lungs belting. She is stumbling, standing, swearing at the sky. She falls towards me, cradling my head as we collapse in mud. Her lips screaming mute at the vanishing dot. I can't hear what she says. I can't hear.

The car, the hospital. She's pacing as they shine things in my ear. The whistle is almost gone and she's shouting to herself, not looking at the doctors. They ask me to repeat words: dog, cat, tomorrow. I am not to look at their mouths and guess, just repeat their words. I shake my head, because it brings her closer, pushing them out of the way to hold me. Because it makes her say, 'See, see, I told you, fuck. The fucking fascists.' She holds me all the way back to the car. One hand on the steering wheel, the other in mine. 'Enough,' she says. 'This is it, this is fucking it.'

'Emergency meeting,' she's shouting from room to room, building to building. My hearing is returning as she rounds them up.

I'm sitting beside her at the confession table as she explains. I make myself pretend not to hear. 'Hawker Harrier Jump Jets.' 'The military base, they're doing it deliberately.' 'The industrial military complex.' 'The nuclear early warning system.' 'It's a deliberate strategy to destroy us.' 'They've got our phone tapped.' She gestures at me. 'Look at her, she's gone deaf, they couldn't even help her at the hospital.'

And I want to nod and have her hold me again but

realise that if I do they will know I can hear, so I stare at the floor.

'What is the point of our haven here if they can do this to us? We have to do something, now!' she shouts.

Eva rose slowly from her seat then spoke.

'We shall do something. We shall all pray that this anger does not visit us again. The anger within us, Jenna, not that which is without.'

My mother's face.

'Let us join our hands in the circle,' Eva said, 'and help Jenna let go of this anger.'

And my mother broke down.

She held me tight that night. Whispering to herself, lists of things to do. I confessed to her that I could hear and apologised.

We started secreting food away and other things. Stealing from the kitchen. Twenty cans of beans. Fourteen of peaches. One torch and four sets of Duracell batteries. HP4. A shortwave radio with three sets of batteries. HP7. A gas canister, a box of matches, all three books of *Lord of the Rings*, a roll of Sellotape. Ten packets of aspirin. A can opener. A roll of aluminium foil to Sellotape to the backs of the old doors I'd built into a tepee to stop the radiation. A copy of *Protect and Survive*. Fifteen bottles of water. But the iodine tablets, the bandages and penicillin, we couldn't get, like it said you should. The lady looked at me funny when I went to the chemist in town and asked her and showed her all the money I'd saved up. One pan for pee and one for poo and one for washing-up. A roll of extra-strong black plastic bin bags for the empty cans or for anyone that died. A sharp knife, for protection, in case the sick people tried to take over our bunker. Everything was all set and I was counting the days. I'd nicked some sunglasses, two pairs, one big, one small, from Woolies, so me and her could look at the mushroom cloud after the flash.

One day after I ran away from school she came and found me in my bunker.

'They chasing you again? Should we move to a new school?' she asked.

'We have to build a wall between us and them,' I said.

'Well, don't build your wall too high,' she said. 'And make sure I'm on the right side of it, eh?'

It was maybe four months since Eva had banned the radio in the kitchen and my mother was talking all the time but not listening, rehearsing arguments, swearing at herself, pacing about. Papers and flyers were all over the floor. Ban the bomb and the march. The tabloids too, she wanted to hear it all, even bad words. She made me read them to her: 'Ugly butch dykes snogging each other in front of children.' 'Smelly unhygienic protest camp lezzers.' 'Hysterical women terrorists.' 'Mad Marxist Lesbians.'

'We should join the peace camp,' she said and explained that they weren't really lezzers and what the hell did it matter if they were anyway? Bloody tabloids. I was glad that her anger was back.

There was one night like the old ones when I used to read her the self-sufficiency manual. She'd had a migraine and skipped her work in the kitchen; she asked me to read because she couldn't focus.

Cruise watch. Peace protesters, CND and affiliated organisations have set up a road patrol across the country to check on the secret movements of Pershing 2 US cruise missiles, transported across the country by road, in violation of the Salt 2 Anti-Proliferation Treaty.

'Yeah, yeah, yeah,' she said, 'but where are they? Tell me about where they are — does it say? All of it. They're here, I can tell they're here already.'

I went through all of the papers and found a line about ships and containers being moved to Dounreay. 'I knew it,' she was shouting. Dounreay was only ten miles away.

She got me to read more from the CND pack, D for Dounreay.

The remote area of land in Caithness has been confirmed as the Soviet's second blast target, eradicating in one blow the UK nuclear stockpile and the experimental fast breeder reactor that has for so long been manufacturing weapons-grade plutonium for international sales, while masquerading as an experimental energy plant.

She punched the air. She yelled, 'Yes, yes. We were right,' she said. 'We were right.'

'She took me in her arms and danced with me.

'Blast zone number two,' she said, 'not bad, eh? For a bunch of old hippies, eh?'

I couldn't understand why she was so happy.

She was energised for the first time since Jono had gone. She slaved all day in the kitchen then stayed up all night writing letters to the government, to CND, to local politicians, signing petitions. She had this plan to rally all the people of Ithaca for a protest march to Dounreay. Finally, all the late nights took their toll and she stopped turning up for kitchen duty.

One lunchtime, nothing was ready and all the folk were in a panic. They asked her what to do but she told them they should think for themselves. 'We don't believe in leaders here,' she said, and winked at me.

The minutes were ticking till the food blessing and I was scared. My mother walked around looking at what everyone had done. It was a mess, there had been no menu plan. There was this woman from Germany – she'd cut twelve carrots in maybe two hours. My mother stood and watched her slowly, contendedly, start on her thirteenth.

There were forty people to feed. My mother sat down on the bench, head in hands.

Lunch was late and the cabbages were undercooked and the baked potatoes weren't even half done but Eva blessed it all anyway and talked of the devotion that went into each meal.

My mother sipped some water and stared at Eva. Confession time began. Eva told everyone she'd been struggling with a great inner need for intimacy, but that she'd crossed a bridge today and realised that all attachments were just shadow memories of the old ego and its cravings. She had decided to forgive herself for her weakness and in so doing had learned to be grateful for these challenges which reminded her again of her faith.

People sighed and nodded; my mother joined in. I feared that all would go back to how it had been before. The petitions and reading, all wasted.

There were thank-yous and Eva nodded to the Japanese woman to her left. My mother was twitching, gritting her teeth.

The woman said she had been struggling with guilt feelings over an abortion that she'd had so that she could be free to come here. And Eva told her that to seek the self is the most selfless task and the most difficult. Self-forgiveness is the start of everything.

And my mother said nothing.

Then there was the man from Holland and his great need to forget and the woman from Sweden and her inability to forgive and the man from America with his need to love himself more. I nudged her under the table, but she only sighed and stared at her hands. I was furious with her, sensing how angry she was and her not saying a thing.

A jet passed overhead, shaking the room, and no one could speak. It was then that she looked up, just before the silence returned. She smiled at them all.

221

'I forgive the jets,' she said.

The others were confused.

'Good,' Eva said.

'Not only do I forgive them, but I love them.'

Eva was silent, the others exchanged discreet glances of confusion.

'I am grateful for the jets,' she said, 'because they remind me of where I am and make me present in the moment.' She paused. 'And I am grateful for the carrots.'

She paused for so long that even Eva was fidgeting.

'I watched a woman . . . Simone, cutting carrots today. And it took me back to when I started in the kitchen. She was cutting this carrot so slowly. And I understand this, like this carrot was important, of course carrots are important.'

Eva looked down at her own hands, flexed a fist shape then released.

'You know, you have this carrot in your hand, and you marvel at how this thing can grow, how it is full of vitamins, how perfect it is . . . this carrot.'

Then she shook her head, fighting herself or the smile maybe that was rising.

'And you have this knife in your hand and you marvel at knives and the Iron Age and the craft and the history of knives and . . . weapons.'

Eva had to say something – 'We are happy for the food we receive.' And there were nods, but that didn't stop her.

'And I respect Simone and her incredible inner focus in the face of the exterior pressure of actually feeding forty people, but . . .'

She lowered her face. Then it started, her hand reaching for mine to try to control it.

'I'm sorry,' she said, 'but cutting carrots isn't going to save us from the bomb—'

'Purposeful endeavour,' Eva interrupted. 'It is not the carrot but the act.'

'Listen to yourself. We can't even feed ourselves. Folk here are always sneaking out to the supermarket in town, to buy Coca-Cola, for God's sake.'

'We could all consume less,' Eva said.

'Yes, and we could all work harder too, no doubt,' Jenna said. 'I do the work of three people already.'

'Perhaps you want to do the work of three people. Perhaps you should just take time to consider why you feel the need to do that.'

My mother's hand trembling in mine.

Eva raised her voice. 'We thank you for your work, Jenna, your long hard work which is an example to us all on our inner journeys. Thank you, this session is over.' Eva stood.

My mother gripped Eva's arm and stopped her exit. She spoke slowly and quietly.

'Perhaps, Eva,' she said, 'we should all be like you: an example to everyone else. Perhaps *you* would like to volunteer to spend tomorrow cutting carrots as part of your inner journey.'

Eva pulled herself from my mother's grasp. 'Perhaps you should consider your tomorrow, Jenna.' Her eyes couldn't meet my mother's. 'I think it's time, I think we all do, for you to reconsider why you are here.' Eva strutted out and the others ran to catch up with her.

We sat there in silence, staring at the big empty table.

'Carrots,' she said, 'fucking carrots!'

Her laughter filling the empty room.

An hour later she'd hitched our old caravan to the back of the Beetle, and that was the last I saw of Ithaca.

*

It happened again on the way along the corridor. Like nausea with no sickness, rushing at you from inside. Giddy

223

emptiness. It chased you back to your room. Sitting staring at the dripping of a tap. The silence between each drip growing around you. You tried to force it away.

It came then. Not tears but a wail. Low like a man. From the pit of your gut, this moan, hollow.

My God, what is this?

Tears without object, fear without words. No thought of your daughter. Crying at nothing. At the emptiness of the room which seemed like your future.

That you could start again. That none of your life so far counted for anything. The dripping of the tap. The wallpaper like a hotel room. Marianne's shoes neatly arranged next to her brochure.

You stared at your feet. Your trainers. You tried to breathe it away. You went to the sink to turn off the tap, to turn it on, to wash your face. There was Mia's toothbrush. The word on it was REACH. Her tube of toothpaste read *Kingfisher, Bicarbonate of soda paste for natural whitening.* Cold sweat running down your arm. It started again. Wailing at the sight of a toothpaste tube.

You knew that this would happen to you from now on. Catch you by surprise while eating, walking, waking. Déjà-vu with no end. Nightmare of a world in which everything has stopped. Waking to find yourself alone in an abandoned city. Terrible silence. It has many names, this feeling. Suicide survivors call it lucidity or detachment. Lucid detachment. You iron your clothes and are moved by the absurdity of the iron, you go to the kitchen and are wordless before the enigma of the stove, you take the pills and turn on the gas and marvel at the smell. A final loving smile which no one sees. You know this.

If you stay any longer the silence will overwhelm, you will fall fathomless into the gap between sounds and words. Will never be able to put a sentence together, will become like Eva.

You must break it, bring it all back together. Words in their proper place. Bag in bedroom. Feet on stairs. No good-byes to these people you loved for a day, an hour. Bag on back seat. Key in lock. That's you now. Yes, keep on. Key in ignition. Finger on on-button on mobile phone. Foot on pedal. Eyes on road. Hands on wheel. Wheels on road. No goodbyes. Left or right. Go now or you'll never have the strength.

Ithaca in your rear-view mirror. Her postcard in your glove compartment.

You can't drive to Sasa like this. First, you need to be calm. Drive to Wyster. Just a trial run. Join the A9 there. Safer than the back roads. Don't think about the absurdity of roads. Follow the other cars. Stop at a store there, shop for shopping, fuel for the long drive. You have to get home.

Bushes, lines, bends in road. Miles and traffic lights, sign – car park – Somerfield – petrol station. Fill up the car with unleaded. Do it now. The green handle. The nozzle in the hole.

It is done and paid for and you have held it together. The stench of the gas took you out of yourself, the rituals of politeness at the checkout. Take a minute to breathe, stare through the windscreen at the people in the world. You're decompressing, the car your chamber. Get ready to start.

Through the windscreen people pass by, benign, indifferent. They look nothing like the children you knew, who terrorised your every day and waking dream. They walk past in trainers and in heels, with fake tans and tank tops, with shopping bags and boxes, happy with their purchases. The light seems to glow in their hair, as if they are a living advertisement. You are a fool for having come here.

But then a man, shoulders stooped beneath the weight of two shopping bags. He is bearded, with remnants of long hair. Crossing the car park not using the footpath. How could it be? Follow him to see better, overtake to see his face. Past the public toilets. Follow slowly, watch the way he stumbles.

You pass and it is. It has to be. Park the car just ahead of him. The words have to match the pictures. Put the name to the person. Everything has to mean something. Push the window button for your window. Say his name.

Pete?

Thanks, he said, and did not recognise you. You asked, Where do you live? He said a certain street, you said, No problem, just say left and right, I'm sure it's on my way. His accent had become more Scottish, he seemed almost local. You drove him to his door, he thanked you and said goodbye, but you held his bags, you pushed for the moment. He looked up at your face. Another breath.

'I know yer face from somewhere.'

'I'm just . . . passing through.'

'Ye'll stay for a wee drink,' he said. 'I'm sure . . . you mind me of someone.'

Inside. You kept him talking as he stopped at the turntable for a second, set the needle on and headed into his kitchen, leaving you alone in his room with Crosby, Stills, Nash and Young. You told yourself to stop naming the things you saw. The pizza box on the sofa, the empty wine bottle by the seat worn thin, the rows and rows of books thirty years old and untouched for as long. The copy of *Kapital*, of Kerouac, *Brave New World*, *Ariel*. The teeming ashtray in its circle of ash on the threadbare rug. You tried to keep him talking, to work slowly up to the questions, but all that came from the kitchen was the clinking of bottles. You tried to block out the album, which you knew was called *Déjà Vu*.

He called through. 'You want a drink?'

'I'm driving. Heading off in a min.'

You worried that you replied too abruptly, that you should have been more accommodating to his habit. Thirty

226

years of the bottle. He would need his drink to loosen up, then you would hit him with it. You would have to time it right so that he wasn't too drunk by the time you revealed who you were, asked your questions. Keep talking to keep him talking.

He entered with two glasses of red wine even though you'd told him you were driving. 'There you go, nice to meet you, not often I get a guest.' You took the glass, moved the pizza box from the fusty sofa and sat waiting for him to sit. He set down his glass and almost fell back into his seat, like he knew after so many years that it would support his fall. You watched his hand reach for the glass, without looking, as if he knew exactly where it was. Taking a gulp that was half a glass, getting up again to go to the kitchen. You tried to block out the lyrics for *Our House* and waited for him to come back through with the bottle.

You kept the chit-chat going. Telling him about the drive north, how there were new bridges at Inverness and Dunster, skipping anything that would upset him, not mentioning Ithaca, or Jono, or what you knew of Saphie, telling him you were on a little holiday, not putting any pressure on him, while he rolled himself a cigarette, slowly, humming along to the music, then stopping as if concentrating on it was more than enough for him to handle. The drunken fool, can't meet your eye. Your face is no longer your own. You could go now and he would never know.

Tell him your name, Rowan.

It is said.

'Rowan,' he repeats.

The things that occur then, even as they do, you fight for words to describe them: an old man holds a woman in her late thirties. An old drunk weeps. A once second father is reunited with his lost daughter. There are hugs, then laughter then he asks about your home, your life. His avoidance of certain names – Jono, Saphie.

227

Top up his glass, ask him the question, Rowan.

'A few wee questions about Jenna, that's all,' you say as you play with the postcard in your pocket. His silence making you talk faster.

'Everyone told me it was the second week in September, but that didn't make sense because there was the card and . . .'

He refills his glass and offers you a drink yet again, then he notices that the bottle is almost empty.

He gets to his feet and you see the effort it takes him to balance and you grow anxious. You hear him unscrew the second bottle and you know you have to confront him before the wine reduces him to incomprehensible tears.

'I mean, maybe you don't know the exact date, but you see, I've been—'

'Fluff on the needle,' he says and you watch him so slowly bend over and blow with his big drunken lips on the needle then set it back down in the middle of *Woodstock*, then lift it again and set it, so slowly, on *Almost Cut My Hair*.

Nothing for it. You tell yourself this is it now. You get to your feet, your hand into your pocket, you stand before him, the postcard in your hand. This is it now.

'She sent this. If you look at the postmark. It was mailed from Wyster.'

He looks you in the eye before he takes it in his hand. He looks at the picture, fishes in his shirt pocket for his lighter and relights the fag.

'Wyster, see? So she must have been here after she dropped me off. The thing is, Pete, I need to know, did she come here to see you? Then, I mean . . . after?'

He motions for you to sit as he falls back into his chair.

'Aye,' he says. 'Yes.'

'After she left me . . . she came here?'

He inhales deeply and nods.

228

You cannot contain it, this hot rush that makes you want to laugh.

'Really? Oh my God, did she say she was going to . . .? Did she seem depressed or—'

He shakes his head again. 'No, no, no.' He looks hard at the back of the postcard.

'I knew it, I always kind of knew . . . So when did she come here? D'you remember the date? I mean, of course you don't, but how long was it after her . . . accident? Cos the thing is, if you look at the date, can you do that, just look at the date?'

You watch him with the postcard, the focusing takes all his concentration.

'Because they said she died in the second week but the date is the twenty-ninth.'

He nods.

'God, that's so . . . And she was here after that. Well, I mean that means . . .'

You have to stop, take a breath before you ask it.

'So, do you know where she is now? Where she went?'

He shakes his head, gets up suddenly. You can't stop.

'Did she stay here with you for long? Did she go back to Ithaca, or London? I had this feeling she went back to London.'

He kneels down at the stereo and starts looking for something. He motions with his hand and you're not sure what it means, is it 'Wait a minute' or 'Stop talking' or 'Something to show you'? He pulls out a box of old tapes. His mumbling is making you fumble for words.

'. . . because she said we were going home and London was her first home. And she must have known Angus would get me back to her parents, so if we were both in London, then . . .'

He pulls tapes out of the box. Throwing others back in.

229

'And it's understandable, forgivable, I even had this theory, I know it sounds silly, that she was in hiding somewhere after the nuclear thing, cos there were these people in jail after that, I mean, it's daft but . . . if you think she still is, because she would be old now, I mean, she might even have . . . of natural causes . . .'

He exhales the smoke with a sound that sounds like Ah. He has something in his hand, holding it out to you. He shakes it for you to take. A tape. An old tape. Handwriting on the cover. But why?

'She had a box of them in the car,' he says, then touches your shoulder. 'Our band – we were pretty damn fine. She was going to move down south for good, she said, she came to pick up a box of tapes and some books before she went.'

He tries to get you to sit down then, to have your glass of wine. You stare at the tape cover. The names of the songs. What has this got to do with anything? He tries to tell you where it happened, the Berriedale Braes: trucks went over there all the time. Terrible road at night.

'She was headin' back south to pick you up,' he says. 'She was rabbiting on and on about you, worrying if you were OK with Angus, she left in a hell of a hurry with all these big plans for you both.' He reaches for your glass and drinks it.

'But the date on the fucking card!'

He shakes his head. Speaks as if each word requires his full concentration. You try to block him out.

'I just found it lying about in the flat,' he says. 'She must have forgotten to post it before she ran off. Oh, this would have been a week, maybe more, after. Just lying on the floor there by the sofa and a stamp on it already. So a few days later, maybe a week – I hadn't heard a word from her, you see – so I put it in the post myself.'

The carpet spins before your eyes.

'You OK, love? Have a drink,' he says, placing a hand on your shoulder.

*

Most modern cruise missiles, including the JASSM, have a precision guidance system that allows them to hit small targets. Before it is launched, a photograph of the target is loaded into the missile's computer.

That was the way it was in that last year, sitting beside her in the Beetle, reading for her, with the book on my knee and the torch in my hand, as we drove to Greenham Common, to the Collective bookshop in Edinburgh, to this or that demonstration in Glasgow.

As the missile approaches the target, an infrared camera in the nose takes a picture and the computer matches it to the stored image.

Driving through the night, the caravan clinking behind us, swaying in the wind, trying to pull us down into the ditches. Reading the facts made her so angry, she said, it stopped her falling asleep at the wheel. It was my job, but I'd dose off and she'd jab me.

'Keep reading, sleepyhead, you want to get us both killed?'

A cruise missile is so accurate that it can be aimed not just at a building but a door or window.

No matter where it was I always seemed to wake up looking out of the little window, seeing other vans and caravans and combis, painted multicolours just like ours. There would be laundry hanging on bushes by some roadside. And all the women and kids in their tie-dyes and floral dresses, charity-shop jeans, the long hair and dirty feet. The peace signs and the noise all the time, the talk talk talk.

We had to piss in the bushes because there was no toilet.

231

The caravan stank of boiled rice and mould and sweat and hash. She covered the walls with flyers and maps and posters and there was always socks and T-shirts lying round or strung from the ceiling. No one seemed to own any of them, they just threw on what they found in anyone's caravan. Dog hair, fag ash, Indian rugs, patchouli, black T-shirts washed grey. There was no space to move and I had to hide most of my things from her. The pop magazines I'd hoarded, some knickers I'd nicked and old mementoes from Ithaca. There was a tiny stove and the gas canisters always leaked. When I got my period, I could smell it everywhere and just wanted to be alone but there was nowhere to hide. I couldn't wash because the shower was communal and I could never sleep because of the meetings going on into the night in our caravan. I constructed a curtain between my side and hers, out of one of her old dresses. She said I was being territorial, like the USA. I said, Fuck off. Smelly hippie.

It was called Faslane. We were camped across the road from the perimeter fence of the nuclear weapons base. The pigs would move us on, we'd drive a hundred yards and park up the road, then come back the next day. From one lay-by to the next. It was some legal loophole and our people liked to laugh at it, but I saw the pigs with their walkie-talkies and yellow vests and truncheons and knew they'd get us one day.

The Social Services came too, rooting about, asking for our names and ages. I'd been maybe nine months without school. When they came the third time Jenna said I had to go, just for a while, to throw them off the scent.

I thought it might be better than Wyster Primary, but it was worse. Shit, in a really shit run-down town. The kids looked even poorer than us.

I was kind of expecting it anyway, the names – tink, gyppo, hippie slut – and it didn't really bother me any more because Jono had taught me Protect and Survive. Duck and

Cover. Keep your head down. I didn't want friends anyway after he'd gone. I kept my mouth shut so they couldn't laugh at my accent. I actually took an interest in the lessons.

I was light years ahead in science because I knew about the Bomb from my mum. I hated English and art – what was the point in such things anyway when the Bomb was going to go off. All the other kids were 'walking dead' as she said. 'Dead already.' They just goofed around all the time in class, like there was a tomorrow. I stole a textbook for science class on physics. She'd get me to read it out on our drives. U235 and 238. The manufacturing of plutonium, carbon rods and electrons, sodium-cooled and water-cooled systems. She was looking for points of weakness, she said, ways to get into the plant. With a school textbook I worked out how to build a bomb.

On the school bus I tried to ignore their whistles and curses from the back. I sat down the front by the driver, picturing them all turned to ash by the flash. The problem, though, was my breasts. My mother didn't believe in bras and she'd say sticks and stones, then be too busy to listen when I tried to tell her. I was an early developer, but it was more the nipples. They stuck out, like hers, and because I didn't have a bra, the cheesecloth shirts would rub at them. The boys would laugh and shout, 'Gies us a feel, Tits.' That's what they called me – Tits. Gyppo Tits. 'Hey, Tits,' they'd shout. 'Stinky tinky Tits.' 'Gies a flash.' 'Get yer tits oot fir the boys.' 'Gies a wee grope, eh?' 'Fuckin' tits on that, lads!'

'I've got a knife,' I'd say. I did, I'd kept Jono's penknife with me.

'Aye, right, big fuckin' deal.'

'You want to see it?'

'Naw, show us yer fuckin' tits.'

You don't have to use the knife, Jono had said, just flash it at them once and they'll leave you alone. It was called deterrence.

Meltdowns were statistically more likely than the government acknowledged, my mother said. 'God knows, it might just take a core leak or accidental explosion to show everyone the danger.' Maybe, she even wanted it to happen. I was allowed to sit in on the meetings. I was old enough to make that choice myself, she said, like I was old enough to smoke weed, though I had to hide the Embassy Regals I stole from the corner shop because she didn't believe in multinational tobacco conglomorates. She hated everyone who had money. We had so little; I was amazed we had any. Somehow she bought a photocopier for the caravan and got a phone line put in. She had to get some part-time work so the plans could go ahead, she said, office cleaning and temping, all low-key, below the radar. She was organising a big thing with help from Tina and Roz and Jambo and Tobe. Tobe had kind of become her boyfriend but she didn't want to talk about that either because she was too busy with the plan. Always her lists, schedules and reports of sightings of missiles, maps with red marker lines drawn on roads where the convoys were expected to be travelling. They had to be kept on the move so the Russians wouldn't be able to target them. The roads, that was the one weak point in their plan, she said. Because roads were public highways. It was in breach of the Geneva Convention to transport nuclear weapons on public byways. She was reading up on international law, British transport law, planning a case for the European courts, a petition, a demonstration. That was the way she talked. Never listening to me, just making plans. Talk talk talk. All the time getting more and more frustrated, talking about the need to stop talking and really *do* something.

And she'd changed too. After so many years of silence she couldn't keep the words in, she was hungry to learn everything. She even cut off her hair. I was there when she did it. Her long raven hair that went all the way to her thighs. I don't know why it upset me so much, sitting there watching her hacking away with the kitchen scissors, right to the roots. I begged her not to. She said it was just so much history, and just in the way all the time. She said she didn't want to look conspicuous, it was the eighties now, she had important work to do and had to blend in with the rest of society. When she finished she asked me if the back was OK, and it wasn't. She asked me to take the scissors and finish it off. It felt wrong. But she insisted. I thought she looked hellish, like one of those lezzer protesters who chained themselves to military fences. When it was all done, she looked at herself in the little mirror above the sink. Lost in herself, touching her cheeks, sucking them in. I got a sense of what she was feeling, how the hair had always softened her features, how now she looked older, harder. She put on a fake smile for the mirror then broke into laughter.

'Shit,' she said, like she'd read my mind, 'I look like a bloody dyke!'

She was going to throw the hair in the bin. It was all over the floor like a rug. I asked her if I could keep it. She said if I tidied it up for her I could. I tied it in elastic bands, and kept it in my box under the bed with Jono's old penknife and my stolen copy of *Protect and Survive*. It filled the box, spilled out over the edges.

Every week it was the same. The pigs would move us away from the perimeter fence and a few days later we'd move back, and they'd move us on again. There had been arrests and court summonses for trespassing, breaches of the peace. Tobe used to roll up the pig paperwork and use it for kindling. When they were talking, some nights, I would walk the mile back to the base. Nosing around the wires. The three sides, the other bound by the loch where she said the nuclear submarines came in. Twelve-foot-high alarmed security fences with coils of razor wire and surveillance cameras on tall stems. All by myself, looking through the wire, nothing to see. Just this big expanse of concrete, as big as a football pitch. It was all underneath, she said. Tunnels, bunkers, secret rooms, corridors, computers with files on everyone and everything everyone did, the NATO early warning system, the silos with intercontinental ballistic missiles, Tomahawks and Shadows. It made me laugh sometimes. That maybe she was wrong. Maybe there was nothing under there at all. And all they'd been screaming at was just some weeds and grass and daisies pushing through the gaps in the concrete.

I'd walk round it, through the bracken and peat, not touching the fence. If you touched it they would come, she said. The pigs with their dogs. They cut through the handcuffs that she and Jez and Kim and Jambo and Tom fastened themselves to the fence with, then put new ones on and piled them into the vans, leaving us kids behind. I didn't mind being left alone. I was used to it. The other kids were too small to hang out with anyway. I'd go back night after night just walking round the fence in the dark. Lying down on the heather, looking up at the sky. You could see lights blinking through the clouds. Planes from Glasgow Airport. Sometimes I'd just stay there and put my hand inside my jeans and touch myself till I felt good again then just lie there some more. Listening to the birds, feeling the breeze from the loch, trying to picture little things, electrons, the splitting of the atom. Something so small, you can never see it, but with such power.

I didn't see much of her then. She slept most nights with Tobe in his caravan and so I was left alone with the photocopier and the flyers and books and this trippy tape Tobe had got us into. He was younger than her, looked like a tramp but had this soft posh voice and these dreadlocks. He'd leave his weed around sometimes so I'd sit there in the caravan, skinning up.

236

Those days, she'd look at me strangely. Like she knew I was stoned, like she knew I was touching myself. Looking at my breasts. Hers were droopy by then. I remember thinking she should have worn a bra all those years and that if I didn't get one soon, mine would end up like hers. She didn't like it when I was left alone with Tobe or when he told her he couldn't believe I was only eleven. She told him not to hug me so much, it wasn't like we were living in a fucking hippie commune, she said. She didn't like the music I played. I stole some tapes by Duran Duran and Frankie Goes to Hollywood from Woolies. Other times she'd look up from her papers and see me sitting there bored and she'd shake her head, like she couldn't believe I was related to her. She didn't laugh much then. Droopy Tits, I'd mutter sometimes as she went past. Stinky tinky Tits. She was too busy to even notice. She'd unhitched the car from the caravan and had been doing a lot of driving then, by herself.

One night she came back from her disappearances and me and Tobe were in the caravan getting high, listening to Frankie. She pulled him outside and started shouting, 'Emergency meeting!' I thought it was about me. She told me to leave because the caravan wasn't big enough for everyone. I told her to fuck herself because it was raining, so she let me stay.

'Quiet, quiet,' she shouted at them all. And she told them she'd been lifted on the street in Glasgow. Interrogated. No phone call to a lawyer. Drug-tested. Strip-searched. Internally searched. This deliberate policy of intimidation. They had her name. How there must be a plant in the camp. I laughed at that. A plant, yeah, the weed. She saw me giggling and shouted out that peaceful protest was no longer enough.

I looked over at Tobe and she caught me, like she thought we'd been messing around behind her back.

'We're just setting ourselves up for failure here,' she

said. 'We can dig in and get arrested again and again, but it's pathetic to see our failure as a sign of righteousness. We have to move to direct action!'

I thought it was dumb. Do what? She'd screw this up just like she screwed up Ithaca. Her eyes were staring past the others to me. She must have seen it on my face.

She had some ideas, she shouted. The convoys – it would take a lot of planning – they would need to be a team – build a network across the country – stop them in the road – not the base – set up a roadblock, a barricade – lie down on the road – hijack the trucks – the world press.

'Wait, wait, wait,' someone said. 'We're not talking . . . violence, are we?'

Then it was the usual round of debate. Ends or means. Same old lame old shit. Gandhi and passive resistance. Violence only leads to more violence. Stupid bloody hippies.

She was getting exasperated. 'I need a show of hands if we're going to move this forward,' she shouted.

They all hesitated. Fuck it, I thought. I put my hand up. The others turned. Tobe laughed, he'd had most of the joint. He put his hand up. No one else did. Her eyes said, 'Traitors!' It was all my fault. What happened then.

It was maybe a week later at school. This kid called Ferret kept leaning over to me and staring and sticking his finger in and out of his fist, then pointing at me, mouthing, 'Fuck, fuck you,' then licking his lips. Laughing with the others, then punching his hand mouthing, 'Dead, dead meat.' I wasn't scared. I told him he was a prick, I had a knife, I'd cut it off, but I didn't have the knife that day.

All day drawing mushroom clouds on my jotter cover, checking the time, trying to ignore their stupid whispers and this sign they were all making of a finger going in and out of a fist. Then this girl, Shona, came up to me, this little weed who always sat at the front and tried to be my friend, even though I told her she was fucking dust already, she

238

said I should tell the headmaster because they were going to rape me at four o'clock. I told her to fuck off but she said they'd been planning it for days and were going to follow me on the bus and when I got off they'd do me.

Then it was French and arithmetic and physics and the four o'clock bell. I got panicky, clumsy. I was afraid of the bus. I made the mistake of standing at the teacher's desk, waiting for them all to go. They made the hand sign at me again as they walked out. She was packing up her things. Frenchie, that's what they called her, the physics teacher. I wasn't sure if I would, if I could, tell her. I just needed some time.

'Yes, what is it, Rowan?'

'Miss.'

'Yes, Rowan. C'mon, I haven't got all day.'

'Miss, I was wondering about cruise missiles, Miss.'

'We don't do nuclear physics till third year.'

'Yes, but, Miss, it's just . . . do you think that it's possible, Miss, if they crashed on the road, that they'd leak, Miss – or is there some kind of fail-safe device?'

She sighed, put her bag on her shoulder.

'I told you we don't do nuclear physics till third year.'

But, Miss. I was about to tell her. About the bus and the fist and finger sign.

'But, Miss, if the fail-safe system was damaged, then there'd be a meltdown, right? And the core would leak and you'd have contamination for a hundred miles, right?'

'Really,' she said, looking at me head to toe. 'You people.'

And that got me: what people?

'If you want to fit in here, Rowan, I suggest you stop assuming that you're better than everyone else.'

I saw red. She was heading for the door. I saw it on her desk. She was fishing about in her bag for the keys. They used the class for biology too, they got to cut up frogs in third year. She couldn't find her keys. A scalpel, among the pens and paper clips. She was checking her watch, going into her bag again for the keys. She didn't see. I grabbed it and slid it into my bag. They weren't in the corridor outside. Or on the stairs as I walked down with her.

You people, she'd said. And I thought, yes, 'we people', we will survive and you will die. You're all dead already. Four o'clock, they'd said, you're dead.

When she left my side and walked into the staffroom and I had to walk the narrow corridor to the front door alone, and saw my bus pull away, and then saw them out there waiting for me, I wasn't so scared because I had the scalpel in my bag and Jono had taught me how to run.

They caught me at the bike sheds. Woodsy rolled up his sleeves and twisted my arm up my back. Ferret started groping my breasts. Sean was getting his cock out, saying hold her down, make her do a blow job. All of them laughing like little kids at their big grown-up words. I kicked Ferret in the balls and bit Woodsy's arm, but I was cornered. They seemed nervous for a second. A split second, between the first explosion and the second. Pick your moment, said Jono. Flash it at them and they'll run. My free hand in the bag, I grabbed the metal handle.

I pulled it out, but they were too close to see. Woodsy aimed to take a swipe at me and it flashed before me – Jono's face in the mud, Jono's face in the flashing lights. I swung my hand round to protect my face. It felt like nothing. Like a flash of wind. Like a brush through hair. Like nothing, I waited for his fist to land but there was nothing. I opened my eyes and he was staring at the blade, backing off, then holding his hand to his face. Then this line, thin like a hair, growing red from his wrist to elbow, then the skin falling open like a page. Then the blood surging, spraying his face. The sound and his eyes, screaming.

*

240

Her face, flashing in the light as they dragged me from the panda car. 'Are you her legal guardian?' they asked. The hour I spent then outside the caravan, as the Social Services threatened her with words: juvenile – court – detention – custody; as the pigs tore through the caravans, scattering our things in the dirt. The others crowding round, screaming that they didn't have the right, or bloody search warrants. 'We know our rights.' They huddled together in little groups whispering about me. Tobe tried to fight his way into the caravan, pushing a pig to the ground, two of them on him then, knees on his back, face in the mud, handcuffs. And voices running, 'Pigs, fuck the pigs!' A pig leaving the caravan with our bag of grass. Others carried away the computer, the books, the papers, taking names and flash photos, pushing their way into the last caravans, smashing down doors. You have the right to remain silent.

She sat alone then, after they carted Tobe and Rod and Kim and Jambo away, clutching the steering wheel of the Beetle, in the dark.

I'd nowhere else to go. All the caravans were gutted. No one who was left would speak to me. I stood there maybe twenty minutes, twenty feet away, staring at her as she stared out the windscreen at the road. It started raining. It shook me from my daze. Somehow, I got the guts to go over and open the door. She didn't turn to face me as I collapsed onto the seat beside her. There were seconds then, terrible, my head against her leg, wailing, struggling to speak, choking on words. 'If I'd never been born, you'd still be in Ithaca now. It was my fault, wasn't it? I'm sorry, sorry. I wish I was dead.'

Her hands floated above my head, then a breath and I felt her touch.

'Shh, shh, it's OK, it's OK.' And she said my name.

In fast breaths, I told her about four o'clock and the blade then questions ran at me – Were they the same people that took Jono? Was it true he stabbed a kid in that detention place? Was it true what he said – that we had the same dad? Would they take me too?

'Shh, shh,' she whispered in time with each stroke.

'Mum,' I said. And for once she didn't tell me not to say that word.

She lifted her hand, then started up the car. I didn't understand. What was she doing? What about the caravan? All our things? She put it into gear, flicked the headlights on.

'Where are we going? Where are we going?'

'Home,' she said. 'We're going home.'

*

Get to the car. Just go. Stupid idiot. What did you expect? He gives you a little story and a sorry. He said listen to the tape as he tried to kiss you at the door. He thought he was a musician and so he gives you music, as if it would be an answer to anything. Stinking socialists with their hippie music. Pathetic. Weeping with the wine and the old songs, every day for years. Fucking drunk. No way he could have remembered what happened. The date. The state he was in. He was too drunk even then.

Put the key in the ignition.

Three-point turn. Checking over shoulder for blind spot. Signal.

If she was alive she'd be like Pete or Eva. Thank God she is dead.

First gear, second, third. Out of the estate. Foot to the floor. Go home now to your baby. She is four hundred miles away and all you have to show for this is some stupid fucking tape in your pocket. Hundreds of these tapes he made, gave them away to everyone for free.

An hour to Inverness. Turn on your mobile, tell Josh you're coming, you'll do anything, anything to make amends.

God, you've been such a fool. Don't even look at the main street. The people, so similar to the seventies, the clothes not so different, the teenage mothers, the unemployed men standing by the post office cashing their giros.

You are stuck at the lights. The junction on the main street says North or South.

It seems wrong. So sudden, going home with nothing. A car honks behind you. The lights are green. It needs some kind of closure as your self-help books say.

You hit the indicator to go north. It's only ten miles away. The place on the postcard. Fifteen minutes' travel and maybe ten spent there just looking and saying this is the end. To go and see the power station again, to put some end to this stupidity.

Accelerator. Follow the sign north to John o' Groats. The road getting narrower, the land flatter, the glare from the sea reflecting back the white grey sky. Get it done. Keep to a safe fifty miles an hour. The turn-off at Wyster; the road changing from A to B. Which your mother said the nuclear convoys would come down, where you stood with her for hours, days, waiting for the missiles and never saw a single one.

The tiny fishing villages with no fishing boats. The telegraph poles that lead to the end of nowhere. The crofts, abandoned for three hundred years. Get to the nuclear centre, have your wee cry.

The trees thin. You remember this, as the land runs out as the winds get stronger as you get closer to the cold north coast. You feel it, shaking the car. The wind that won't let anything live. Not even sheep now. No grass. Nothing to be done with this wasteland. Some things are like that. You have wasted your time looking for answers like she wasted her life trying to grow things in this soil. Not even memory can live here.

Slow down, watch out for farm vehicles. They can come out of nowhere.

You weren't focusing, your wheels clipped the verge. See how easy it is. The roads are so tight, so many bends. See, this is what must have happened. Maybe she was upset when driving, she wasn't focusing, and it was an old car, the brakes bad, she often said that if she'd had the money she'd have got them fixed. See. She died in an accident. Everyone else accepted it, but you couldn't, could you? That things happen without justification. She had to die for a reason because you could never find one to live for. All this time it has not been about her at all.

Then it's there on the horizon. Many times you had seen it but each time it seemed just as alien. The perfect white dome of Dounreay. For two whole miles it holds your eye. As tiny as a spot then like a full stop.

A tourist bus wants to overtake you. It's single track. There are things called passing places. You slow down and let them pass. Fine. You see, things are there for a reason.

Stop here. This could be the field. She said not to get too close. They had cameras, telephoto lenses. They took down vehicle registration plates if you got too close. MI5, the FBI. Drive to the next passing place. It must have been where she parked that time.

Get out. Look at you. Stand on the grass verge. What did she tell you? She talked about the nuclear threat. No. It was something rather strange. You can't recall exactly but you think she might have said, 'Actually, it's quite beautiful, the perfect circle.' The empty moorlands and then the white dome. This building that housed every horror in the world. 'It looks like an egg,' she said, 'for a huge, impossible bird. I had no idea it would be so pretty.' A curlew flew overhead then, circling you both, crying out its name, curlew, curlew.

'We should go,' she said. 'Don't want to disturb her. We must be near her nest.'

Look at you – tourist in a passing place. Trying to cry

and failing. Just getting back into your car. It's too much and not enough.

Go to Dounreay, stop at the security gate. Ask them if there are tourist tours. Pay your ten pounds. Get shown round. But then, even then, what will you see? Corridors and old computers and metal and more signs. You'll be standing on top of the nuclear core with tourists with cameras and the guide will tell you that far below, beyond twenty feet of reinforced lead and steel, nuclear fission is taking place. But all you will see will be the painted floor, the signs in red and orange, the faces of the other tourists and the bored expression of the guide. There will be no heat or vibration or noise. Nothing – you can't see an atom. They weren't producing power, your mother said, they were making the Bomb. You can't see a lie.

You take the turn before Dounreay to John o' Groats, the most northerly point on the British mainland. It's stupid, you know it is. To seek the end of your travel at a place with a sign that says The End.

The tourist buses. The Last House Hotel. The End of the World gift shop.

Get out, stand there and let her go. Go down to the beach that your mother said was the most contaminated in Europe. The leukaemia clusters in Ryster, Thorston and Wyster. There are these little shells from sea creatures, on the beach, she said. Groatie buckies, buckies from John o' Groats. The tourists are told it's good luck to find them, they are so rare these indigenous creatures, their shells. The tourists, she said, look through the stones for a souvenir, then go and eat their lunch at the Last House Hotel and put their fingers contaminated with medium- and high-level radioactive waste into their mouths.

Get out of the car. She never let you come here before, didn't want you to be contaminated. There was that kid in your school that died of leukaemia. You can't remember his name.

245

You don't care. The tourists are already down on the beach. This is the end, then you will go home to your child.

You walk past the heritage museum with its advert for realistic historic waxwork depictions of a real Highland family and there is a rack of postcards – Highland cows against the power station. Exactly the same picture as the one on your mother's card. The impossible blue sky. The white dome. Fifty of them on the rack. A promotional picture, taken in the fifties when it was new. She came here, like you, to try to mark the end of the nonsense, to have her wee cry. She bought the first postcard that came to hand. She wrote it to her parents and asked for more money. You'll tear the damn thing up when you get back to the car.

Walk towards the beach. You want to put your hands in the contaminated water. You want to search with Sasa, through the stones and pebbles and seaweed for groatie buckies, because they are lucky, and you will make sure she washes her hands before you get to the hotel to eat chips.

You have to have your cry before you can go back to her. You cried in Ithaca. Why can't you cry here? What will it take?

Walk away from the tourists to the beach into the wind. Feel the cold salt wind in your eyes. It makes your eyes water. Keep on. Make yourself. Feel your feet on the shingle and stand by the very edge of the water.

Picture what she's doing right now, she's with a childminder, they're splashing about with paint together because you abandoned her. Cry, go on. Do it. Get it done. Think about her first day at school, her first friend. Make yourself cry. Look out at the islands and the North Sea. Think about your poor crying child, all the things you could share with her, when you explain the sea to her, the clouds, her first Christmas when she can open her own present. Her first sentence. Her first pet. Her first visit from the tooth fairy. That's it. Look out

246

at the tourists, down by the beach, there must be a child among them. Her first school report, her first taste of solid food, her first night crying over homework, her first thunderstorm. Think of yourself holding her. But no children on the beach, no parents, only old people, so old. They travel to the ends of the earth to see them all before they die. How sad it is to be old, look at them standing there staring at the beach, looking at it as if it was a memory already. You have to cry here and be done with it. Cry for the loss of her then. He will never let you see her again. Think of her first time in the front seat of a car, her first time in a supermarket choosing her own yogurt, her first best friend, her first boyfriend, her first time coming second, her first recurring nightmare, her first CD bought with her own money, her first copy of *On the Road*, her first time reading your old books to try to understand.

Your eyes are dry.

The sign above you says Johannesburg 9,873 km. New York 5,198 km. Sydney 16,687 km. Arrows with the words on. A big board with polaroids, worn and torn, held on by tacks, flapping in the wind. Moscow 2,435 km. Kyoto 8,935 km. All posed the same, hugging each other beneath the sign. No children. All old people. Hong Kong 9,344 km. Sao Paulo 9,991 km. London 816 km.

You are inside the car again. Sad phoney fuck.

Put it in gear. Go back to your family. Make what little story of survival you can.

Minutes and miles and you are accelerating. Useless selfish bitch. It'll be a hard drive but you deserve it. Go on, punch the steering wheel. Do it. God, you are shit. One night in a hotel to rest, that was all you needed. Idiot. And you did this.

You have offended his sense of order. Restraining orders. Two-hundred-yard perimeter round the house. He will quote it in court that you have a history of this and that, that your mother abandoned you too, that he doubts, and his lawyer will back this up, that you were ever 'capable'. He will have recorded Charlie, to use her as evidence.

There are no cars at the junction so you head through. The moorland and more of the same, the turn-off for Ithaca. Speed past it.

It was your fault for choosing him. You should have married someone who understood. You should never have married at all.

Dunster and Lyster. The end of Caithness where it hits the Highlands, where the roads narrow, the bends multiply. The sheer drop at the braes where she went over. Slow to third when it comes.

You will be there for Sasa. Her first experiments with make-up. Her first poem, her first song that she learns at nursery, her first swear word, her first time when she locks herself in her room, her first time in detention, her first pyjama party, her first sunburn, her first lie.

The road widens but there are blind bends. Slow down.

Her first time talking back, her first cigarette, her first text message, the first time she puts her head underwater, her first time lost in a shopping mall, her first story she made up herself, her first moments going on a bicycle all by herself.

All the things you told yourself back there to make yourself cry. Stop pushing down on the accelerator, it won't make them go away.

Her first glass of wine, her first time reading Germaine Greer, her first temp job, her first revolutionary organisation, her first pair of heels, her first orgasm, her first tube of Canestan, her first quarter of hash, her first time blaming you for everything.

My baby.

Now it comes to you, as you get closer to her, minute by mile by minute, all that you might lose and might have lost already. That you have done to your daughter exactly what your mother did to you. Your past will be her future. No one should have to live your life again.

You are not going to cry. Get a coffee after the braes. You just need something, to stop this voice telling you what will happen. Some noise other than the thrum of the wheels, the click click click of the indicator. The radio, turn on the radio, but it is, you know this, always like this, too far north. No reception. The CD then, only his Moby compilation and his *Sounds of Tropical Rainforests*. It sends you to sleep, you will not fall asleep at the wheel again, ever.

It's in your pocket.

Just some old hippie songs. You'll probably know the words.

Go on. It'll make you angry if nothing else. Some crappy compilation of all Pete's favourites, some Joni, some Joan, some Bob. *Both Sides Now* – Crosby, Stills, Nash and Young, and Baez and Joplin and Mitchell and . . .

Go on, Rowan. Reach for it.

But you're scared, aren't you? They leave them some-times. Suicides. Like letters. Last words on a tape.

Slow down.

Don't be silly, it's just a tape, what's the harm in it? Music to help you drive. Slow down to second.

You are safe, parked in a lay-by. Push it into the music console.

A crackle and hiss. You are waiting for her voice, talking to you. This tape that he'd kept for nearly thirty years knowing that one day you would come.

Turn off the engine to hear better. Still nothing, just the hiss then a clunk. A guitar, then a bodhrán, an old folk song. It's Pete, Pete played the guitar and the banjo and the bodhrán. Two bars and you are waiting for her voice but it doesn't come. You breathe again. You open your eyes.

It's just Pete. And Pete accompanied by Pete. He gave

249

it to you like you were some record producer from down south, like at the age of sixty-five he was still waiting to be discovered.

It's laughable. You start up the car and leave the tape on. Pete's guitar is not great. You laugh to yourself. Pete and your mother and the whole folk-music thing. You're glad that Pete's big revelation amounted to this – amateur cover versions.

The road sinks downwards, you feel the bonnet dip, the pull of gravity even before you see the signs telling you to slow on the bends. As you turn the steep narrow you glimpse the sides rising above you. You are a hundred feet down and the walls of stone amass above. A sheer drop to the sea. The road winds its way back on itself as you drop three hundred feet then up again. They should have built a bridge. Three braes like this. You don't know which one she went over.

So easy to understand that it was an accident; it was a miracle that you survived it on the way here.

And actually, as you climb to the top of the brae and there are no cars, no mistakes, the bit near the end when Pete does a guitar solo, it isn't bad at all, actually.

You take the next slope down in third and see the sandbanks for the trucks that lose control. You go down to second. Only one more brae to go, till the straight road south and the song ends. There is crackling again and you thank Pete for this, as his guitar starts up again. The second song seems familiar but the arrangement different. What is it? A Dylan cover? You're safe in third.

At the end of the fourth bar, a little harmonic on the higher strings.

Can ye no hush yer weepin'?
A' the wee lambs are sleepin'

250

She's here, filling the car.

> *Birdies are nestlin', nestlin' the gither*
> *Dream Angus is hirplin' oer the heather*

Her voice so strong, so young. Reach for the off button. No, not yet. Hold steady. The bend is hard, use both hands. Shut up, shut up!

> *Dreams to sell, fine dreams to sell*

Reach the top, the road will be straight and you can turn her off there, just twenty seconds till you have a hand free. Turn her off!

> *Angus is here wi' dreams to sell*

The sounds of saliva, parting on her lips, the intake of breath, full lung, before the note. Closing your eyes and hearing her voice so close to your ear. The deep falling darkness, the terrible intimacy, breathing in the warm roundness of her song.

> *Hush my wee bairnie an' sleep without fear*

She carried you through the dark, taking your weight.

> *Dream Angus has brought you a dream my dear*

It had been a long drive. You were tired, sleepy. She fumbled for a tape while she drove, there were many in the glove compartment, she grabbed the first one she found. She was startled to hear her own voice coming at her from the speakers. She shouted at you to turn it off. That is the last thing you remember. Turn it off.

251

Hear the curlew cryin' o
An' the echoes dyin' o

You see her now behind the wheel, after she dropped you off, hours later, days maybe. Alone, she wanted to hear her voice again, to face it down. She tried to sing along but her voice faltered and she couldn't recall what passion or naivety had once made her sing like that.

Even the birdies and the beasties are sleepin'
But my bonny bairn is weepin' weepin'

A moment comes to her, everyone is together. The note is so pure and strong, filling her chest and the hearts of all as she holds onto the very limits of her breath. To live in that note with the others, to make that note last for ever.

Dreams to sell, fine dreams to sell

You see her weeping then. She tried to wipe her eyes to see the road. She reached to turn off the tape but made a small miscalculation as she leaned.

Angus is here wi' dreams to sell

Your eyes are wet. Wake up, Rowan. The wheel wrenches itself from your hands, spinning. Her voice becomes a whisper over the scream of the skid.

Hush my wee bairnie an' sleep without fear

A violent thud and wheels spin in the air. Lift your feet from the pedals. There is nothing you can do now. Listen to her lullaby. Close your eyes, my wee bairnie. Hush, hush.

the road home

'THERE WAS SPLINTER and Tommy and this girl called Debbie. I don't know what Splinter's real name was, maybe Sinclair, maybe it rhymed. Debbie's name was . . . yes, I'm sure her name was Mackay. She was very pretty. I saw her the other day in town, with a baby, I think it was her, or her daughter. I'm sure her name was Mackay. Debbie.'

'Debbie Mackay? Is at e hairdresser, Rab?'

'Na, at's Denise.'

'Could be Tony's lassie? Naw, she's a bit yownger, Denise Mackay, ye sure it's no Denise? She's a Sinclair now, her man's Wullie.'

'This would have been, oh, 'seventy-eight.'

'Zat a fact now, cos, if ye da mind me sayin' ye da look it. If ye da mind me askin' – how old are ye?'

'Thirty-nine.'

'Weel, at's why then. I wiz a few years yownger than ye, at's why ah canna mind ye. Bit Debbie, ah should ken a Debbie. Ye ken a Debbie Rab?'

'Denise's mither mibbe. Debrah.'

'Right enough, aye. It'll be Debrah. Fine wuman, Debrah. At'll be her, right enough. So ye kent Debrah at e school, eh?'

'Yes. Sorry, so Debbie's kid is called Denise?'

'Aye, no, bit Denise'll be, wit? Must be in her twenties now. Aye, Debrah takes care o' e little eens now cos Denise's at e hairdressin'.'

'Debbie is a grandmother?'

'Aye, aye. Same age as yersel right enough. Three is it no, Rab?'

255

'Three grandchildren?'

'Aye. At'll be Debrah right enough. Ye huv any little eens yerself?'

'Yes, actually, I do.'

'Biy or a lassie?'

'A lassie. She's eight, nearly nine months.'

'Is at no lovely? A wee lassie. Always wanted a wee lassie but I got this thing here! Is at no right, Rab.'

'Get aff!'

'Wit's she called, yer wee lassie?'

'Ailsa. Sasa, for short.'

'Bonny name fir a lassie. A wee lassie, eh? She'll be bonny lek her mither then.'

'Yes, she is, very bonny, more bonny than me. I was just driving to see her.'

'Weel, ye just gee her a call when we get to e toon. Ye can use ma phone if ye lek. Aye, come in, and we'll get e polis cos they'll hev to do a report, bit dinna worry, we'll take care o' all at, and ye can huv a wee wash and a cuppae tea and ye'll be right as rain and ah'll git Mike tae come an tow e car oot and ye'll be fine. Chust a culpa more meenets and we'll be there.'

'Thanks. Look, I'm really, really grateful for the lift and everything. You've been so lovely.'

'Nah, least we could do fir a local lassie. Ah mean, ye wir lucky, awfy lucky. I said tae Rab, did ah no, Rab? Ye fair flew. We was just comin' up e road and we seen ye, goin' over the edge, is at no right, Rab?'

'Aye, right enough.'

'And I says, Rab, I says, she wis lucky she never went over on her side cos if she did she wid hav rolled, over e edge lek.'

'Really? You think so?'

'Oh aye.'

'Fir definite, aye, seen it afore, ye wid hav rolled, a

few times, and crushed, cos you wis doin', what da ye say, Rab, what ye think?'

'Bout sixty.'

'Really? Was I?'

'Aye, bout sixty. Fer flew ye did, aye, ye wis lucky it wis where it wis and no a bit afore, ye wis lucky it was just e field. But still, a hell o' a drop. Bout, what ye say, Rab?'

'Twelve feet.'

'Aye boouta twelve-feet drop, anyway, and you seen e chaset? Hell o' a bang, ye seen it, bent lek a, lek a . . .'

'Lek a banana.'

'Aye, right enough, Rab, lek a banana. And e sun roof, ye see it? Popped open, cos e chaset was buckled.'

'Aye, a write-off.'

'Right enough, Rab. Total write-off. Ye wis lucky ye jist walked oot. I couldna believe it when I seen ye just standin' there in e field lek. Lek, I says tae him, she must huv a guardian angel. Did ah no, Rab?'

'Aye, ye did.'

'Ye sure yer all right? No a bit stiff or at? Cos, ye know, it can take a while afore ye ken if there's anything wrong wi ye. Lek, if you feel sleepy or at. Yer no feelin' sleepy, headache or—'

'No, fine, really, still feel my toes.'

'Ye must huv been a bit, a bit feared though, a drop lek at.'

'Well, actually, to tell you the truth. I was—'

'Ah'd huv been feared, ah'd be a nervous wreck.'

'— I, uh. It sounds silly. But I just, I just kept my eyes closed and there was the bang and I must have thought this is it. Then everything seemed to stop.'

'Yer life flash afore yer eyes. No?'

'No, not at all. Bit of a disappointment, really. Just this sense, when I opened my eyes. I don't know. I just felt so incredibly, it sounds silly. So incredibly happy.'

257

'Right enough. Ye wis laughin' when we seen ye. Hummin' a wee tune too. Wis she no, Rab?'

'Aye, she wis.'

'It wis maybe e shock. Ye wis mibbe in shock.'

'No, I don't know. Maybe. Sorry. I just can't stop. Am I still grinning? I feel like I'm grinning.'

'Right enough, aye.'

'Am I? Really, I don't know why. I just can't stop. Why I just feel. I want to. To laugh.'

*

Johnny and Rab and Johnny's wife Sheila and biscuits and cups of tea. Then the police came, and Rab told them the story and there was more laughter – 'She fer flew, aye, she did' – and he told it again like it had already become a proud part of local legend. Sheila was so lovely, and the police too, the way they didn't do a breathalyser. The way they asked the questions.

'And so you were going how fast, would you say?'

'I was, I think, sixty, maybe less. Is sixty OK?'

'It's fine.'

'I'd just come out of the braes so I must have been in third at most because of the gradient and I had the tape on. I was trying to turn it off when it happened.'

'Yer sure you're OK? We could call e doctor.'

'No, I'm fine. Really.'

Then it struck me. That the voice had gone. That for the first time in so long I was calling myself 'I'.

'Fine, really, I am.'

Then the garage man came, they were talking to him at the door, and Johnny told the story again and the garage man told his story about getting the chains out and how the tow truck got stuck in the mud and it was a hell of a job. The car was fit for the scrappy, that was all. There was something familiar about his voice. I couldn't see him, he was at the door with Johnny. Then Johnny invited him in to meet me.

'Is is Mike Sinclair,' he said. 'Ye ken, lek, Mike an e mechanics.'

Mike play-punched him and said, 'Get aff,' then he turned and I saw it, as he leaned over to shake. The scar down his cheek. Jono ripping his face.

Mike, Spike, Sinclair, Splinter.

'How ye doin'?' he said. His hand there, waiting. 'It's Rowan, right?'

I took his hand, scared that he'd read my face. Johnny interrupted.

'Ye mind her at e school. She wis at e school, be e same time as yersel.'

I tried not to look at the scar.

'No, no, sorry, ah canna mind ye, sorry. It's Rowan, right? No, sorry, ah canna mind ye.'

He wasn't lying. I didn't know how I felt. Not relieved, maybe angry at first. That this person who had caused us so much pain, couldn't even remember my face.

He was laughing, embarrassed as Johnny went through the dates, the names.

'How can ye no mind, ya numptie? She used ta ken Debrah. Debrah Mackay.'

'Aye, aye, ah ken Debbie weel. But ah'm, sorry, sorry, I just canna mind ye at all.'

Then it happened. They were all laughing together and it came to me: how stupid I'd been; of course – they'd had children and grandchildren, and twenty years of work and unemployment and troubles of their own and that day, even though it had scarred him for life, it was just one single day and he had even in time come to forget and forgive the source of the scar. It happened as we all laughed together. Somehow I forgave the child in the laughing face

259

of the man who had pulled my car from a field; and forgotten me.

*

One, two, three, four. The time is 7.17, and I've been travelling for nine hours. The things I've seen, little one, passing my train window: horses running, shadows of clouds on snowy mountain peaks, the lines of telegraph wires making a rhythm.

Only an hour till I see you again.

I'm counting breaths to try to calm myself.

Eighteen, nineteen, twenty. A thousand cars trapped on a motorway now and the fear quickening as I get closer to you. The names of stations flashing by. The train doesn't stop in these places; they don't count in the scheme of things. I have lost count. I must start again.

One, two, three, four, five.

He will have changed the locks.

If he wants a divorce, and social workers come to write assessments of me, to have organised schedules for my visits, and only then accompanied by another adult, I will accept. I'll make those minutes with you mean more than the days he denies me. I'll teach you songs, though I know the words to none. We'll learn them together.

He'll have had you in front of the TV while I've been away. You'll have seen too much. I'll tell you about how I grew up without a TV; about making pots from mud; of how there's mud up there in the Highlands called peat, made of dead trees, and how coal is peat that's been compressed over millennia and diamonds are made from coal, but as old as the earth.

The pylons multiply as the train accelerates; I can't count them.

And there are things I'll never tell you: like how a

moment with you, watching you painting, or playing, or dressing up – these things are as good as it'll ever be. We parents are too busy with our plans and our futures even to see you. As you learn that red and yellow make orange and that the letter 'Y' looks like a tree, as you stand before the mirror and realise that the other child who waves is you. That when you try to kiss her on the mouth she tastes of glass.

Wastelands of concrete and mud. Bulldozed scraped earth.

The speed obliterates, a passing train slams its wind against me.

Four more stops to London King's Cross. I close my eyes and breathe and try to picture your chest rising and falling against mine.

And if he shouts when I enter, I'll insist that we don't do this in front of you. There are things a child shouldn't see. If he won't be calm, I'll accept and walk away and wait till he is quiet.

Brand names pass by – McDonald's, TK Maxx, Toys R Us – England is no longer England.

I see myself watching you every day as you grow older. I watch you at your nursery, going in and out of cars. I see them pick you up and drop you off. I watch you through a fence, waiting for the moment when they turn their backs for just a second and I will run with you in my arms.

I'm rushing through tunnels, violent flashes of dark. I must be on the outskirts. I need more time.

My phone has no new messages. It's a bad sign. He's given up on me. Must sense, in some way, that I'm coming home.

St Albans, Hemel Hempstead, Barnet, Harrow, Golders Green. The energy it takes to rise and fight each day. I see my mother trapped in the city in the sixties, suffocating in the sunshine.

261

Start again. Count the breaths, one, two, three, four.

London King's Cross. Already the others are fighting for space, trying to get out first, cursing each other. Such violence. I want to drop out of time altogether and just be old, to be a grandmother, to be a mother again.

Close your eyes, my love. I'll be there soon. Maybe you are asleep already. Yes, he'll be showing you your picture book.

When you're older he might tell you stories about me. About how I left. He'll say you're not to worry – you'll grow up to be nothing like me.

I will not let him relegate me to just another story that they tell you to fill the empty space where I should have been. We shall write our story together, little one.

I'm leaving the station now. I need more time. I could get a room tonight, make a plan. But if I don't come back now, then how will I ever have the strength? I'll postpone. I will. The fear will only grow.

I'm standing at the taxi rank, amid people and their chat. Adverts are all around with leering smiles and sexual poses. Girls are passing in make-up and heels, laughing. How can I ever live here again?

I must take the Underground. But no, I won't be able to stand them, the bodies of strangers touching me, their stink, the desire in their eyes that measure me as I pass, their eyes that are distant, that dream of anywhere other than where they are.

I have to walk then, walk home.

My mother was eight months' pregnant when she left London. She was confused but she felt me growing in her gut and knew we had to escape. I understand now. Soon, I'll take you away.

I'm passing the shops, counting my footsteps, nineteen, twenty, twenty-one.

He'll deny me access and I will come back again and

again. Weeks will go by and the police will take me away. The doctors will inject me with things to make me sleep. It's OK. My sleepy love. It's sleepy time.

I'll have to find a flat for myself and arrange visits through the courts. He'll use our money to get the best lawyer and I'll have to fight him with another lawyer to get access to the account even to pay the lawyer's bill.

Forty-eight, forty-nine . . . Start again.

I could go to him one night and explain. Stand there and see if he has forgiveness in his eyes. One night when you're asleep and he stands in the doorway blocking my way.

Half a mile. Not long now, not long now.

I picture his face at the door. His silence waiting for me to speak.

Can I tell him the truth through a chain lock? Can I just come in and not talk? Maybe if I wrote it all down for him, started at the very beginning with my mother.

Two streets to go.

De Beauvoir Road. The home we picked because of the school catchment area. I'm at number 12. We live at number 44. I'm counting them as I walk. 18, 20, 22.

I'm standing at our door. The security light has come on. A light meant for burglars. My keys are in my hand though he said he'd changed the locks. The lights are off in all the rooms. I'm looking at your little bedroom window upstairs. There are the curtains he and I picked out from Ikea together. Not pink but beige because we agreed that too many girls' things were pink.

It is 20.32. You'll be fast asleep now.

I picture him having a stiff drink before answering the door.

I see him on the other side, praying for me to go away.

I see his face, holding you after my knocks have woken you. He will have carried you to the doorway. Maybe you'll

263

be grumpy and not reach for me, maybe you'll cling to him and cry and hide your face from me. Look what you've done to her, he'll say.

I see him calling the police.

I see myself months later, living in some bedsit, signing on, muscles weak from not eating. Drawing pictures of you, plans for our escape. Making a cup of camomile tea, to calm the nerves; then soaking the towels in the sink and folding them to plug the gaps under the doors and windows before I turn on the gas.

I see that my mother foresaw all of this, long ago.

I'm standing on the doorstep. The doorbell sometimes doesn't work. You have to hold your finger against it hard. It was put in by the last people, we said we would change it.

Please let him forgive me.

The security light goes off even though I'm still here.

Knock then, I should knock.

If he won't let me see you again, then I'll write it all down, for you, not for him. I'll send it to you, when you're older. The whole story of Ithaca.

I breathe and stare at the door with our name on it. The name I took, which was his, which is yours now.

I make my hand into a fist and raise it to the door.

I forgive. Everything. I have to. I do.

I forgive even you, Mother.

I knock.

I have nothing, nothing but love for you.

The sound as I strike echoes on the other side.

My little daughter with my mother's eyes.

Please forgive me.

I close my eyes and wait.